NEVER SPEAK OF IT

CAROLYN RIDDER ASPENSON

Severn River Publishing
www.SevernRiverBooks.com

ISBN: 978-1-64875-656-6 (Paperback)

ALSO BY CAROLYN RIDDER ASPENSON

Jenna Wyatt Series

How They Were Taken

Never Speak of It

Before the Next One Falls

The Rachel Ryder Thriller Series

Damaging Secrets

Hunted Girl

Overkill

Countdown

Body Count

Fatal Silence

Deadly Means

Final Fix

Dark Intent

Foul Play

Trusted Lies

Grave Pursuit

To find out more about Carolyn Ridder Aspenson and her books, visit severnriverbooks.com

To Erika, Morgan and Justin
Let's be honest, you won't read this one until after I'm dead either.

1

I walked into my office to find Jack Parks sitting behind my desk, yanking open and then slamming closed each drawer. Repeatedly. We hadn't known each other long, barely enough time to establish trust, but that didn't faze Parks. Boundaries were optional to him, a truth I learned the moment he barged past mine like speed bumps in a Publix parking lot.

He looked up at me with sheer horror in his eyes. "Don't you have any Wite-Out?"

I tilted my head and narrowed my eyes. What would come next, a quest for floppy disks in my filing cabinet? "Wite-Out? Seriously?"

"Yeah. The stuff you use to white out things on a piece of paper. Hence the name Wite-Out."

I pursed my lips and gave my head a quick shake, hoping to communicate my opinion of his ridiculousness telepathically. "Don't you have your own office? Why are you here?"

"I needed a printer." His eyes flicked to his cell on my desk. "Where's the Wite-Out?"

"News flash, Parks. This isn't 1994. We've moved on to backspace keys and PDFs."

"If they don't sell Wite-Out anymore, they should." He ran his hand across his cropped hair. "I'm screwed." He continued ripping through my desk for something he'd never find.

"I don't know if they sell it anymore because I haven't used a typewriter in years." I gave Parks a hard eye roll. "Maybe before you turn my desk into a crime scene, you could ask how my morning went? Just a thought."

He massaged the back of his neck. "Good morning, Jenna. How's your day going so far?"

I smiled. "Thank you for asking, Jack." I called him by his first name instead of his last, feigning a politeness he knew I didn't have, at least not with him. "It's been fine if you don't count being cut off by a car held together with duct tape, stubbornness, and someone's last three bad decisions."

Parks acted interested, but the side of his head, nearly hitting his shoulder, said otherwise. "This morning? Or are we talking about a lifelong pattern of poor driving and questionable decision-making?"

"A lifelong pattern, but today? I'm one existential spiral away from weaponizing my Bronco."

That annoying smirk twitched at the corner of his mouth. "Do tell."

"Finally, something about me catches your attention."

"Everything about you catches my attention."

"Whatever. I was two lanes over from my exit, merging like a responsible adult, when this beat-up blue Honda, probably older than me, swerves in front of me like he's playing some race car video game."

"Race car game," he repeated, complete with an eye roll. "What are we talking? Mario Kart or Grand Theft Auto?"

"That's not the point. Stop looking for something you won't find and pay attention."

"My bad." He raised an eyebrow. "Did he signal?"

"Oh, absolutely. About thirty seconds after the fact. And then, genius that he clearly isn't, he slams on his brakes. I had to swerve into the next lane to avoid turning him into a hood ornament. Almost hit a guy in a Lexus who gave me the finger and mouthed something that looked like 'psychopath.' Which—fair. But still."

He wanted to smile. I could tell. "And you still made the exit?"

"Barely. I took it on two wheels and a prayer. Pretty sure my tire alignment's out of whack now."

"And that Bronco's brand new." Parks laughed, full-out. "This is why Leland warned me to never let you drive."

I narrowed my eyes. "I drive like a woman trying to survive Atlanta traffic without committing a felony. This guy came out of nowhere."

"That's what they all say right before blaming it on the GPS." He tilted his head, that smug cop-sense kicking in. "Do you think it was intentional?"

I snorted. "If it was, the would-be assassin needs to retake Homicide 101. It's just frustrating. Like you said, my Bronco is brand new. I'd like to keep it in one piece for a while."

"Who've you pissed off lately? You have a way of bringing out the worst in people. Maybe they're coming back for justice."

"I only piss off criminals. I don't do that with normal people."

He raised an eyebrow but said nothing.

I laughed. "Fine. Do you want the alphabetical list or the one sorted by motive?"

He grinned. "All right, then. Next time we're on a case and someone tries to run you off the road, try not to blow a tire. I don't think your insurance covers hostile witness retaliation."

"Noted," I muttered, grabbing the coffee I'd forgotten I had. "Remind me again why I chose this life over real estate or some cushy office job?"

"Because they don't come with me."

There might have been some truth to that, but I wasn't about to admit that out loud.

"By the way, she called again."

"Who?"

"Your Harvard buddy, Riley Chatsworth." He dug through my top drawer again. "You really don't use Wite-Out?"

I set my bag on the credenza behind my desk. "There's this thing called the backspace button. When you're in a document on your laptop," I stressed the *on your laptop* part, "and make a mistake, you hit that button, and your mistake magically disappears."

"I know that, wiseass, but I've already printed it."

"Correct it and reprint it." I laughed. "And get yourself a printer. The UPS Store is making bank off you."

"Not if I use yours." He winked at me. "I'll get one eventually."

"Please, and seriously, will it kill you to stay on your side of the building for a change?"

"I rented here first," he said. "Can't fault you for wanting to be near me, so I'm just appeasing your desires. Like I do with most women."

I ignored that, even though I kind of wanted to fire back. But poking that bear would've guaranteed an R-rated response, and I wasn't in the mood to spar with someone who always took it too far. "Why does she keep calling you?"

"Because you won't return her calls. She said it's important. I told her I'd do my best to make you call her back, but no promises."

"You talked to her?"

"She's called five times in the last week. What was I supposed to do?"

"Ignore her like I have." I opened the credenza, dug through a container of ancient office supplies I had collected over the years, found a bottle of the white stuff, and tossed it at him. "I'm not sure it's still liquid."

He caught it without even looking . "I knew you wouldn't let me down." He dotted the stuff over something on his document while saying, "If she's calling me that much, it's bad, Wyatt. Call her."

"I will when I have time." I eyed my desk and flicked my chin up as a hint. When he didn't move, I finally said, "May I have my desk back, please?"

He pushed out the chair and stood. "What's your beef with her, anyway? She steal your boyfriend or something?"

"Or something." I sipped the coffee I had picked up on the way to the office and set it back on my desk. "She almost got me kicked out of Harvard Law."

He whistled. "Damn. What happened?"

"It's a story for another time."

I clicked on the radio. The brief static gave way to the crisp, authoritative voice of a national news anchor. "A shocking development from Atlanta, Georgia. Authorities arrested Riley Chatsworth, chief executive officer of Paramount Assurance Corporation, the leading insurance company in the United States, for the alleged murder of Gregory Hoover, president of Tellion Technology, a former PAC client."

Parks and I made eye contact.

He mouthed, "Wow."

PAC didn't just sell insurance. They weaponized it. Their reputation as the biggest player in their market had changed when insurance became a political talking point. Many believed they held life-and-death decisions in boardrooms while pretending to be paper-pushers. Rumors that they stalled claims and waited until someone either gave up or died had made the news multiple times.

Were those rumors true? If so, Hoover must have pushed back, and maybe pushed too hard.

The anchor's voice remained crisp and controlled, but each word landed with the precision of a blade, cutting through my focus and dragging me back into a storm I hadn't expected to revisit.

"Chatsworth, a prominent figure in the insurance sector, was taken into custody early this morning outside her Atlanta office by APD. Reporter Emily Garcia has more. Emily."

"Thank you, Sarah. Yes, the arrest of Riley Chatsworth may come as a shock to the public," Garcia said, her tone smooth but giving off curiously weighted vibes, "but according to APD Chief Johnston Baylor, there are startling allegations tying her directly to the high-profile murder. He added that his top detective made the arrest."

My lungs forgot how to function for a second. The pressure in my chest wasn't just from the words. It was from what they *meant*. From the past clawing its way back into the present.

Garcia's voice filled the silence again. "Hoover was found deceased in his Milton, Georgia, home, with a gunshot to the head. Investigators say forensic evidence discovered at the scene led them directly to Chatsworth."

I stared at the radio, half hoping sheer disbelief could rewind time or change the outcome. But no amount of disbelief could undo what I'd just heard, or the ugly truth that I might be involved in it, whether I wanted to be or not. Riley Chatsworth had just become headline news, and the byline belonged to me. Or she wanted it to.

Memories of Riley from our Harvard days flashed through my mind.

We had once been inseparable, challenging and cheering each other through grueling law courses until that bitter fallout over her dubious moral choices. I hadn't seen her since graduation, and the attempted contact and news report fractured the old wound, leaving it raw and bloodied once again. My ex-husband, Nick, once told me I carried a grudge longer than an old-school mob boss. He wasn't wrong.

The reporter dived deeper, detailing the public and police scrutiny surrounding PAC's aggressive business tactics under Riley's leadership, hinting at a motive rooted in the fierce corporate falling-out with Tellion Technology.

"Police aren't commenting on the specifics of the evidence but have confirmed finding the murder weapon in Ms. Chatsworth's home at the time of her arrest."

I swallowed hard as the questions burned my throat. The friend I thought I knew. But did I ever really know her? Could she have crossed a line that sharp, that final? One I thought she already crossed years ago? If she had, murder topped her crimes against me by a long shot.

"This arrest has sent shock waves through the business community, with Paramount Assurance Corporation's stock plummeting and Tellion Technology calling for a thorough investigation into its former medical carrier's practices. Ms. Chatsworth's attorney has stated that they will fight the charges and this is a wrongful accusation aimed at tarnishing her reputation. Mr. Hoover leaves a wife and two children to mourn his death."

The silence in my office wasn't peaceful, but poised, like it held its breath, waiting for a punch I wouldn't see coming. "This doesn't make sense," I said. "She's been trying to talk to me for weeks, but she was just arrested for murder?"

Parks grabbed his keys from my desk. "She's either psychic and knew it was coming, or someone is out to frame her."

"I don't believe in psychics, but the second option, I can believe."

"What about the third option?" he asked.

"She did it?"

He nodded. "Looks like you just found our next client."

I cocked my head to the side. "Our?"

"I'm playing receptionist for you already. I think I deserve a spot on the team."

I leaned against the cool glass of my office window, staring down at the traffic, the people unconcerned about whom the police arrested or framed for murder. I envied that kind of ignorance. The easy, detached way of going about life without a clue. But I didn't get to be that person. I'd never been that person.

The memory of Riley's betrayal, once distant, surged forward, vivid and sharp.

We sat in the stark, hushed exam room, the students collectively anxious and panicked, their breathing the only sign of life. I had caught a movement from the corner of my eye. Riley, glancing at my test. I ignored it. Her glance and the guilt I didn't want to feel, choosing to focus on the exam. That decision, small and silent, sparked my near expulsion from law school. The proctor's voice shattered the silence, and everything after that rewrote our friendship in ink I couldn't erase.

"Ms. Chatsworth, step outside, please."

The room held its breath. Riley's chair scraped loudly against the floor as she stood. She shot me a look of desperate appeal. Though I wasn't with her, it would come out that, in the hallway, confronted by the proctor's stern inquiries, she crumbled, spinning a tale that implicated both of us, but primarily me.

She had blamed me for offering my answers when she had expressed concern about passing the test. She claimed I had purposefully angled my paper in her direction, when, in fact, as a left-handed person, I always angled my paper that way.

I vigorously defended myself to the administrative board, using what I had learned from law school as an example of my future potential, but cheating was a serious charge at Harvard Law, so they kicked my case to the dean.

A week later, as my goals and status at HLS swung from a threadbare rope, the professor, Edmund Blackwell, dropped the allegations against Riley, claiming his proctor had made a mistake.

I learned that Riley had slept with the man to clear her name. She hadn't pushed for me, but Blackwell called me in and said he saw potential in me, and if I screwed him too, he'd do me a favor. I told him the board would love that story.

Back in the present, I pressed my forehead against the glass, the cold seeping into my skin. Anger simmered beneath the surface, like a slow boil. How could she? After everything, after nearly destroying my career before it even started, she dared to reach out to me as if nothing had happened.

The office door clicked open, and Parks entered. His face clouded with concern.

"You need more Wite-Out?" I asked.

He laughed. "I saw you standing here looking a little crazy, so I figured I'd better stick around." He waited for a rebuttal of some sort, but when I didn't respond, he asked, "Are you okay with this?"

The question hung between us, heavy and fraught with implication. What was I going to do? Riley was in serious trouble. Despite everything, she had been my friend once, my closest confidant. Could I turn my back on her again, when she needed help more than ever? After all, she had turned her back on me and moved on without looking back.

"I don't know," I admitted, the uncertainty gnawing at me. "Part of me wants to help her, but another part thinks she did it."

"You can't forget what she did, can you?" Jack finished my thought with a gentle voice. He steadied his gaze at me. "You don't have to decide anything right now. Let's just see how things unfold. Maybe more information will come out that will help you decide."

My thoughts drifted back to Harvard, to the moment I learned of Riley's accusation. I remembered standing in front of the disciplinary committee, my future hanging by a thread, fighting to prove my innocence. The memory stabbed me sharply in the chest, reminding me of the pain and humiliation I had endured because of her lies.

Parks's phone erupted with a ring. He snagged it and moved his eyes to the screen. "It's her." His gaze locked on mine. Could he read the turmoil rioting through me? "Your call, but I'm right here with you," he said.

"I'm fine." I snatched the phone, sucked in a steeling breath, and slammed my finger down on the answer icon, then put it on speaker. "Hello, Riley."

"You must have seen the news," a man said.

"Who is this?" I asked.

"Riley's attorney, Harris Taylor."

I glanced at Parks. His eyes widened. Taylor had earned the title of the top criminal defense attorney in the southeast. And he was. His services cost a pretty penny because he could create reasonable doubt in a jury who saw video of his clients murdering their victims. Of course Riley would choose him. She had the money to pay him.

"Mr. Taylor, what can I do for you?"

"Ms. Chatsworth would like to see you. She's at Fulton County Jail. When can we expect you?"

"Why?" I asked, though I already knew the answer. "Why does Ms. Chatsworth want to see me?"

"Police arrested her for the murder of Gregory Hoover, and she insists you are the only one who can prove her innocence."

"Isn't that your job?"

"We will work together, Ms. Wyatt."

"I'm going to need some time to think about this, Mr. Taylor."

"Given your career with the Georgia Bureau of Investigation, you're aware of the urgency in this matter. I understand your office is in Roswell. I'll expect you at eleven." He killed the call before I said no.

I stared at my phone as if by not moving, I could make those last ten seconds disappear. But I couldn't. And they wouldn't. Besides, I knew up close and personal that doing nothing never erased the past.

I stared at my phone, then at Parks, trying to focus on the outrage instead of the twist in my gut. "Can you believe the nerve of that guy? Telling me I'll show up? Screw that BS."

But it wasn't just his tone. He assumed I'd come running, that I was still the girl Riley could use and discard at her convenience. And the worst part? A small, traitorous part of me wanted to go. Wanted to see Riley's face. Wanted to hear her say it. That she was innocent. That she was sorry. That I had spent years holding that grudge for no reason.

"We have to go."

I leaned against my desk, suddenly aware of how flimsy that barrier felt between me and the mess unfolding. "We? We have to go?" I wanted to say no. I needed to say no. But the part of me that hadn't let Riley go was already halfway out the door with Parks beside me.

"I've been getting the calls."

I forced the issue, not only to convince him, but to show myself I could do things without him, even though in that moment, I wasn't feeling that. "Because I refused to answer mine."

"Come on, Wyatt," he said. "This is big, and you know it. You need to hear what she has to say."

"So, it's me, not we."

"Here we go again. We both know we're better as a team. I'm tagging along. If I have to take pictures of another idiot cheating on his wife, you'll be bailing out my ass for assault charges."

"On the husband, I assume."

He grinned, already at the door and holding it open like a challenge. "Let's move, partner."

"I'm not your partner," I fired back, even as I scooped up my phone and stormed out with him, knowing full well that he was.

Every rational part of me screamed to walk away. But I couldn't. I couldn't not do it, and that scared the hell out of me. Because wanting to help her meant I might still care, and caring meant I was vulnerable again, and I hated that more than anything.

We arrived at Fulton County Jail an hour later.

"Have you ever been here?" I asked.

He smirked. "As a visitor or guest?"

"Either."

"Visitor, yes. Guest, no, thank God. The place is dangerous."

"Most jails in major cities are."

"Fulton County is one of the worst in the country," he said.

I agreed.

The interior greeted us with the sharp scent of disinfectant and a heavy sense of foreboding.

"This smell sticks to your clothes," I said.

"Industrial cleaners usually do. We used them in the Navy."

"You used them? Are you sure you were NCIS? It sounds like you were scrubbing toilets."

He whistled low. "Ouch. I'd say something about you being fired from the Georgia Bureau of Investigation, but I've got a heart."

I laughed. "Right. I forgot about your sensitivity issues. My bad."

An officer sitting behind bulletproof glass scrutinized us. "IDs and purpose of visit," he demanded through the intercom. We pressed our identification against the glass and informed him of our appointment with Riley Chatsworth. He checked our names against a list, waved his hand to dismiss our IDs, and motioned for us to proceed through the metal detector.

We placed our belongings, including our weapons, into the trays. Then Parks cleared the detector without issue, as did I.

"You'll get your things back when you leave," the officer said. "Though I don't know why you'd pack heat here. You know you can't take them inside."

"Have you been in your parking lot lately?" Parks asked. "Or across the street?"

"Hmph, I guess you're right about that," the officer said.

Another officer escorted us down a series of sterile, echoing corridors. Each door in the deeper parts of the facility required a badge swipe and a solid push to open. The air cooled, the atmosphere grew more controlled, and our steps echoed down the empty halls.

He brought us to a closed door, opened it, and motioned for us to enter. "You'll meet her here. Someone will bring her in shortly. No physical contact." He pointed to the camera on the ceiling. "We'll know." He gestured for us to take a seat before exiting.

"Friendly guy," Parks said. He stood against the wall and scanned every corner of the room, looking for what, I didn't know.

I took the chair facing the door. "Thirty minutes," I said. "She gets thirty minutes."

"Yes, ma'am."

Fifteen minutes had passed before Harris Taylor walked in. "Ms. Wyatt." He eyed Parks. "Mr. Parks. I assumed you would join Ms. Wyatt." He handed me a file, dropped another one on the table, then set his brief-case on the floor. "Thank you for coming." His politeness landed like a warning. Lawyers didn't thank you unless they were about to bury you beneath a battle they thought they might lose. Taylor never lost, so Riley must have looked guilty to him, too.

The door creaked open, and a guard led Riley into the cramped room. He left the shackles on her ankles but removed the cuffs from her wrists.

She sat directly across from me. "Jenna, thank you for coming."

I steeled my eyes at her. "I've got thirty minutes."

"Ms. Wyatt," Taylor said, "my client has been allowed bail, but with conditions. Rest assured, you'll have all the time necessary to find Greg Hoover's true killer."

I leaned back and crossed my arms.

"I'm not a bodyguard, and I don't babysit."

"We have someone to handle her supervision. She is also required to wear an ankle bracelet and, of course, cannot leave the state."

I pushed back my chair. "That all sounds great. Good luck in court."

Before I had the chance to stand, Riley said, "I didn't do it, Jenna. And the only way to prove that is to find the person who did. I know what you're thinking. That this is just like before, but it's not."

My jaw tightened. "You have no idea how I feel." If she thought drag-ging up the past would soften me, she was wrong. Dead wrong.

"I didn't mean—I just know how important that's been to you. Please, Jen. I can't do this without you."

There it was. The real reason she called. Not remorse. Not clarity. Desperation.

And she knew exactly which nerve to strike.

I ignored her and spoke to her attorney. "Mr. Taylor, may I have a moment alone with Ms. Chatsworth, please?"

He glanced at Riley, who nodded.

He tipped his head slightly to the side. "I'll be outside."

Parks followed.

I studied her the way I had studied every suspect, and the way I'd studied her after the betrayal. Tracking every twitch, every subtle shift in tone. But this wasn't law school, and I wasn't the one she'd betrayed. It was a murder investigation, and she was on the wrong side of the table.

Her rapid blinking, the way she clutched her arms and fidgeted, all signs of nervousness, an emotion that worked for innocence or guilt. I needed more. I wouldn't help her without knowing the truth, and I didn't trust her to tell me. I only trusted my gut.

"Did you kill Gregory Hoover?"

She stopped blinking and set her forearms on the table. "No."

"The police found you with the gun."

"I just got home and found it on my counter. I picked it up, and then they knocked on my door. When they told me about Greg, I told them it wasn't mine, that someone must have broken into my house to set me up, but they didn't believe me." She spoke in a polished, practiced tone. She was too careful. Too aware of what I was looking for. Even her body movements appeared practiced. As an attorney, she knew what I needed to see to believe her. "Jenna, I know we have a past, and I'm sorry for what I did, but I didn't murder Greg."

I stared at her, surprised that the hurt hit harder than I expected. "You lied about me once. Boldly. Publicly. Why should I think you're not doing it again?"

She didn't flinch. That almost made it worse. Her mouth trembled, just slightly. "Because that lie cost me something I couldn't replace." She swallowed hard but held my gaze. "We were best friends, ones who finish each other's arguments. I wrecked that. And I've hated myself for it ever since. But this? This isn't a lie. I didn't kill him."

She drew in a shaky breath. "And I need someone who can see past the headlines. Someone who won't stop until they know the truth. That used to be you, and I know it still is."

We'd had that kind of friendship. She had been the only person to break through my walls until Nick. And since she screwed me over, I hadn't allowed another woman to get that close.

My breath caught in my throat. I closed my eyes and let my gut lead me to where I needed to go. "You better be innocent, or so help me, Riley."

"I wouldn't come to you if I wasn't. Listen, I know you have no reason to help me. If our roles were reversed, I'm not even sure I could do it, but I'm asking you to trust me. I won't betray you again."

I cleared my throat. "I'll do it, but not without Parks, and we need to know everything. Every detail of every second leading up to his murder."

God, I hoped I wouldn't regret that.

Tears slipped down her cheeks. "Thank you. Thank you, Jenna."

I opened the door to allow Harris Taylor to come back in. Parks and I shared a look. I gave a slight nod, which he returned. Taylor sat while Parks closed the door and stood beside it.

"We're prepared to pay you the daily rate Jessica Steadman paid with a sixty-thousand retainer."

"How do you know what Mrs. Steadman paid?" I asked.

"I have been on retainer for the Steadman family for many years."

I glanced at Parks, wondering if he was thinking the same thing I was. That woman should've gone down for what she did. Not even a slick attorney like Taylor could've saved her. But Steadman had connections and no soul.

"I'm only doing this with my partner. Equal pay for the both of us." I glanced at Riley. "Can you afford that?" She'd had a trust fund and had hired the most expensive attorney in town. I thought she could.

Taylor bent down and whispered in her ear, then stood and said, "My client is fine with that."

"Great." I pushed back my chair to stand again. "When is she being released?"

"We're waiting on the paperwork," he said. "It should be within the hour."

I handed him my card, though I doubted he needed it. "Two p.m. Bring the babysitter. I'll need to vet him."

Taylor's upper lip curled. "He's with my firm."

"Good, because I'm vetting you too."

I pointed a finger at Riley. "You better be telling me the truth."

"Jen," she said, "you were always the one person who could see through lies. Even mine."

Parks yanked the door open, and we bolted like the place was on fire.

He gently rammed his shoulder into me as we walked to the car. "You called me your partner."

My lip curled. "No, I didn't," I lied.

"Yes, you did. You said, 'I'm only doing this with my partner' and got us equal pay." He bumped me again. "I feel special."

I tipped my head back. "Fine, I did. What else was I supposed to do? You forced me into it by driving me here."

He laughed. "I haven't known you long, but I can guarantee nobody forces you to do anything."

I smirked. "Damn straight."

We made it about three blocks from the jail before my phone rang. The display showed *Unknown Caller*, which normally meant spam or someone trying to sell me solar panels I didn't want.

I hit accept and clicked speaker involuntarily. "Wyatt."

A pause, then breathing.

I cut the call. "Do you think the companies that hire telemarketers realize they do that?"

"Do what?"

"Breathe into the phone like a psycho from a horror movie. It's like they want us to hang up on them."

He crawled forward with traffic, stuck in a relentless loop of stop and go. "You'd rather talk to them about your car warranty or health insurance?"

"Well, no, but—"

My phone rang again. Another unknown caller. I eyed Parks.

"Maybe it's the supervisor calling to apologize for the psycho breather?"

I clicked accept and speaker once again. "Wyatt."

Silence again for a moment, then a voice, distorted and filtered. "Stay out of it."

"I'm sorry. I didn't get that," I said.

Parks glanced at me and then back at the traffic.

Another pause. Then, "Walk away. Both of you."

I sat back against the seat, contemplating what to say. Parks's jaw clenched as his posture stiffened. He hated veiled threats as much as I.

"I'm not sure I know what you're talking about," I said. The goal with calls like that was to keep them talking and hope they'd say something to give away their identity.

"This is bigger than you can handle," the voice said. I struggled to determine the caller's gender. "Walk away before you get hurt."

I gave Parks a look. He tapped on his phone, probably pulling up one of those apps to trace the number. It would lead nowhere. Calls like that left trails impossible to trace in our situation.

"Got it," I said. "Thanks for the warning. Question, though, do you threaten all private investigators, or are we just special?"

"I'm giving you a chance. You won't get another one."

The line went dead.

I stared at the screen. "Well, that was subtle."

Parks muttered something that sounded like, "Unbelievable," and yanked his vehicle into a half-empty church parking lot with a view of the highway.

He killed the engine and turned toward me. "I got a recording of it." He replayed the call. "Is your cell phone number public?"

"Not intentionally, but anyone can find it if they look hard enough. Isn't yours that way as well?"

"Yes, but they didn't call me, Jenna. It could be someone close to Riley or someone inside PAC. Hell, could be someone in law enforcement."

I hated to think it could be law enforcement, but every field had bad guys, and big-name murders often involved all sorts of bad guys. "We're being watched," I said aloud, just to hear it out in the open. "Or Riley is."

"Makes sense since we just left the jail." Parks leaned back in his seat and drummed his fingers on the steering wheel. "Someone might be watching us."

I looked out the window and spotted a silver pickup rolling past, and a black sedan parked crookedly across from us. Neither looked suspicious, but then again, that was the point. "If someone is, we should go," I said. "It has to be someone that knows I'm connected to Riley."

Parks didn't move.

"Jack," I said, softer this time.

He looked at me, his jaw tight. "You good?"

"No." I forced a smile. "But I'm used to that."

He pressed the button to start the engine again. The low hum of it filled the tense silence between us.

As we pulled back onto the road, he said, "This changes things."

"I know."

"We still taking the case?"

"Hell yes," I said. "I don't scare that easily."

He nodded like he expected nothing less. "You realize we might be walking straight into something worse than a cover-up."

"We probably are."

He flipped open the center console, grabbed a stick of gum, and held one out. I took it. We drove in silence, the tension in the air thickening. I chewed, but it didn't help. My fingers kept tapping against my leg, sharp and constant, counting down to the big finale coming.

2

Parks dropped me at the office and headed out to grab coffee and Chick-fil-A sandwiches, fuel for whatever came next.

The door clicked shut behind him. I exhaled, letting the silence reclaim the room. But his energy still pulsed in the air, sharp and electric. Parks didn't just enter a room, he took it over. And even after he was gone, he never really left.

I hadn't meant it when I told Taylor I planned to vet him, but since he'd mentioned being on retainer with Steadman, I decided to go ahead. I dialed a number I knew by heart, but it went straight to voicemail. "I need intel on Harris Taylor when you've got a chance. Thanks."

I'd left my thermos in the car. It was a weak excuse for a break, but I grabbed it like a lifeline. I had just a few precious minutes to process what I knew would be an emotionally taxing investigation.

I grabbed my key card and tugged the office door shut behind me. The building's security system wasn't fancy, just electronic access for tenants, simple but effective. It usually worked. Usually made people feel safe. Even me.

I pressed my card against the key card reader. The light flashed red.

I tried again. Nothing.

"Come on," I muttered. "Just work." I shook it, gave it another shot. Still red. Still no beep. "You've got to be kidding me."

I turned it over in my hand and checked the chip. No visible damage. I tried again but still nothing.

"Okay. No big deal. Battery's low. Or maybe the system glitched."

I pulled up the tenant portal on my phone but found no flagged issues. The log even showed my key card had unlocked the front door to the building earlier that morning. I pressed it again, this time holding it longer. Finally, on the fourth try, the green light flashed. Chirp.

So much for peace. The thermos didn't matter anymore, and I didn't bother getting it.

"Don't be dramatic," I muttered.

Still, a chill crept up my spine. Had someone tried to mess with my key card?

"Stop being paranoid."

Riley's arrest, the visit to the jail, it all stirred up the old dust in my head. Or maybe I'd just spent too much time around Parks, who treated suspicion like oxygen.

I blamed him, but it didn't help.

I scribbled a reminder on a sticky note, *Replace key card. Check entry log.* My phone rang, but my eyes stayed on the key card.

One red light. One small glitch.

Nothing, right?

Unless it wasn't.

I answered the phone without a greeting. "Thanks for returning my call."

"My pleasure."

Leland Seymour ran the Georgia Bureau of Investigation, where I used to work, until he fired me. Rightfully so. I'd spent most of my life chasing a ghost, the one who abducted my five-year-old sister, Molly. He knew it. He warned me it had taken over my life, but I didn't listen, and it cost me first my marriage, then my job.

In hindsight, firing me might have been the best thing Leland ever did for me. He claimed it was one of those "this hurts me more than it hurts you" things, and he was right. Without that fallout, I never would've taken the case that made my career: tracking down the man who kidnapped Jessica Steadman's daughter and murdered her husband. I didn't know she'd kill him. But I almost couldn't blame her. If Molly's killer had still been alive, I might have done the same.

"I need your opinion on Harris Taylor."

"You saw the news."

"Yes, but he contacted me. Riley wants me to help them find whoever killed the Tellion guy."

"You spoke to Riley?" The surprise in his voice wasn't surprising. He had become a father figure to me over the years, and he knew our history.

"Don't sound so surprised," I said. "I'm taking her case."

"Am I in one of those alternate universes or something?"

"Or something," I said.

"Are you partnering with Parks?"

"Why does everyone have to use the word 'partner'? He's helping me."

I could hear the grin in his voice. "Thank God."

"What's that mean?"

"Means you two make a good team. I'd hate to see what you'd do to Christopher with this one. You know the law better than him."

I laughed. "I just wanted to understand the law."

"Most people buy *Law for Dummies*, but you went to Harvard."

I hated when people mentioned my Harvard education. I wasn't superior because of it or at all, but I did push the limits. "I'm not most people. You think a case like this will get the assistant district attorney?"

"I'd bet on it. He's good. You'd better get solid proof she didn't do it."

"I know."

"Do you think she's innocent?"

I hesitated. "I do. And I hate that."

"Jen, you've got good instincts. Trust them."

"It's not my instincts I don't trust. It's her."

"It's been a long time," Leland said. "Maybe you should cut her some slack?"

"She almost cost me everything."

"But it didn't happen. Yet you're still holding a grudge."

"Maybe, but I'm trying to keep it separate."

"How can I help—within the GBI limits?"

"Can I trust Taylor?"

"Yes."

"He's Steadman's attorney."

"I know, but I'm confident if he knew the truth, he wouldn't be."

I trusted Leland more than anyone. Maybe he was the only person I trusted. "Thanks, Pop."

"My pleasure. Oh, the wife is upset you haven't come to dinner in a while. We need to get a move on that."

"Yes, sir."

My real father bailed shortly before Molly's abduction. My mom barely functioned after her disappearance, so I raised myself. Leland stepped in when I didn't even realize I needed him. Not even Nick, my ex-husband, had done that.

I tapped out a text to him asking if I could meet him at our daughter Alyssa's ballet class instead of picking her up. I no longer cringed at the thought of talking to him, but it didn't give me a warm and fuzzy feeling, either.

Got a second to talk about tonight?

He didn't bother responding, instead, called me. "Hey, I'm out of town, but Heather can drop her off. Do you need her to stick around, or can you get Alyssa home?"

"On second thought, I'll pick her up," I said.

"Heather doesn't bite, you know."

"I know, but I might."

"Got it," he said. "She's moody, anyway. The pregnancy is doing a job on her."

I would have liked to have done a job on Heather when I learned she'd had an affair with my husband, but as much as I couldn't stand the home-wrecker, she wasn't the only reason my marriage had failed. She simply finished what I had started. I owned my part in the destruction of my marriage, but she could have waited her turn.

Parks returned with our food and coffee. "Here you go, partner."

I dropped my chin to my chest and shook my head. "I'm never going to hear the end of this, am I?"

"Probably not." He glanced at the window. "Maybe we should merge. You've got a bigger office."

"And Wite-Out."

"That'll close the deal for me."

"There is no deal, Parks."

"Maybe not yet." He cocked an eyebrow but didn't argue the point. "I'll check in tomorrow."

"Yes, sir."

He nodded and turned to go, then paused. "Hey, one thing."

"What?"

"That Taylor." He scratched the side of his neck casually, but I caught the shift in his tone, just enough to create a mental bookmark.

"What about him?"

"I'm not sure." He leaned his shoulder against the doorframe. He hesitated, then added, "He didn't ask a single question about your qualifications. Just assumed you'd take the case."

"Because Riley insisted, and he's the top defense lawyer in the state, if not in general. I'm sure he knows every PI in the business."

"Or Jessica Steadman recommended you."

"It's possible, but I spoke to Leland. He assured me if Taylor knew the truth about Jessica Steadman, he'd drop her as a client. Besides, we're good, and we were all over the news from that investigation. Who wouldn't want us?"

He flashed a quick grin and reached for the doorknob. "Taylor plays chess. Let's just make sure we're not the pawns." Then he was gone, the door closing with a soft click behind him.

I stared at the papers on my desk for a moment as his words still hung in the air. It was nothing—just a comment. Parks had a habit of tossing those out, little breadcrumbs that didn't feel like much until you looked back and realized they led somewhere. Taylor was slick, but he was Riley's problem, not mine. Still, I reached for my phone, pulled up the encrypted notes app I used for sensitive info, and typed one word with a question mark.

Taylor?
Then I moved on.

I had rented a small space with two offices, a small breakroom, and a small conference room with the money from the Steadman investigation. I hadn't kept her bonus, what I considered hush money, but I'd earned the money she'd paid to find her daughter.

Parks took his usual stance against a wall, arms crossed, silent but observant. The muscle, a beefy guy with cropped hair and enough tattoos to make a biker gang jealous, stood on the opposite side. They played a game of who would look away first, and so far, no one had lost. Taylor settled into the chair beside Riley. He adjusted his cuffs with the air of a man who had never lost a case and didn't intend to start. Riley exhaled, letting her shoulders drop slightly as she glanced at me. If she thought our meeting would be easy, she was in for a rude awakening.

I leaned forward and folded my hands on the conference table. "Let's start simple, Riley. Tell me about your life these days. What's it like to be Riley Chatsworth, trust fund baby, Havard grad, and corporate executive?"

She blinked. "You make me sound like an elitest."

As Leland always said, if the shoe fit. "You said it, not me."

She turned toward Taylor. "This is the part I warned you about." She smiled at me. "You know I've been fortunate to have the things I do, but I worked hard to get where I am today. Very hard."

"I think I read online that you're getting married. Robert something or other? Are you planning a big wedding or something small and private? If you're not in prison, that is."

"Robert Vance." Her voice tightened. "And there isn't going to be a wedding. We're not engaged anymore."

"Oh?" I fought back a smile. Riley had never been good at maintaining romantic relationships. She preferred bed-hopping over commitment. "What happened?"

Taylor made a sound in his throat and shifted in his chair.

Riley ignored him. Though visibly uncomfortable, tucking loose hairs behind her ears and glancing at the table, she answered, "We wanted different things."

I tilted my head. "Like what?"

She tapped her freshly painted nails against the tabletop in a rhythm that barely masked her frustration. "He wanted to retire early, live in Aspen, ski all day, invest in startups, things like that."

"And you didn't?"

"I did not. I want to work. I'm too young to retire."

I lifted a brow. "Why? You've got a trust fund. Your father left you enough money to live three lifetimes without lifting a finger, and Vance is a multimillionaire. Why would you bother working?"

"You know me too well to ask that."

"I don't know you at all."

"I'm still her," she said. "And tell me this, would you quit your job under those circumstances?"

"Probably not, but I don't have your kind of cash, and I don't have a lot of hobbies."

"You used to," she said. "When you could at least pretend not to be obsessed with your sister."

I pressed my lips together and pushed back the anger building in my gut, then I turned to her attorney. "Mr. Taylor, I suggest you advise your client to refrain from pissing off the people hired to prove her innocence."

He leaned toward Riley and whispered in her ear again.

Her posture stiffened. "I apologize." She waited for me to acknowledge it, but when I didn't, added, "Not everyone who inherits money wants to sit around and do nothing."

"Fair enough. So, work is your passion?"

She hesitated. Her gaze flicked away for a beat before returning to mine, and then she nodded. "It gives me purpose."

"Must be a hell of a purpose to make you give up skiing in Aspen with a rich fiancé."

Her lips pressed into a thin line. "What are you getting at?"

"We were friends a long time ago until we weren't. If I'm going to work for you, I need to know everything, and that starts with a basic reintroduction." I pointed to the door. "You're welcome to hire another private investigator if you'd prefer."

She looked at Taylor, who nodded once.

"Go on," she said to me.

"You just said you're the Riley I knew back in the day. Does that mean the one who loved a good time?" I leaned back and smiled, letting nostalgia color my voice just enough to keep her off-balance. "Remember the parties?" I laughed a little for show. "I do. The all-nighters. The way you could turn any dull law school study session into a night that ended with a hangover and a cautionary tale. What was it everyone called you again? One-more-round Riley?"

Her lips quivered. "That was a long time ago."

I fixed my eyes on her. "People don't change that much."

Taylor shifted. "Ms. Wyatt, is this really relevant?"

I shot him a look. "I need to know who I'm dealing with. You're a smart man, Mr. Taylor. You know that people have patterns. Riley, who I knew as a party girl and a cheating liar, suddenly became the face of corporate responsibility and is now a suspect in a murder investigation. I need to know if this is all a game."

Riley's jaw tightened. "I haven't partied like that in over a decade. I don't even smoke weed anymore."

I nodded slowly, letting the silence between us stretch just long enough to become uncomfortable before asking, "So, no vices?"

She hesitated. "Wine."

"Were you drunk the night of the murder?"

"No. I'm only an occasional drinker." Her eyes narrowed. "Not enough to be a problem. Unlike you."

I deserved that. I had been known to hit a bottle of whiskey or wine more often than necessary but had slowed down to almost a stop to get everyone off my back about it. Since finding out the truth about Molly's murder, the need to drown my emotions enough to forget them had all but disappeared. A therapist would have called it closure, which it probably was, but I called it kicking my guilt in the ass and moving forward with my life. Something I realized Molly would want for her big sister.

She shifted in her seat.

"You always wanted to be the center of attention," I said finally, the old bitterness curling at the edges of my words. "The life of the party. You hated being alone. These feelings are hard to change."

She swallowed hard. "Maybe I grew up."

"Maybe," I agreed, watching her closely. "Let's talk about Greg Hoover."

Taylor straightened, but I didn't break eye contact with Riley.

Her hands clenched into fists in her lap. "I didn't kill him."

"You've told me that. How well did you know him?"

Her throat bobbed in a swallow. "He was a client. We engaged professionally, as would be expected."

I watched her as the word hung in the air like a challenge. "Right. A client."

Riley's face remained impassive, but the pulse at her neck betrayed her. She knew I believed there was more to it, and the pressure it put on her, the fear of my saying it out loud, pulled her into a panic.

That confirmed what I'd thought. She and Hoover had a thing.

Taylor cleared his throat. "This line of questioning—"

I cut him off with a palm toward him, then glared into Riley's eyes. "How long were you sleeping with him?"

The color drained from her face. Taylor stiffened beside her. His eyes narrowed. Parks, still silent, exhaled sharply. Though the muscle didn't even flinch, one might have called that a *mic drop*.

I let it sit there, watching the weight of my statement settle over her, the way her carefully constructed composure cracked just slightly under the truth. I was right. She hadn't told anyone. Not even her own lawyer. So, what else had she hidden?

Taylor broke the silence. "May I have a moment with my client, please?"

"Of course."

I grabbed my coffee and motioned for Parks to leave the room with me.

He closed the door behind us. "Holy shit. How did you know?"

I couldn't wipe the smile off my face. "I know Riley. Like I said, most people don't change."

"That was a big risk, putting that out there like that. What if she drops us?"

"She won't." I gulped down the last of my coffee and tossed the cup in the garbage can underneath my desk. "She needs us, Parks. For all her faults, and all mine, we know each other. And she's right to believe I can find Hoover's killer."

He took two large steps toward me, then, standing close enough for me to feel his breath, looked down into my eyes and whispered, "*We*, Jenna. We can find his killer, partner."

The door opened. Taylor cleared his throat. "We're ready."

"Great," I said, bounding toward the conference room. "Let's get this party started."

I softened my expression for the next half of our conversation. Riley needed to feel comfortable, or she'd lie, and I didn't have time for that.

"You told me you came home and found the gun on your counter."

"Yes."

"Where had you been?"

"At work. I stay late most nights."

"Can anyone prove that?"

"I asked for videos from the security cameras," Taylor said. "They should be at my office now. Let me give them a call." He stepped out of the room.

"The police took your clothing, I assume?" Parks asked.

"Yes, and they searched my home."

"Back to when you left work," I said. "Your company is in the 191 Peachtree building, correct?"

"Yes."

"I've never been, but I assume it has twenty-four-hour security?"

"Yes. It maintains twenty-four-seven on-site security services."

"How does it work? Do you need a key card to access? Is there a check-in desk?"

"Visitors are required to check in. Employees have ID key cards."

"Did you leave through the front of the building? Say goodnight to the person at the desk?"

"No. Our elevator goes straight to the parking garage," she said. "If I drive, which I normally do, I use that elevator."

"And bypass security," Parks said.

"As I said, I use a key card, and there are videos, like my attorney said."

"Was anyone else with you? Did anyone see you leave the office?" Parks asked.

"No."

He pushed back from the wall and moved to stand behind me. "Do you own a gun, Ms. Chatsworth?"

"I do not."

"Anymore," I said.

I held off dropping the bomb until Taylor returned.

"My office said the cameras weren't working," he said.

"Not at all suspicious." I cleared my throat. "We're just discussing if Ms. Chatsworth owns a gun." I smiled at Taylor. "Are you aware that your client won the National Rifle Association Pistol Championship in 2010?"

He eyed Riley. I wondered if he had begun to regret taking her on.

"I haven't shot a gun of any kind in years," she said. "I've been focused on my career. I don't even have my carry license."

"According to the news, Tellion Tech is a former PAC client," I said. "How long did you work with them?"

"For ten years," Riley said. "They left us six months ago."

"Why?" I asked.

"They had a fifteen percent increase in high health claims, and multiple subscribers with life-limiting illnesses. It required us to increase our rates to meet their needs."

"So, you charge more for terminally ill patients. Got it."

"No. They require more care, thus they cost more."

"I guess it depends on the way you look at it, but I do understand. We all know insurance isn't cheap these days."

She leveled a dagger-sharp stare at me. "It's not all going into my pocket."

"I'm not saying it is." I jotted down a few notes.

I asked Riley, "And were you sleeping with Hoover after Tellion dropped PAC?"

Her eyes shifted to Taylor. He nodded once.

"For about a month."

I locked eyes with Taylor. "Her affair is going to get out. I need to know everything, or we can't do our jobs effectively."

"Continue," he said.

"How long were you two involved?"

"Ten years."

I heard Taylor swallow.

I gritted my teeth and said, "Wow. That's a long time to work at breaking up a marriage."

She glared at me. "You don't understand."

"He has two kids," Parks said. "Five and three years old."

"I'm aware," she said. "There were breaks in our time together."

I snickered. "He sure kept busy, didn't he?"

"The relationship started out as a fling," she said. "My team and I took his team out to dinner. Dinner turned to drinks. People left, and it was just us. It wasn't intentional."

"It's always intentional," I said. Nick had once said the same thing about him and Heather. *It wasn't intentional.* As if a tornado had ripped their clothes off and locked them together.

"Did his wife know?" Parks asked.

"Yes, but not until recently."

He pursed his lips, then said, "He hadn't told his wife for years? Are you sure about that?"

"No, I'm not."

"Right. You met someone and got engaged in that time as well. Seems a little odd for a ten-year-long fling."

Her gaze flicked to me. "As I said, we spent time apart, but that didn't mean it wasn't serious. I ended my engagement for Greg."

Parks cleared his throat. "Did Hoover know why you ended the engagement?"

"We discussed it, yes. We wanted to be together. He even told Evelyn he wanted a divorce."

"Was this before or after Tellion dropped you?"

"Before."

"What happened next?"

"We continued seeing each other, but out of respect for his wife, we kept our relationship private. He met with an attorney. I ended things with

Robert. We planned to be together. To get married." A tear slid down her cheek. "Why would I murder the man I loved?"

"But you broke up," I said. "Why?"

"He broke it off. One day out of the blue he came to my place and told me it was over. I asked why multiple times, but he just said it had to end. I begged him to stay, but he left without giving me a reason." She cleared her throat. "I came to learn he hadn't left his wife and hadn't filed for divorce."

"You learned this how?" Parks asked.

"She told me." Her posture stiffened. She wasn't shaken. Riley Chatsworth didn't do shaken. She was pissed. "Evelyn threatened me," she said flatly.

"Threatened?" I leaned forward and rested my arms on the table between us. "How, exactly?"

She sighed and shifted in her seat. "She showed up at my place a few weeks ago and banged on the door."

"She came alone?" I asked.

"Yes. She made sure of that."

"Meaning?"

Riley's lips pressed together before she said, "Meaning she waited until Greg was out of town because she didn't want him finding out."

Interesting. That meant Evelyn wanted control of the narrative. "What did she say?"

Her jaw tightened, but then she exhaled sharply. Fixing me with a cold look, she finally said, "She said Greg would never be foolish enough to dismantle his life for someone like me, just a stupid little fling."

Parks let out a slow breath but didn't say anything. Neither did Taylor, who had barely looked up from his legal pad.

I caught the pain in her eyes and felt something like empathy forming in my chest. "Did you believe her?"

Her chin lifted. "I told her that stupid little fling lasted ten years, just two years less than her marriage." She swallowed. "I know Greg loved me. I don't know what happened, but I know he wouldn't have ended things without a reason. Was that reason Evelyn? I don't know, but if it was, she threatened him into staying. He didn't stay because he wanted to."

"That had to sting, though," I said.

Riley's mouth curled slightly, like she knew what I was doing, but she didn't take the bait. "She was desperate. She wanted to put me in my place."

"What place was that?"

Her fingers tapped against her arm. "Beneath her."

Parks asked, "What else did she say?"

She hesitated, just for a second, then sat up straighter. "She said Greg wasn't stupid enough to ruin his life for me. That he had his fun, but he'd never actually leave her. She wanted me to know that loud and clear." Her fingers tightened against her sleeve. "She called me pathetic and delusional if I thought I was anything more than a mistake. That Greg would never risk his reputation, his career, or his family, for someone like me." She closed her eyes for a moment and said, "She just kept saying that, over and over."

Parks cocked his head to the side. "Someone like you?"

Her jaw clenched. "I'm assuming she meant a stupid little fling."

Evelyn saw Riley as less than something disposable. "She didn't just want to insult you," I said. "She wanted you intimidated."

She exhaled a quiet laugh. "She failed. Her threat fell on deaf ears."

"Why do you call it a threat?" I asked.

She went still. "She made it clear that it was."

"What exactly did she say?"

She hesitated again, then met my gaze. "She told me to stay away from Greg and her family. She said if I didn't, I'd regret it."

"Did she say how?"

Riley's tongue flicked against the inside of her cheek before she answered. "She told me I didn't know what she was capable of."

A heavy silence filled the room until Taylor said, "A jury would consider that reasonable doubt, but I need more than that."

"You need the killer," Parks said.

"I do."

"What did you take that to mean?" I asked Riley.

"I don't know."

"You didn't ask?"

Her eyes flashed. "What was I supposed to say? 'Gee, Evelyn, could you clarify how you plan to ruin my life?'"

"Jenna, let's not twist her words," Taylor said.

"I'm not twisting them," I said, keeping my eyes on Riley. "I'm trying to understand them."

She held my gaze for a beat too long before exhaling. "She didn't clarify. But she wanted me to know she could make things difficult."

"Did you believe her?" Parks asked.

Her fingers drummed against her sleeve again, a tiny, anxious tell. "I didn't not believe her, but I didn't exactly write her off as a bitter wife."

"Was that all?" he asked.

She exhaled sharply. "She threw a drink at me and left."

Parks frowned. "She brought a drink with her?"

"No," she said, annoyed. "I was holding a glass of wine when I opened the door. She grabbed it out of my hand and dumped it on me."

Parks muttered something under his breath, but I focused on Riley. "So, just to be clear, she didn't physically hurt you?"

"No. She didn't even touch me."

"Did you tell her husband about any of this?"

Her face darkened. "I left a voicemail asking him to call me. I didn't think telling him through voicemail was the best way to handle it."

I studied her. "And?"

"He never returned my call." Her nostrils flared. "I think she threatened him as well."

"She needed control," I continued. "She didn't just want Greg to stay. She wanted you to know she was the reason he wasn't leaving."

"She was desperate," Riley muttered, crossing her arms tighter. "But that wasn't my problem, and I don't believe he stayed because he loved her. I know he didn't."

"Maybe not," I said. "But if Evelyn was desperate enough to come after you, what else was she willing to do?"

Riley's jaw tightened, and for the first time, I saw something close to hesitation in her expression. She knew something more.

Parks looked at me with his eyebrow raised. He saw it too. "Riley, did you keep seeing Greg after that?"

Riley's fingers flexed against her sleeve. "No."

Parks tilted his head. "No?"

Her eyes flicked between us. "I told you. He had already ended it."

"That's not what I asked. Did you see him again?"

A pause. Then: "Once."

Bingo.

Taylor cleared his throat. "She already stated their relationship ended before Greg's death."

"I heard her," I said, still watching her. "But I also think she's holding something back."

She didn't deny it.

"Riley," I said slowly, "what aren't you telling us?"

Her mouth pressed into a tight line.

"Yeah. That's what I thought."

Riley glared at me. "It's not what you think. I wasn't with him again. I just saw him. We didn't even talk."

My gut screamed that we were circling the truth, but my head refused to let go of the past. I wanted her to be lying. I needed her to be lying because if she wasn't, that meant someone else out there was smart enough, cold enough, to orchestrate the murder. And I was already a few steps behind.

But her silence wasn't like what I remembered from law school days, when she was calculating. This one carried weight and emotion.

And damn it, my gut betrayed me. I had started to believe her. I knew we weren't done there. Not by a long shot. "If you can't tell me the truth, then you might as well leave right now." I looked at Taylor. "Your client isn't being honest with either of us. Don't you consider that a red flag?"

"I went to him, okay? At his apartment in Midtown. I checked his location on my phone and used my key." Tears welled in her eyes.

"Yet you didn't talk to him?"

"He was in his bedroom, and he wasn't alone."

I almost felt bad for her. "He was with his wife."

"No. It wasn't her. I couldn't see well enough to identify the woman, but it wasn't Evelyn."

"Let me get this straight. You checked his location on your phone, drove to his place in Midtown, let yourself in, saw him in bed with someone else, and left." I eyed Taylor. "You've got a lot on your hands with this one."

"I didn't kill him."

"That's what you said, but that right there could be the key that locks your jail cell."

"I know. That's why I need you to find the real killer."

Parks said, "What about Robert? Maybe he found out about your affair and wanted to hurt you the way you hurt him?"

"He didn't have to find out," she said. "I told him."

"Sounds like motive to me," he said.

"He wouldn't do that. He doesn't like to get his hands dirty."

"That's what paid killers are for," he said.

"What about other people?" I asked. "Have you had confrontations with others? Maybe a disgruntled employee? An insured person?"

"I'm the CEO of the biggest health insurance company in the United States. I'm threatened on a regular basis, especially since COVID, but nothing's ever come from any of them."

"When was your most recent one?"

"I'd have to check, but I believe it was about our denial of an experimental drug treatment."

"Mr. Taylor," I said. "We need access to Ms. Chatsworth's laptop. Do you think you can get it?"

"Chandra can get it, but it's all on the cloud," she said. "I can access from any computer, but Chandra would be the one to go to for these things."

"Who's Chandra?" I asked.

"My executive assistant."

Taylor slid a file folder across the table. "Here are my notes from my meetings with Ms. Chatsworth for your review."

"Thank you. One more question, for now. Why were you calling me before Hoover's murder?"

Her eyes shifted between mine and Taylor's. "Because I wanted you to find out who the woman was."

No way in hell would I have taken that job.

3

I tossed the folder onto my desk and sank into my chair, stretching out my legs with an exhale that carried more frustration than I wanted to admit. "She's lying about something," I muttered as I rubbed the bridge of my nose.

Parks leaned against the edge of my desk, arms crossed, eyes fixed on me.

"Of course she is," he said, voice even. "The real question is why."

I hated when he did that, stated the obvious but made it sound like a challenge, like I wasn't already five steps ahead. I rested my elbows on my desk and pointed at him. "You could at least offer me some theories."

He smirked. "How much time do you have? I could come up with a couple hundred, maybe?"

I scoffed, but he wasn't wrong. Riley Chatsworth had dodged just enough questions to make me suspicious, but she was good—too polished, too in control. I knew that game because agents played it all the time.

The desk creaked under his weight. "You got in her head, which I'm assuming was your goal."

I glanced up at him with one brow raised. "That supposed to be a compliment?"

His mouth twitched. "Maybe."

For a beat, the office fell into silence with just the hum of the air vent and the distant murmur of traffic outside. We needed to get started, to at least put together a plan, yet neither of us even suggested it.

He rolled his shoulders, the tension from the interview probably still hanging on him too. He pushed up his sleeves, and for the first time, I noticed the lean muscle in his forearms. I shouldn't have noticed. But I did.

"You're staring," he said, low and quiet.

I blinked and straightened in my chair. "Stare mode. I was thinking."

"Sure." He pushed off the desk and walked to the window to peer out at traffic.

I wasn't sure what annoyed me more—the way he acted like nothing ever got under his skin, or the way he always seemed to know when something got under mine.

"I knew you didn't like her," he said after a moment. "But I didn't realize the intensity of it."

"Not intense enough to not take the case, if that's what you mean."

"That's not what I meant." He turned back and watched me carefully. "It's personal, more so than what you claim."

I didn't answer. He already knew he was right.

Parks stepped closer with his hands in his pockets, posture loose but eyes sharp. "You want to tell me why?"

I held his gaze, frustrated that I felt the slow pull of something I refused to name. "Not really."

Something flickered across his face, amusement, maybe, or just understanding. "Didn't think so."

The silence between us stretched again, that awkward, something-was-happening kind. I should have looked away. I almost said something about it, but instead, I held his stare a second too long.

"She slept with a professor to stay in school."

"Wow." He sounded surprised. "That's a romance novel waiting to be written."

"It was disgusting and desperate."

"But she secured your stay too."

"She didn't do it for me, Parks. She did it to save her own ass."

He tilted his head slightly, like he was waiting for me to say something else. "Did you?"

I blanched. "What? No. He tried, but I threatened to go to the board."

"So, he dropped the accusations against you too."

"Yes."

Parks grabbed his jacket off the chair and headed for the door. "You don't want to be late picking up Alyssa." His voice had softened, not quite an order but not really a suggestion either.

I should have let him leave, but something stopped me. "Parks."

He paused, put his hand on the doorframe, but didn't turn around.

I hesitated. What the hell was I doing? "Good work today."

His fingers drummed against the frame once before he glanced over his shoulder with a knowing look in his eyes. "You too," he said. "See you in the morning. I'll bring the coffee."

And just like that, he was gone.

I let out a slow breath and leaned back in my chair, staring at the door long after he'd disappeared. A woman, middle-aged, with a wiry frame and fury carved into every line of her face, yanked on the door, but it was locked. I walked over and opened it for her, even though I knew I would regret it.

I knew her better than I would have liked, but in situations like that, it was best to act like I didn't. "What can I do for you?"

She charged over, whipped her finger toward me, and shook it ferociously. "You've got a hell of a nerve, you know that?"

I'd heard that before but acted surprised regardless. "Excuse me?"

"You heard me," she snapped. Her voice trembled not from fear but from rage. "I saw your name in that article about the Steadman case. It said you're a PI now." She glanced around my office. "And look at you, setting up shop like you didn't destroy my daughter's life."

I stood fully, palms flat on the desk, and steadied myself. I continued pretending I didn't know her. "Ma'am, you'll have to explain—"

"You don't remember me? I'm Valerie Crandall. My daughter is Trina Crandall."

"Right." I acted as if it had all just clicked. "Trina Crandall. Didn't we arrest Miss Crandall for armed robbery and trafficking methamphetamine with intent to distribute?" Her kid broke the law and got caught, but it was my fault.

"She was innocent."

Every mother's first thought. "As I believe you said back then too, but a jury determined otherwise."

"She was a child!" Her hands shook. "A child!"

"Ma'am," I said with a tone I thought empathetic, but I doubted she would have agreed. "With all due respect, Trina was twenty-one at the time of her arrest, and if my memory serves me well, which it always does, she was caught with a stolen Glock in the waistband of her jeans and a gym bag full of vacuum-sealed packets of meth in the back seat of a car parked behind an abandoned building near East Point."

"It wasn't hers. She was holding it all for a friend."

I'd heard that more times than I could count. "Ma'am, that's the universal excuse for everyone caught with drugs or a weapon."

Her face reddened. "Are you calling my daughter a liar?"

I worried she might stroke out, but I had learned compassion and facts could and should go together in incidents of that nature. "I'm saying a court tried, convicted, and sentenced her to twenty years without parole for her crimes. If she had been holding it for a friend, she should have named him."

Valerie took a step forward with her fists clenched. "She was just a kid. A *kid*. And you," she jabbed a finger at me, "you made sure she never had a chance to grow up. You paraded her in front of the press like some kind of monster. Now you're sitting here with your shiny office and your coffee mug and your second damn career like none of it matters."

I motioned toward the chair across from my desk, but she didn't sit. "I'm sorry you're upset, but I am not responsible for your daughter's bad decisions."

"You destroyed my family. Do you know that? You ruined our lives while you've been out here living yours."

"I'm sorry you feel that way—"

"No, you're not!" she shouted. "You of all people, you lost a sister. That's what they said. A little girl. Kidnapped. Gone forever. So, you *know* what it feels like to lose someone. Yet you still did that to me."

"That's not the same thing."

"The hell it isn't!" she snapped. "You took my baby!"

I let her rage stand for a moment before speaking. "My sister was kidnapped and murdered at only five years old. Your daughter was convicted by a jury, Ms. Crandall. Based on evidence. She had a public defender and was convicted. The decision wasn't mine."

"Oh, please," she sneered. "Like your report didn't set the whole thing in motion. They threw the book at her because of *you*. You painted her as some cartel queen. She wasn't. She was scared and stupid. She was in the wrong place with the wrong people."

"She had a stolen firearm in her possession," I said evenly. "The same Glock used in an armed robbery in Doraville four days earlier. If you don't recall, that was confirmed through ballistic testing. She had over two pounds of meth packaged for sale. That wasn't wrong place, wrong time. It was a deliberate choice."

Valerie's face flushed deep red. "She didn't even know the gun was loaded! She told the truth. It wasn't hers."

"Fine," I said, though I knew the truth. "That may be true, but it doesn't change the fact that she was in possession of it, and that's what the law sees."

"She was only twenty-one!" she screamed. "Barely old enough to drink, and you locked her away like she was some serial killer."

"I didn't lock her away," I said, tone still calm, though I was growing tired of the drama and her continued attempt to defend her guilty daughter. "I followed the evidence. That's what my job was. And the jury found her guilty on both counts. The sentencing was handled by the court, not me. Must we continue this?"

She slammed her hand on the edge of my desk. "You could have said she was cooperative. You could have said she was scared. You could have asked for leniency!"

"I wrote exactly what the evidence showed," I replied, keeping my voice even. "I included her statement. I included the surveillance video of her handing a bag of drugs to a known dealer. I included the dashcam footage from the patrol officer who found the weapon tucked into her waistband."

Her eyes welled with tears, but she didn't back down. "She didn't deserve twenty years. No parole. You made sure they buried her."

"It's not my job to make that decision."

She gritted her teeth. "She's twenty-two. She'll be forty-two when she gets out. Do you know what it's like to visit your child in prison every month? To hear her say she wishes she'd died instead of gotten caught? To know she's in there with murderers and God knows what else?"

"I live every day knowing my sister never got a second chance. Molly didn't get to grow up. She didn't get to make stupid mistakes, to risk losing from playing with the big dogs like your child, and you know what? No one was held responsible for that. And never will be, because he died before we caught him. Your daughter has a chance to continue her life down the line. My sister had that chance taken from her."

Valerie's shoulders shook. She finally slumped into the chair across from me with hands limp in her lap and tears running freely. "She was a good kid," she whispered. "She was funny. She was so smart. She wanted to be a vet."

"I'm sorry," I said. "But your daughter made choices that had consequences."

Her head snapped up again, her anger flaring once more. "Don't you dare say that. Don't you sit there and pretend like this is on her. You could've stopped it."

"Okay, we're done here." I stood, walked to the door, and opened it. "If you truly believe that, then I suggest you file a formal grievance against me and the GBI. The records are public. The trial transcripts are available. But I will not apologize for doing my job."

Valerie stood slowly. "Do you sleep at night knowing you took my baby away?"

"I sleep knowing I did the right thing based on the law and the evidence. That's what justice is. Not feelings. Not wishes." I held the door open. "Have a nice day."

She said nothing as she walked past me. But I knew the tears fell harder as she crossed the threshold.

When the door clicked shut behind her, I stood there for a moment, the echo of her pain still hanging in the air. Then I walked back to my desk and sat.

Grief had a thousand faces, but justice never came without someone bleeding.

The late afternoon sun blazed across the pavement as I stepped outside. The heat wafted over me and curled off the asphalt in hazy waves. I immediately began to sweat. I smelled grilled burgers from the pub down the street and the sharper tang of exhaust fumes from cars that crept through Roswell's downtown traffic. Atlanta's rush hour started at 2 p.m. and never ended. I dug into my bag and grabbed my key card just in case I needed to figure out how to lock the door with it. I didn't. The lock did what it was supposed to, automatically lock. I stuffed the key card back into my purse.

I slid into my Bronco and exhaled sharply from the sweltering air and burning leather and pressed the ignition button. The engine thrummed to life and vibrated under my grip. I reached for the radio, but my fingers hesitated over the dial. Something tugged at my senses, a quiet prickle at the back of my neck. I flicked my gaze to the rearview mirror and caught a black sedan idling across the street. Its tinted windows swallowed any glimpse of the driver.

"Relax, Wyatt," I muttered. "Not every car in Roswell follows you." Still, a thread of unease coiled in my gut. I pulled onto Canton Street, the familiar rhythm of the afternoon filling the space around me. Pedestrians wove between parked cars, and laughter spilled from patios lined with string lights already on even though the sun wouldn't set for hours. Life happening, moving forward, because that's what it did. I wondered how Evelyn Hoover and her two children would get through it.

I checked the mirror again. The sedan followed at a comfortable distance, unhurried and unobtrusive.

"Coincidence," I said, gripping the wheel tighter. I tapped my fingers against the leather at the light for Woodstock Road and watched the car through half-lowered lashes. The light flashed to green. I eased forward. So did the sedan. My pulse quickened.

"This cannot be happening again." I made an unnecessary turn onto Norcross Street. The sedan mirrored me. I sucked in a breath through clenched teeth. "Okay, buddy. Let's see if you're following me or I'm just paranoid."

I swung a right onto Alpharetta Street, then an immediate left onto Magnolia. The car mimicked every move. I swallowed hard, gripping the wheel so tightly my knuckles blanched.

I tried to convince myself it wasn't a replay of the Steadman case and the way they knew my every move before I made it. My stomach twisted into a knot.

"Not again," I muttered. "Not this time."

I angled my rearview mirror for a better view. The black car remained steady, not closing in, not hanging too far back. Careful, but controlled. Following me like a pro, only not professional enough for me to miss it.

I scanned the street ahead to plot my next move, then jerked the wheel to the left, cutting across two lanes to take a last-minute turn onto Mimosa Boulevard. Tires squealed. Horns blared. My heart slammed against my ribs. I checked the mirror. The sedan followed, smooth and unfazed.

"Damn it." My breath hitched. I forced myself to focus. The afternoon rush thickened as cars clogged intersections and limited my opportunities. I calculated my options. The best-case scenario was to circle back toward Canton Street and possibly lose them in the congestion, but if they anticipated that—

No. I needed a hard out.

I took Canton to Holcomb Bridge toward 400. Traffic moved at a decent clip because of the green light. I braced myself, kept my speed even, and still pretended I hadn't noticed the car, though my lane switch before might have given me up.

The light turned green. I floored it and weaved between slower cars. A truck driver blared his horn, and another one flipped me off as I cut in front of him. I checked the mirror. The black sedan kept pace but was still a few cars behind.

I yanked the wheel and jerked onto the on-ramp for 400. My tires bit into the pavement and gripped the curve. The highway stretched ahead with cars crowded like sardines in each lane. I merged between a box truck and a sedan as my heart hammered against my ribs.

"Come on," I breathed. My eyes flicked between the road and my mirror. "Follow me."

The black car continued straight, passing the entrance ramp completely.

I let out a breath so sharp it stung my lungs.

Traffic pressed around me, swallowing my Bronco in a sea of brake lights. I glanced at the mirror again. The sedan had vanished, lost in the mess of vehicles streaming through Roswell's surface streets.

Still, my fingers remained tight around the wheel. The unease lingered like an itch beneath my skin. Maybe they could merge onto 400, or maybe they had never followed me at all.

"Maybe I'm losing it," I muttered. "I'm talking to myself, so it's possible." Or maybe, just maybe, they wanted me to know they had been there, watching me.

I made it to pick up Alyssa without a tail and hoped I'd just made something out of nothing, but I didn't take any chances. The Bronco rolled to a stop a few homes down from Nick's. I kept my foot on the brake and scanned the area for the sedan or anything that looked out of place. I'd lived there long enough to know what fit in and what didn't, people included.

"Hey, Jenna. You look great," Heather said when she opened the door to my former home. "Is that a new shirt?"

I glanced down at the black button-down I'd had for a few years, then up at her. "Heather?"

She shifted her weight from side to side. "I'm just—"

"I know, trying to make conversation, and I appreciate it, but I don't want Alyssa to be late for ballet."

She offered me a half-hearted smile. "Come on in. I'll get her."

"I'll wait out here."

She left the door open and walked toward the kitchen. Heather had tried to make amends, but I wasn't ready, but not because she had Nick and I didn't. I had lost some of the bitterness for her responsibility in things, but I still struggled with the idea of her having more time with my daughter than I did. My problem, not hers. I had fought Nick for equal custody but ultimately realized it wasn't an option because of my job, but if I had time during his days with Alyssa, he had come to a place where he would let me have her without a fight.

Alyssa ran to the door and wrapped her arms around my legs. "Mommy!" She looked up at me. "Did Heather tell you I'm the star of the recital?"

I crouched down and squeezed her shoulders. "She thought you should tell me." Heather hadn't mentioned it, so I assumed. "You'll have to tell me all about it on the way." I picked her up and held her for a moment, then set her down and summoned the biggest smile I could for Heather. "I'll have her home after dinner."

"Take your time."

I clipped Alyssa into her booster seat while she rattled on about the recital. "It's called Twinkle Toes, and I get to kiss the audience!"

I feigned shock as I stared through the rearview mirror at her. "Kiss? Boys will be in the audience!"

"Ew. Not a real kiss. I'm blowing them one, and then I get to do a curtsy with everyone else behind me. I'm the star."

"That's going to be so amazing. I can't wait to see it."

"It's next week. Oh, mama, you have to stay in your car during practice. Ballet Master Jasmine says it's a surprise."

"I'll wait right outside my car for you."

"Okay. She will come outside when we're done, so you don't have to worry about me, okay?"

"Baby, I will always worry about you."

Her brows pinched together, her nose scrunched up slightly, and her head tilted to the side. "Why? I'll be with Ballet Master Jasmine."

"I know, but moms worry about their kids. It's just what we do."

"Oh. I worry about you sometimes too."

"You don't have to worry about me, Liss. I'm pretty darn tough."

"I know, but I miss you, and you miss me too, right?"

My heart shattered like glass. "Every single minute I'm not with you."

"See? I worry because that's a lot."

"I have Bob, remember?"

"Yes! And I know he loves you, so that's good."

"Then it's settled. Don't worry about me, okay?"

"Okay." She kicked the back of my passenger seat. "Can I tell you a secret?"

"You can always tell me anything, Alyssa."

She whispered, "I worry sometimes about other things."

No parent wanted their child to worry about anything. "About what, baby?"

"Esther Boone wet her pants last week during class. The boys laughed at her and got in big trouble."

"Poor Esther. She must have been embarrassed."

"She had to go home. The next day we all had to bring extra pants and undies just in case it happened to us."

I tried not to smile. "You're worried you're going to have an accident too."

"I don't like being embarrassed."

"No one does, but I don't think it's going to happen. I was in school a very long time and that never once happened, so I think you'll be okay."

She looked out the window. "I hope so. Heather made me take my red leggings as my pants, and I don't like wearing those."

"I think your red leggings are super cute."

"You do?"

The surprise in her tone made me smile. "I do."

"Can I tell you another secret?"

"Of course."

She leaned forward in her booster seat and whispered, "There's a man who always sits outside the coffee shop Daddy takes me to on Saturdays. He wears a suit and has a really fancy watch. He's always looking at his phone but never buys anything."

I glanced at her through the rearview mirror. "Did your daddy or Heather talk to him?"

"Nuh-uh. Daddy doesn't talk to people at the coffee shop. Neither does Heather. They say that's our special time together."

My stomach burned at the thought of Heather spending that kind of time with my kid. I should have been happy she gave her that attention, but I'd have to get by the jealousy of it before that would happen. "That sounds fun. A lot of people do work for their jobs at coffee shops sometimes instead of their offices. Maybe he does."

"Maybe. He smiles at me a lot. He looks nice. Maybe he could be your boyfriend? We can go there and see him."

"What does he look like?" I asked. Not because I wanted a boyfriend, but because I wanted to know who my kid noticed and if he had noticed her too.

She shrugged. "He's like daddy. Tall and dark hair."

Daddy wasn't what I would have called tall, but to someone tiny like her, it made sense. "Maybe we'll go by there sometime, but I don't have time for a boyfriend right now, sweetie."

"Heather says if you had one, you wouldn't spend so much time worrying about her. I think it's nice you worry about her."

I chuckled, knowing that wasn't what Heather had meant. "I guess I'm just a nice person." I turned left and then said, "If you see him again, do me a favor, okay? Point him out to Heather and tell her I'd like to know exactly what he looks like."

"Okay!"

A fancy-dressed man with a nice watch at the coffee shop. Could have been anyone, but of course, my hackles shot up, and I worried he was there because of me.

I headed straight home after dropping Alyssa off from class and a quick slice of pizza at Johnny's. Bob met me at the door, meowing as if he hadn't eaten in weeks. He darted to the kitchen and sat by his bowl. I set my things on the counter and grabbed a can of cat food from the pantry. His meowing escalated. "You're not starving, Bob. Be patient." I grabbed his empty bowl and replaced it with a clean one. He let out a sharp, sassy meow in response.

"Here you go," I said as I set the saucer on the floor. "Eat slow."

Bob didn't listen. He never did.

A quick shower, a change into sweats and a sweatshirt, and my long hair twisted up into a clip at the top of my head, and I was ready in under ten minutes to fall onto the couch and relax before my world focused on Riley Chatsworth.

The familiar tap hit the door just as I padded down the hall toward the couch. "Parks," I muttered. I swung it open, and there he stood, file box in hand. "You're supposed to let me know you're coming. That's what the gate system at the entrance is for. What if I had a guest over?"

He smirked. "You mean I've got competition?"

"Like you'd even have a chance." My eyes followed him as he walked into my apartment. I slammed the door shut.

He set the box on my coffee table, took a seat, and opened it. He removed a file and set it beside the box. "It's the autopsy report."

I snatched it up and plopped onto the couch. "Already? So much for a night of relaxation before kicking into high gear."

"Sorry about that, but you know these high-profile cases get preferential treatment."

I scanned the report. "Minimal bleeding from the gunshot wound even though the heart was pumping before being shot."

I flipped the page and narrowed my eyes. "Significant arterial blockage, signs of ischemic damage, pulmonary edema. His heart was a disaster waiting to happen."

"Managing two women at once for that long would kill most men."

I whacked him on the arm. "Nice."

He shrugged. "One woman at a time is hard enough."

"Says the king of one-night stands."

He pushed his shoulder into mine. "There's a reason for that."

"Really? Please, share that with me so I can understand how men justify one-nighters."

"Just looking for the hardest one to take on."

"Weak." I went back to the report. "The coroner said he had a heart attack, right?"

"Yes. DA doesn't care about the heart attack, though. He cares about the murder one charge, and he'll get it however he can."

"You don't think they're covering up something? Like maybe this Hoover guy died and then someone shot him?"

"Because murder makes the news, and a heart attack doesn't?"

"Maybe?" A chill worked its way up my spine. "Something's off about this whole thing. I just can't figure out what." I didn't trust Riley, not fully, maybe not at all. But I trusted the feeling in my gut when something didn't add up. And nothing about Hoover's murder added up.

"Convenient, huh?"

"Too much so." I stared at the report, then scooted to the end of the couch. "So, someone comes into Hoover's house and shoots him to frame Riley. Why?"

"Maybe Evelyn did it."

"But then she'd have to drive all the way to Midtown, get into Riley's place, leave the gun, then drive back. I don't think that fits."

"It's happened before," he said. He stood and walked into my kitchen, poured himself a glass of orange juice, and sat on the opposite side of the couch. "And it doesn't look like anyone broke in, so whoever did it had access to the home."

"How'd you get the box?"

"I called Taylor after I left the office and said we needed two copies of everything they had. According to the guy who delivered it to me, it's most of what the prosecution has, but they're withholding some things from him."

"He already filed a discovery request, and the DA compiled everything this fast?" I peeked into the box. "That's rare."

"It's Harris Taylor. They don't screw around with people like him."

I sifted through the papers. "Did they say anything about the 911 call?"

"Not yet."

I set the papers on the couch. "We'll need that eventually."

"I'll call Taylor first thing tomorrow. For now, why don't you grab a bunch of your sticky notes and highlighters, and we'll go through this."

"All right, let's start with the police report and break it down." My hair bun slipped to the side. I removed the clip and set it on the table, letting my wet hair hang over my shoulders.

"Yes, ma'am."

I ignored that. "Mrs. Hoover called 911 at exactly 10:34 p.m. She reported arriving home to find her husband unresponsive in his study. She couldn't find a heartbeat. The report says she sounded panicked but coherent."

"Why didn't she say he was dead when she talked to the operator?" he asked. "It was a head shot. She had to know."

"I'm assuming she was in shock, but that's to be determined."

Parks's eyes fixed on me rather than the report. "Probably."

Why did that staring make me uncomfortable? "What are you staring at me for?"

"Because you look cute with your hair down like that."

My eyes locked with his for a few seconds before I dropped them back to the report. "They were on the scene by 10:42 p.m. Eight minutes to respond, which isn't bad, considering their station's location. The first officers on the scene found the front door slightly ajar, which Mrs. Hoover claims was her doing when she ran out to meet them."

"Two officers immediately secured the perimeter while the others entered the house," Parks said. "They found Hoover in his study with a single gunshot wound to the head, no sign of a struggle. The study was described as orderly, except for the chaos directly around his body, a knocked-over chair, things suggesting he might have been taken by surprise." His gaze lingered on me a moment too long as he waited for a response.

"According to the officers' observations and Mrs. Hoover herself, nothing was missing from the house. The officer says it looks like a targeted hit, not a robbery gone wrong."

He stretched his legs. "That sounds like a professional job more than a jilted girlfriend or angry wife."

"I agree," I said.

"Makes me wonder who stood to gain from his death."

"There's a nanny listed as being upstairs with the kids. She claims she didn't hear anything." I continued reading. "In Mrs. Hoover's initial statement, she said she believes Riley had a motive and the means to kill him, citing the breakup and her access to a weapon."

"That sounds planned," he said. "How would she know Riley had access to a weapon? And what about getting inside the house?"

"I don't have an answer to the gun question. She claims her husband recently told her Riley knew the garage code, and that she asked him to change it, but he hadn't yet."

"Convenient," he said.

"I agree." I pushed my hair behind my ears. "If Evelyn didn't kill him, maybe she knows who did. We need to do a deep dive into Hoover's background, his business dealings, and personal grudges."

"Interesting," Parks said, scanning the report again. "No one asked where she had been at the time of the murder."

"Poor policing," I said. "Happens often, unfortunately."

"I would have been kicked out of NCIS for that rookie mistake."

I removed the envelope with the crime scene photos from the file and flipped through them. The wound close-up captured my attention. "Did you see this?" I showed him the photo. "The wound is practically clean."

"I did. I know."

"It's strange. He had a bad heart. I guess that might have something to do with it."

"Agreed," he said. He removed the arrest warrant and affidavit from his folder.

"The arrest warrant and affidavit have more info," he said. A grim expression tugged down the corners of his mouth as he scanned the papers. "You're not going to like them."

"You already went through all this? Why didn't you tell me?"

"Just briefly, while you were at ballet with your daughter. I don't have a photographic memory like you, so I'll need to go over it a few times to piece things together."

I studied a picture of the weapon. "She could shoot this gun with her eyes closed. Where's the silencer? There had to be one if the nanny didn't hear the shot."

"I thought the same thing. We'll need an answer to that. But Riley's fingerprints are all over it, Jenna." He drummed his fingers on the arm of the sofa. "Read the thing. Tell me what you think."

I read the document quickly and then looked at him, shocked. "She lied to us. She said she found the gun on her counter."

"She did say that."

I snorted and tossed the page onto the table. Irritation prickled beneath my skin. "What a piece of work. She hasn't changed at all."

Parks sighed. He leaned back and stretched his arms behind his head.

"I'm not defending her, but she could have a reason for lying. Either way, we've got a serious credibility issue on our hands."

"If she's lying to the cops, they'll crucify her on the stand. And if she's lying to us, that's even worse."

He flipped through his copy slowly. "Hoover's wife made the call at 10:34 p.m. The police got there minutes later, found Hoover dead from a single gunshot wound to the head. No forced entry, no immediate signs of struggle, and they sealed the scene right away. Like I said, it all feels like a setup."

I reached for the initial responding officer's report and skimmed it again.

"It's not going to change since you read it the first time," Parks said.

"I know that, smartass. I'm just seeing if I've missed anything. But it's odd to me that the wife is okay enough to point the finger directly at Riley. As for the nanny, she was watching TV in her room with her headphones on so the kids didn't wake up. What's your thought on that?"

"How does she know when they need her?"

"Probably has cameras." I ran my hand through my hair. "I don't know what or who to believe."

"We'll get a better handle on who's lying and telling the truth."

I let out a heavy breath. "I'm not sure any of them are."

"Here's the thing. Hoover had a complex network of connections and plenty of rivals. If we don't find anything to move on, we'll have to talk to them, but right now, Riley's deception is glaring. She said she picked up the gun, so we know how the residue got on her hands."

Frustration boiled inside me. "But why would Riley risk everything and shoot Hoover in cold blood, then just casually leave the murder weapon lying out in the open on her kitchen counter?"

"Exactly my question," he said. "She's either panicked and stupid, or someone placed that gun intentionally."

"She's got a Harvard law degree. She knows better than to leave the gun out in the open."

I rubbed my forehead to ward off a headache forming behind my eyes. "Unless she's counting on that logic to save her. Think about it. If it looks too staged, people might think she couldn't possibly be that careless."

He nodded. "Could be. Or someone wanted it precisely this way to frame her. Which circles us right back to Hoover's wife and her perfectly timed tip."

I yawned. "We need to talk to Riley. No more subtle questions. If she can't look us straight in the eyes and explain this convincingly, we've got a much bigger problem than we thought."

"Subtle? Not a word I'd associate with anything you do."

I shrugged. "Valid point."

Parks stood. "We'll hit her with the contradictions and watch her carefully."

4

Parks walked into my office carrying two coffees again. It had become a thing.

"Do you really have an office, or did you break into someone else's and pretend it's yours?"

"If I said I didn't, would you give me some space in this one?"

"Not in a million years, Parks." I had just finished printing several articles I found on the internet as well as background checks on Hoover, his wife, and, of course, Riley Chatsworth.

He eyed the two stacks of papers on my desk and then handed me a cup. "You've been busy."

"Couldn't sleep, so I came in early."

"You should have called me. I would have come then."

I handed him one of the piles. "I'm a big girl, Parks. I can work on my own."

"Partners, though. Remember?"

I tipped my head back. "Remind me to let you work for free next time."

He grinned. After skimming the papers, he looked up at me and asked, "She filed for a legal separation?"

"Twice, but neither filed the maintenance action."

"Georgia requires that for a legal separation, right?" he asked.

I took a sip of my coffee. "Yes. Without going to court for it, the separation isn't legal."

"So, she filed, but changed her mind?"

"Could have been just a threat."

He studied the two petitions. "The most recent one was about a month ago."

"Which makes me think that's why he dumped Riley. Because his wife threatened to leave him and he didn't want to lose half his income."

"No, she threatened to take his money but not divorce him. She wanted her lifestyle, but she didn't want him to be free."

"And the only way he could be was to break up with Riley, then divorce Evelyn on his own, without the legal ramifications of the legal separation," I said.

"He'd have to pay something in the interim," Parks said.

"Right, but he would have the upper hand. If she made the first move, it's possible she wouldn't get as much."

"Is that what you did with Nick?" He smirked. "Kidding."

"I don't need Nick's money."

"At least not since Steadman paid us so well."

"Remind me to vet our potential clients better next time."

He pretended to shoot me with his finger. "Our potential clients."

I rolled my eyes so hard I felt it. "Did you call Taylor yet?"

He removed his cell from his pocket. "Doing it now."

"Don't," I said. "I want to talk to Riley without him." I grabbed my bag. "Let's go."

"You planning to call her on the way?"

"Nope."

He grinned. "This should be entertaining."

"I'm hoping for informative and truthful."

"Come on," he said. "I'm driving."

The morning rush hour traffic crawled down 400 toward the city, giving

Parks the opportunity to switch radio stations a million times to "find the perfect rush hour music."

"That's what Spotify's for," I said.

"I like a variety, not the same playlist over and over."

"Yet you listen to SiriusXM, where they play the same tracks on a loop every day."

"Drink your coffee," he said. "We need you human for this interview."

I laughed. "What am I now?"

He chewed on his bottom lip, then said, "I'd rather not say."

"That's probably a smart move."

Parks had one hand on the wheel and the other draped casually over his thigh, but his eyes flicked toward the rearview mirror every few minutes like he wanted to make sure no one had tailed us.

I leaned against the passenger door with my head tilted toward the window. "You good?"

He didn't answer right away. Just gave a little nod and said, "Yeah." The word carried no weight. Just sound.

His phone rang before I could press the issue. He grumbled something about never getting a moment and tapped the screen on the console.

"Parks," he said.

A man's voice came through the car speakers, low, unfamiliar, but laced with something I couldn't quite place. "Cowboy, it's Turtle."

Parks eyed me.

I shrugged, having no clue who that was. *Turtle? Cowboy?*

He looked back at the congested traffic. "Hey, Turtle, you're on my Bluetooth, and I have someone in the car. It's been a long time. You still pretending you can surf?"

"Not anymore, man," he said, but he didn't laugh. "Listen, I got some news this morning, and I'm passing it along."

Parks sat up a little straighter. "What's going on?"

There was a pause long enough for me to shift in my seat.

"It's Commander Nash," Turtle finally said. "His neighbor found him dead in his house this morning. She just called me."

Parks didn't move. Didn't blink, but his fingers tightened on the steering wheel so hard his knuckles whitened. "No," he said, almost too quietly to hear.

"Yeah," Turtle replied. "I thought you'd want to know."

"Yeah, yeah. Of course. Do they know what happened?"

"Said it looks like a heart attack, but they'll do the autopsy."

"What neighbor found him?"

"Cheryl. The one on his right. You meet her?"

"A while ago, yeah. Haven't seen Nash in a few years."

"Me neither. She said she saw his paper still on the porch and went in. Found him on the couch, remote in one hand, dog curled up beside him. EMTs said it looked like he went peaceful."

I glanced at Parks. His jaw worked, but no words came out. His eyes stayed locked on the road, but I knew a storm brewed behind them.

"You okay, man?" Turtle asked.

"No," Parks said, voice rough. "Not really."

"He was tough as nails," Turtle said, trying to sound light. "But his heart —remember how he used to joke that coffee was the only thing keeping it going?"

"Yeah," Parks murmured. "He said if it ever gave out, it'd better be on his terms. I always hoped he was joking."

"We all did."

Parks nodded like Turtle could see him. He rubbed a hand over his mouth, then tapped the steering wheel with his index finger, over and over.

"Funeral details will come later," Turtle said. "I just—I didn't want to wait. Figured you deserved to hear it from someone who gets it."

"Thanks, brother," Parks said, his voice strained. "You let me know if the family needs anything."

"Will do." Turtle cleared his throat. "Hang in there, Cowboy."

The call disconnected.

We drove for a few more seconds in silence. Then he pulled off 400 at exit two and into the first business with a parking lot and shifted his truck into park. He didn't say anything. Just stared out the windshield, his fingers flexing against the steering wheel like he wanted to punch something but didn't know where to aim.

"You want to talk about it?" I asked softly.

He didn't answer right away. "I didn't keep in touch the way I should have," he finally said. "He wasn't just my boss. Hell, he was the reason I made it through my first year. I was fresh out of FLETC, all ego and no clue, and he put me in my place without saying a word. Just had this way of looking at you that made you want to be better." He paused, then asked, "Do you know what FLETC stands for?"

"Federal Law Enforcement Training Centers. Tell me what he was like."

"Quiet," he said. "Sharp. He didn't waste words. Didn't suffer fools. He had a freezer full of frozen burritos and a microwave in his office. Ate one every day he was there. And he knew when to push and when to back off, which made him a hell of a leader and a scary good interrogator."

I let the silence stretch for him. Sometimes the best thing you could do was just sit in it with someone.

He sucked in a deep breath and blew it out. "I was going through some stuff a few years ago," he said. "Personal. Didn't tell anyone. He shows up at my place with a six-pack and says, 'You're not as invisible as you think you are.' We sat on my porch for three hours and didn't talk about any of it. Just drank. Watched the street. But I'll be damned if it didn't help."

I felt something pinch behind my ribs. Parks never got emotional—not that I had seen. Not even close. He was the steady one, the wall I had begun to lean on when things spun sideways, but he looked like someone had yanked the foundation out from under him.

"I'm sorry," I said, because there wasn't anything else to say.

He nodded once, then looked down at his hands. "I think I always thought I'd see him again. Say the stuff I didn't say when I had the chance. That's the part that gets you, you know? The stuff you don't say."

"I know." I had more experience in that than I had ever wanted, and he knew I understood.

He stared ahead. I caught his reflection faint in the glass. Then he reached to the side and shifted into drive. "We've got work to do."

"You sure you're okay?" I asked.

"All good."

I pressed my forehead against the cool window and watched the sea of brake lights flicker in the early haze. A little later, I said, "Bear right here, toward Peachtree Road." I wasn't sure what to do, so I acted normal. It's what I would have wanted in that situation. "I don't know how anyone can live here. The traffic is horrible."

"It's horrible by us too," he said.

"True, but it somehow seems less than this."

"More traffic lanes. At least in some places."

I eyed the affluent district known for its pricey real estate and high-end shopping. "This is Riley territory, all right." Towering office buildings and luxury boutiques lined our route. "She's probably visited every shop around here. It's her kind of playground—expensive and exclusive."

Parks snorted, a smirk playing on his lips as he dodged a particularly aggressive taxi. "Explains why she chose to live right in the thick of it. Nothing like being a stone's throw from your favorite designer stores."

I nodded as my thoughts briefly flicked to Riley's penchant for the finer things. "She used to shop at all the luxury stores in Boston. I'd go with her wearing my Levi's and a T-shirt while she wore every designer on the market. I couldn't afford that kind of clothing, but I went anyway."

"That's what friends do," he said.

"I guess."

As we turned onto Peachtree Road, the upscale façade of her apartment building came into view, its modern lines glaring under the brightening sky.

"There it is." I pointed. "Can't miss it with all those expensive cars parked out front."

Miraculously, Parks found a parking spot nearby. We walked into the building and greeted the doorman.

"We're here to see Riley Chatsworth," I said.

The man's eyes narrowed for a split second before he smiled. "Is Ms. Chatsworth expecting you?"

"We're with her attorney," Parks said. "We should have twenty-four-seven access."

"Yes, of course. I'll need your identification and for you to sign in."

"No problem," Parks said.

Five minutes later, we exited the elevator on the eleventh floor and walked to her unit.

Riley's security person answered the door. "IDs, please."

A familiar voice inside the condo said, "Darlin', they're with the band. Please let them in."

He let us in, and a black Chihuahua proceeded to attack Parks's shoe.

"Off," he said, shaking his leg.

A woman rushed in and swept the dog into her arms. "Sorry," she said. "He's very protective of his home." The dog growled and snapped at her shoulder.

"Clearly," Parks said. "But I'm sure he's different with the people he loves."

"Not at all." She whispered, "He's a tyrant. He loves Ms. Chatsworth, and that's it." She hurried off with the dog still in attack mode.

Tiffani Bateman swept into the room like she'd just stepped off the pages of *Southern Living*, every inch of her polished and poised as usual. Blond hair coiffed to perfection, pearls resting against a pastel dress that belonged at a garden party, not on a bodyguard, which was what I assumed she was. She moved with a confidence that came from beauty queen crowns and cotillion seasons, her syrupy Southern drawl smoothing over every word. On the surface, she looked like she'd offer the bad guys sweet tea and a slice of pie, but I knew better. Beneath the lipstick and hairspray, the girl wasn't some aging debutante; she was former FBI and the female version of 007. She carried herself like a woman who hadn't seen the worst the world had to offer, but secretly had, and walked away without a scratch.

"Well, if it isn't the dynamic duo," she said. "I was so glad to hear Harris hired you to get to the truth."

Harris? She called Riley's attorney by his first name? "Nothing but the best for my college bestie." Despite my effort to hide it, the sarcasm crept through. "What brings you here? We met different security yesterday."

"Harris asked me to step in for this one. He thought Riley would be better with a female lead."

"I didn't know you work for him," I said.

"I'm on a contract, like you." She wrapped me into a hug.

My body instinctively stiffened.

"Darlin'," she whispered. "You have got to let people in. A hug won't kill you."

I wrapped my arms around her and hugged her back. Surprisingly, I didn't spontaneously combust.

"How are you, really?" she asked.

"I'm good, Tiffani. I promise."

"Good. Should we call Harris?"

"Nope," I said. "This shouldn't take long."

"Would you mind if I stayed with you?"

"We're on the same team," I said.

"That we are, darlin'. That we are."

Riley walked out from the bedroom. "Oh, hey. I wondered when I'd see you again."

"Surprise," I said. "This won't take long. We just have some additional questions."

"Then I've got answers." She sat on her leather sectional and faced the large TV hanging on the wall.

Parks and I sat on the other side, facing a spectacular view of the city skyline.

"Nice view," Parks said. "Bet this cost a pretty penny."

"Just a few," she said. "But I love it." She glanced at her dark wood coffee table and added, "I bought it last year. I hope I don't have to trade it for a prison cell."

Thanks for the lead in. I watched her carefully for any micro-expressions. "Then why did you lie to us yesterday?"

Her hat trick of expressions clearly conveyed her feelings. First, a fleeting sadness flicked across her face, showing guilt, then a slight nostril flare for shock, and the grand finale, squinted eyes to feign confusion. "Lie? I didn't."

Parks removed the police report from his file. "You told us you found the gun on your kitchen counter."

"No, I said I put the gun on my counter."

"Is that what you're going with?" I asked.

"I'm sorry. I'm not sure I understand."

"Riley, cut the BS. You lied. You told the police you found it in front of your door. Why change your story?"

"It was an upsetting situation. I wasn't thinking clearly. It was outside. I didn't want my neighbors to see it, so I picked it up and put it inside on my kitchen counter."

"That's a big difference," Parks said. "And it's one that could work in your favor."

"How so?" she asked.

"It's a reason for having your prints on the gun as well as why they found gunpowder on your hands."

A woman walked out from the kitchen carrying a tray of glasses and a pitcher of ice water.

"Or you told them something different to cover your actions." I thanked the woman for the water.

"It's not like that," she said.

Parks took a sip of his water. "Then tell us what it's like."

She twisted her fingers into a knot. "There are things I can't explain."

"Eh." The sound came hard, like slamming a door I had no intention of reopening. My legs moved before my brain caught up. I was up. Done. Ready to walk out the damn door.

"Wait," Riley said. "It's not what you think."

"It never is with you. I told you I needed honesty, but apparently, we have a different definition of the word." I eyed Parks. "If you want to work this, feel free, but I'm out of here."

My boots hit the floor harder than I'd meant, but that didn't stop me.

"I'm afraid they'll come for me next."

I stopped dead in my tracks. Turning around slowly, ready to regret that small move, I asked, "Who?"

She looked at Tiffani and flicked her head to the side.

"No," I said. "Tiffani stays. She's here to protect you, and she can't do that without knowing the full story."

"Okay," Riley said.

I stood my ground, choosing to be ready to bolt over giving her the benefit of the doubt.

"You've got five minutes to prove to me you're worth it."

She exhaled and turned toward Tiffani. "She means that."

Tiffani said, "Then if you don't want to spend your life in jail, it's best you get on with it."

"Greg was friends with Dr. Jessica Moore, a clinical pharmacologist who works for Vireon, the pharmaceutical company owned by PAC."

I checked my watch. "Four minutes."

"Dr. Moore has been working on a clinical trial for a cancer medicine that could replace chemotherapy. Tellion has multiple insured members and dependents with various types of cancers, all stage three and four. She wanted to offer the clinical testing to his patients, and Greg was all for it, until he saw the cost."

"Aren't clinical trials usually free?" Parks asked.

"Only partially. Insurance covers standard-of-care costs during clinical trials. Things like labs, imaging, doctor visits they'd pay for even outside the trial. The trial sponsor, usually a pharmaceutical company or research institution, pays for the experimental drug or intervention itself. In our case, it's our pharmaceutical company, Vireon Pharmaceuticals, so even though they're running the trial, there is a cost to the employer group, and Greg didn't want to pay the increased fees."

"What type of increase are you talking about?" I asked.

"While the medicine itself is of no cost to the employer group or member, administrative costs typically rise for insurers offering access to the trial. More appointments, lab work, case management, prior authorizations, specialized care coordination, to name a few. Most trials increase utilization of services like extra scans, tests, and hospital stays, all part of the insurance plan purchased by the company, which means a higher medical loss ratio.

"It also depends on the phase of the trial, but Moore's experimental treatment, since it's for cancer, is handled slightly different, so the costs associated with it would depend on the type of cancer, the risk of spreading, and the odds of survival. Unfortunately, even with the members at stage three, there is a greater risk of requiring covered services, thus a greater increase in cost to Tellion."

I looked at Parks.

He raised an eyebrow. "Riley, did Tellion's employees know about the trial?"

"I believe so. Greg is very devoted to the health and welfare of his employees and their families. Two of those dependents are under five years old. It broke his heart when he realized he couldn't allow participation in the trial, but the cost risk was too high."

"Can we get their names?" he asked.

"Are you aware of HIPAA?" she asked him.

"The Health Insurance Portability and Accountability Act? I know I sign a form about it any time I go to the doctor."

"That's an annoying consequence of an otherwise important security program for patients' private medical information," she said. The way she explained the details, almost robotic, without emotion, didn't surprise me. "Because these individuals were part of—or connected to—a clinical trial, their contact information is protected under HIPAA and federal research confidentiality rules. We can't release their names or their parents' information without a valid court order specifying what's needed. Once we have that, we'll review it carefully and provide only the contact details authorized by the court, just no medical or trial-specific data."

She spoke in present tense, referring to Hoover as if he were still alive, and the insurance company as an employee. Killers rarely spoke of their victims in present tense, even if they denied responsibility.

"How long does that process take?" I asked.

"In a normal situation, we would drag it out to ensure we follow HIPAA requirements, but since this is a high-profile case, I would think PAC would accommodate a subpoena as quickly as possible."

"Because you're the suspect?"

"Because PAC is a publicly traded company, and the stock plummeted over twenty percent after my arrest made the news."

Parks cringed. "Ouch."

"Not only will I lose my job, I've lost a major contribution to my retirement, and as I've said, I didn't murder Greg."

"Do you have a relationship with Dr. Moore?" I asked.

"Not a personal one, and Greg's refusal to join the trial damaged our professional relationship."

I returned to the couch and sat beside Parks. "How so?"

"Jessica believes PAC should have taken the hit on the increased costs for Tellion, and because I'm the CEO, she blames me for it not happening. She and Dr. Phillips."

"Dr. Phillips?"

"Our chief medical officer. He fully supported the trial, and understandably so. He participated in the treatment's creation."

Parks jotted that down. "Are you the final decision-maker on something like that?"

"No. That is above the CEO's head. If we cover the added medical costs, we're looking at a significant impact—possibly tens of millions annually. Because of that, it goes to the board for the final decision, but to understand the risk, we have to look at the bigger picture. If word got out that we had agreed to a plan design for the trial with Tellion, our other big clients could, and most likely would, request the same option."

"What is the process to make that decision for just Tellion?" I asked.

"It's the same for every risk. Actuarial and underwriting work together to forecast the cost and adjust pricing. Medical economics adds insight on long-term health outcomes and potential savings. Finance and compliance evaluate the financial risk and legal exposure. Finance wants hard numbers before we take it to the board, and that can take some time."

Parks nodded. "So, PAC decides against covering the cost, forcing Tellion to take it on, and Hoover decided to drop the trial option."

"Yes."

"Let me see if I've got this right." I cleared my throat and watched her carefully as I spoke. "You think an employee of Tellion murdered Hoover because he denied the trial, and then this person framed you for his murder."

"I think it's possible."

"And why do you think they'll come for you?"

"My personal relationship with Greg will get out, and when it does, whoever killed him for whatever reason may think I know something I don't," she said. "But it's not just that. Health insurance executives are targets now. It's entirely possible that I will be blamed for another cancer patient's death because PAC won't cover the costs of the trial, and that can be a problem for me."

"How many clients was it presented to?"

"It wasn't supposed to be presented to anyone, but our national accounts team was mistakenly notified of the trial and spread the word. We have over four hundred employer clients and four hundred million members. We have no idea how many clients our reps discussed the trial with, but as of my last day, we had received ten thousand inquiries from companies and members."

Parks dragged his fingers down the sides of his face. "Damn."

"I know this is a lot, and I know I should have been completely honest, but I'm afraid. How can someone find a killer out of a possible four hundred million members and their families?"

I looked at Tiffani.

"Yes," she said. "I'll increase security now." She stood and left the room.

"Riley," I said. "I understand that, but this is the last time you can lie or lie by omission. We can't help you if you aren't honest."

She nodded as tears slid down her cheeks. "I know. I won't. I promise."

I rubbed my temples. "Who else?"

She pursed her lips. "I'm sorry?"

"Who else could target you? Former employees? Friends? Family?" I glanced at her perfectly manicured nails. "Your nail tech?"

"I don't know."

I softened my tone. "I know you don't think your ex-fiancé did this, but I'd still like to talk to him."

"I know he didn't do it. He's out of the country and has been for over a week."

"Who did you say your assistant is?"

"Chandra Martin. Why?"

"What is your relationship like?"

"We are close. Or we were. She wants to move up at PAC, and I had been mentoring her."

"Getting her involved in more than administrative work?" Parks asked.

"Executive assistants do more than administrative work," she said.

I stood and walked around the spacious room. Leaning against the back of the couch, I admired the skyline through the floor-to-ceiling windows and let the silence drag. It made Riley nervous. She pushed herself off the sectional and walked over to the windows, arms crossed tight, with her gaze locked on the view as if it might offer her a lifeline. It wouldn't.

"What does she actually do for you?"

Riley's jaw clenched, and for a second, I thought she'd blow me off. Instead, she sighed and turned, leaning against the glass with her shoulders sagging like the weight of it all had finally begun to hit. "Everything," she muttered.

Parks shifted on the couch. With his elbows on his knees, he watched Riley like a wolf waiting to find the weak spot in a herd of deer. "We're going to need a little more than that."

She laughed, but it was humorless. "She knows what needs to be done before I say it. Schedules, deals, clients, all the things a CEO of a big company needs handled. She keeps me on top of everything, so I don't have to think about anything but the bigger picture. But she handles the ugly things too. Keeps the board off my back when they get nervous. She runs interference when we're negotiating renewals or rate hikes with corporate clients and knows when to back off."

"What about personal things?" he asked. "Does she run errands? Drop off dry cleaning? Does she have a key to your place?"

She stared out the window.

"Riley, level with us," I said. "What does Chandra *really* do for you? And I'm not talking board meetings or emails. I mean the personal stuff. The things no one else sees."

She turned around and stared at me, her expression smoothing into something unreadable. "That's a broad question, Jenna."

"Humor me."

She hesitated, then exhaled slowly. "Chandra manages everything that could become a distraction. Yes, she handles the business, schedules, investor relations, board communications, but it goes far beyond that."

Parks gave a slight nod.

Her voice softened. "She pays my bills. The utilities, property taxes, insurance, you name it. She makes sure nothing lapses or draws attention. She arranges maintenance for my car, the condo, even the pest control. I couldn't tell you the last time I personally scheduled an oil change." Her mouth pulled into a tight smile. "That's the surface. The more complicated things, she handles those, too. Personal relationships when they get messy. If I've misjudged someone's expectations, Chandra steps in. She delivers difficult messages so I don't have to."

Parks blinked. "You mean she breaks up with people."

She gave the faintest nod. "In so many words, yes. She's made those calls. Drafted those messages. Ended relationships—cleanly, quietly. Removed any lingering threads before they became problems."

"Did she end your relationship with Robert Vance?" I asked.

She cleared her throat. "She drafted the email, but it came from me. Well, my email."

"An email?" I rolled my eyes. "What'd you do? Pass a note during study hall?"

"It had to be clear for legal issues. I didn't want anything coming back to me. Relationships at this level, with this kind of money, are complicated."

"I'd think you'd prefer the one-night stands from our Harvard days."

She laughed. "Sometimes, I do."

"Jesus," Parks muttered. "She ever have to clean up anything worse?"

Riley hesitated, then met his eyes. "She's covered mistakes. Paid someone off once—a woman who thought a brief connection meant something more. Chandra made it go away. No drama. No scandal."

"Who was this?" I asked.

"Rebecca Ramsey."

"What kind of something more?" Parks asked.

"The kind you're thinking," she said. "But it wasn't that, not for me. Rebecca misunderstood my intentions. It doesn't matter, though. She won't be an issue."

"Why is that?" I asked.

"She committed suicide."

My eyes widened. "How soon after your situation?"

"Oh, at least a year. She had developed feelings for an actor. They had a brief relationship, and then the woman ended it."

"We'll circle back to that, if necessary," I said.

Parks leaned back and watched her with narrowed eyes. "That's not an assistant, Riley. That's a fixer."

"I prefer to think of her as indispensable. She understands the value of discretion. Of keeping my personal life from bleeding into the professional. Without her, it would be far messier. For everyone."

I nodded slowly. "What about Hoover?" I asked, keeping my voice neutral.

Riley flinched. Her eyes darted toward me. "She knew from the start. I never told her outright, but Chandra sees everything. She kept it contained. Made sure Greg and I never appeared in the same room unless there was a reason. Covered my travel, shifted meetings. If Greg showed up when he shouldn't, Chandra found a way to move me or make it look like a client meeting." Her voice cracked a little. "She never judged."

"Sounds like loyalty," Parks muttered.

"It is," Riley shot back. "Chandra's protected me in ways no one else has. She's cleaned up things most people wouldn't touch."

"What else?" I pressed.

"You know how much we handle? Billions in client money, risk assessments that can tank companies. She knows which clients are unstable, which ones are a breath away from bankruptcy. Chandra monitors all of it. If a client starts slipping, she's the first one in my ear."

"So, she knows where the bodies are buried?" I asked.

A bitter laugh escaped Riley. "She put a few there. Figuratively. We dropped a hospital group last year—they were bleeding claims. Chandra found the data, built the case, handed me the exit strategy. She never blinked.

"She handles our regulatory audits. Flags risk exposure before compliance even breathes on it. When Greg's company threatened to pull coverage two years ago, she had a file on his CFO's gambling habit. We never used it."

"But it was there," I finished.

"Yeah," she said. "She's the only person I trust to know where my leverage is—and how far I'd go to protect this company. When Greg dropped us, she postured it about the trial, not our relationship."

"Was it?" I asked. "About the relationship?"

"As I told you yesterday, it was due to high claims costs and increases in rates. If our relationship was part of the reason, he never mentioned it."

I nodded while processing that. "Not trial increases?"

"No. Members with cancer always have increased claims. It's not uncommon to raise rates in that situation."

"Did Chandra help you maintain your relationship with Hoover?" Parks asked.

She nodded. "She covered for me multiple times..." She stopped and swallowed hard. "The first night Greg stayed over, for example, but there were many others."

Parks's gaze sharpened. "Covered how?"

"Told my driver to clock me at a charity gala I never attended. Told security to wipe the logs." Riley smiled bitterly. "She probably has a file somewhere in case it blew up."

"Smart," I muttered, "and dangerous."

"Would she cover for you the night of Hoover's murder?"

"If I had asked, probably, but I didn't ask." She shrugged. "She's protected me for years. And I took care of her, too. I make sure she's paid better than half the VPs and put her name on bonus lists no one questions."

"Would she kill for you?" Parks asked in a tone like gravel.

She looked at him then, no, studied him. "No, but I think she might make it look like someone else did. And she'd clean up after."

I blew out a slow breath. "We need to talk to her."

"I'll tell her to cooperate. For me."

"Call her," I said. "Tell her to come over and to bring her laptop."

5

Parks and I took a break while waiting for Chandra Martin to arrive. I had suggested Riley contact Harris Taylor as well since she'd admitted to telling us things she hadn't told him. He needed the information to continue building her defense.

"We'll be back in a few hours," I said as we headed out. "That should give you enough time to be honest with your attorney and for Chandra to get here."

"Jenna," Riley said, "I've told you everything I can think of. Chandra will know more."

I nodded once and left.

We hit the sidewalk on Peachtree Road, where the midday traffic crawled past in a steady stream of luxury sedans and matte-black SUVs. Horns blared as impatient drivers jockeyed for position. Buckhead pulsed at lunchtime, refined and loud. Every storefront gleamed like it knew exactly how expensive it was. The area wore its wealth like a badge, a pristine and polished one residents were eager to show off. I squinted across the street at the St. Regis, where Bentleys and Teslas lined the valet stand like trophies. Umi sat tucked in its corner, packed with Atlanta's moneyed elite.

I laughed at all the silk blouses, tailored suits, and faces stretched tighter than a drum.

"You've never been to Umi, have you?" Parks asked. "Those people inside are the norm."

"I hear it's good, but I feel under-Botoxed."

He laughed. "Thank God for that. It's got the best Japanese food this side of the Mason–Dixon line."

"Tell me again why we're not inside drinking?" I muttered.

Parks grunted beside me. "For starters, I gave it up, you're cutting back, and because you said we needed to process."

Damn it. I did say that.

We strolled past The Shops at Buckhead, where Hermès windows glittered with handbags worth more than my car. Women sipping rosé and picking at salads they'd probably never finish crowded Le Bilboquet's patio. I flicked my head toward the women. "I'm so far out of my element here it's laughable," I muttered. "Look at them drinking overpriced wine and barely eating expensive salads. I'm sure they all claim to be allergic to carbs."

Parks snorted. He shoved his hands in his pockets as he followed my gaze. "You think any of them are happy? Their husbands are ghosts. They're either working, cheating, or both. So, they sit here every day, drinking just enough to take the edge off, and I'd bet what's in my wallet they'll drink more later to wash down the Xanax or pop a gummy so they can sleep through another night in a cold bed alone."

I blinked, surprised at the bitterness in his voice. "That's specific."

He shrugged. "I've been around this place too long, I guess. Misery's easy to spot in Buckhead. It just dresses better than our area."

The smell of truffle fries drifted down the sidewalk. My stomach growled in protest, but I pushed past it. There was no way I could eat with Riley's story still fresh in my head. "She's hiding something," I said.

Parks didn't argue. He rarely did when I used that tone.

"You ever think how funny it is that this place drips money, but half the people in those high-rises are one bad investment away from losing it all?"

"Or one dead business partner."

I cracked a grin. "Exactly."

We kept walking as the sun dipped lower and shadows grew longer. Past the boutiques and the gleaming steakhouses, Chops Lobster Bar, Bones, places where men with gold watches and secrets did their worst deals over dry-aged beef. But beneath the glitz, Buckhead's darker side bled through. The condo towers weren't just home to executives and their Botoxed wives. They hid mistresses, drug habits, and bank accounts funneled offshore. More than one deal made on Peachtree ended with a body dumped outside the perimeter. Many of which might never be found.

"This place looks glamorous, but it's all an illusion."

"Yep," he said. "People try to hide behind money, but eventually the bad ones show themselves."

"You think Riley's one of them?"

"A combination of the two. Desperate, lonely woman and corrupt business executive."

"Looks like we feel the same."

Chandra Martin, a young, too skinny, blond-haired, blue-eyed woman who stood around five feet five, sat beside Riley on her couch. They both stood when we walked in.

"Chandra," Riley said, "these are the private investigators I told you about. Jenna Wyatt and Jack Parks. They have some questions for you."

Parks smiled and then walked around the couch. "We need access to Riley's emails. Can you make that happen?"

So much for pleasantries, though I didn't mind.

"Yes, of course." She removed the laptop from her bag, opened it, and tapped a few keys before setting it on the table. "There you go. I've got two screens open. One is Riley's personal email, and the other shows her business ones."

I stared at Riley until the dog ran into the room, barking. The high-pitched yelps hurt my ears.

"Jasper," she said. "That's enough."

The dog didn't care about Riley's command, but he did jump on her lap and lick her on the mouth. She pet him and kissed his nose.

"Can we access each on different laptops?" I asked.

"I can log in on them if that's what you want, but I'll need Riley's approval."

"Of course," she said.

"Why can't you log in?" Parks asked Riley.

"I can to my personal email. I just hadn't thought about it. I use my business email for most things. But PAC will have already removed my log-in and required Chandra to create a new one. They'll have her following up and sending emails to Wallace Bennett, who I assume is acting CEO. Let me get my laptop." She stood and walked down the hall.

Chandra nodded. "Thank God he's got an assistant already, because I refuse to work for him." She glanced at me. "Please prove she's innocent, because I would like to keep my job."

Riley returned with her laptop. "Keep it for as long as you need it. It's my personal one, and I rarely use it."

"Would you like me to save the new log-in for her business email?" Chandra asked.

"Please," I said.

Parks started with the work emails on Chandra's laptop while I scrolled through the personal ones. I sank deeper into Riley's leather couch as her personal laptop warmed my thighs. The inbox swelled with unread messages, many from Jessica Moore. Each subject line hit harder than the last.

"Can I print these?" I asked, eyes fixed on the screen.

Riley stood stiff by the window, arms crossed, gaze locked on the Atlanta skyline. "The printer's down the hall. Chandra, would you grab them for her?"

I clicked print. The faint hum vibrated on my legs.

Chandra moved fast and returned minutes later with the stack of paper. She handed it over with her mouth pressed tight. "I only replied to a few, then I just ignored them," she said. "She sent a few to Riley's work email as well, but nothing like these."

I gripped the pages and skimmed the first email.

Riley—You're gambling with lives. Eliatrixin works. You know it, I know it. We pushed this trial because it could change everything, but you refuse to carry the weight. You let Tellion pull back, and now patients will suffer and die. Do you sleep at night, or do the dead keep you company?

I clenched my jaw as I flipped to the next.

PAC should've approved the full damn trial. Instead, we nickel-and-dimed the care until Tellion walked. Now every exec with a conscience sees what you did. They know you buried this. You should've made it right, Riley. You had the power. You didn't use it.

My stomach soured. These read like threats, not professional complaints. "She sent these to your personal email so they weren't saved on the company server."

"Yes," Chandra said. "I assume that's why."

"Jesus, Riley," I muttered. "She came unglued months ago."

"I haven't read most of them," she said. "I stopped after the first veiled threat."

"Keep going," Chandra bit out.

The tone darkened and the words grew meaner with each email.

You think hiding behind PAC protects you? You're wrong. I built this program. I stood in front of boardrooms and sold hope to dying people. And you, YOU, pulled the plug. I should've gone to the press. Maybe I still will.

My pulse kicked harder. I knew the trial hadn't launched because of the costs, but the emails felt personal. Jessica hadn't written it like a professional; she wrote it like a woman cornered.

I read the next one out loud. "Listen to this. 'Greg Hoover dropped PAC because of you. You think I don't know? You poisoned that deal, same way you poisoned the trial. Now my job is on the line, and I'm trying to clean up your mess while you sit in that glass tower, pretending none of it touches you.'"

I stared at Chandra. "She's threatening her job and to go public. Why didn't you make her read the rest of these?"

"I suggested she do that," she said.

"And I didn't bother," Riley said. "At the time, I thought Jessica was harmless. She's always been emotional. I never thought she might do something to hurt me."

"Jessica knows she screwed up pushing the Eliatrixin trials without the financials to back it," Chandra said. "She thought PAC would fund the additional medical costs to members. She gambled and lost."

I looked at Riley. "She thinks you're the reason Greg bailed. And she's not wrong, is she?"

Riley's jaw locked, but she finally answered. "I told you it was about the costs, and I don't make that decision."

Parks looked up from the other laptop. "But you can influence the board."

"Of course," she said.

"Did you?" I asked. "Did you suggest they not approve the funding because of what it would cost? And if so, does Jessica know that?"

"The numbers spoke for themselves. I just didn't argue to do it."

I dropped the pages on the coffee table. "This can't stay buried. You know that, right? She's too far gone. These start off desperate. They end with threats." I thumbed through the stack, stopping on the most recent message, one barely two weeks old.

I'm done begging, Riley. If I go down, I take you with me. I'll pull every email, every meeting, every dirty secret, including Greg. Let's see how fast your board votes you out once they know what really happened.

"Christ," I muttered. "She's ready to torch it all."

Riley nodded. "Yeah. She is."

My gaze narrowed. "She wants Eliatrixin in front of every major company PAC touches."

Riley let out a harsh laugh. "Of course she does. If that trial fails, she fails, and Jessica Moore doesn't fail."

"She blames you," I said. "For the trial. For Greg. For every shitty decision she made along the way."

"She's not wrong," Riley whispered.

My temples pulsed. I didn't have time for a headache. "What?"

"She's not wrong," Riley repeated. "I didn't stop Greg from walking. I didn't fight harder on Eliatrixin. I let it happen."

"Why?" I asked.

"Why what?"

Had I not been clear? "Why did you let it happen?"

She shrugged. "I guess they were emotional decisions, not business ones."

"Can you explain that further, please?"

She exhaled. "I was upset. I'd heard something before, something personal, and I let that determine my behavior."

"What did you hear?"

"That Jessica had slept with Greg."

Parks looked up again. "Was he?"

She looked at me. "I don't know for sure. I didn't attempt to verify it."

"How did you hear this?" I asked. "Watercooler gossip? A random email you shouldn't have seen? Did someone tell you?"

"Evelyn told me. I didn't believe her at first. I thought she just wanted to hurt me, but the more I think about it, the more I think it might have happened. But only because Jessica would have thrown herself at him. Greg loved me. I can't believe he would have done that on his own."

Right. Because men never let their primal urges rule them. "And you didn't ask him about it?"

"I didn't want to give Evelyn the satisfaction. Even if it was true, I had been dating someone and eventually said yes to marrying him. What right did I have to judge Greg?"

"Why were you dating someone else?" Parks asked. "If you loved Greg, why even go out with the other guy, let alone get engaged?"

A tear slid down her cheek. "I just wanted him to know how it felt. We'd been apart for a while. I started dating. He came back. I kept dating because he stayed married. I know it sounds petty, but I wanted him to feel how I felt knowing he loved me so much and hadn't left her."

I had a lot to say to that, but I kept my mouth shut. She didn't need my judgment.

Chandra printed out two copies of all two thousand emails possibly relevant to the investigation. She had to change the printer ink three times. It had taken hours to go through them, so Riley had offered to buy dinner, but Parks and I declined. I wanted to get back to my apartment and start digging into everything.

"Am I dropping you off?" Parks asked.

"Only if you don't want to go through this stuff with me."

"Order something from DoorDash. It's going to be a long night."

I ordered burgers, fries, and two chocolate shakes.

Parks pulled into the lot, killed the engine, and sat staring at the entrance to my place. I didn't say a word. I didn't need to. He turned to me and watched me with that same unreadable expression he wore almost always.

"We going in?" he finally asked.

"Waiting on you," I said.

"I've got that odd feeling in my gut. Something's not right."

I had it too and let him know. "Better find out, then, huh?"

We climbed out of his truck and headed toward my building. Parks tracked every movement around us. I did the same but kept checking him for signs of something he didn't like.

"If you can get in here without the code, anyone can," I said.

The security on the complex looked good on paper. Keypad and code entry, cameras, but we both knew better. Delivery guys, rideshare drivers, people tailgating, and half of Atlanta's criminals knew how to get past a keypad.

"Everything looks normal," he said. "We're probably just paranoid."

"I'm rarely paranoid, but since my apartment's been broken into before, when my gut tells me to be aware, I'm aware."

"Right there with you."

We walked up the stairs toward the third floor. I felt no creeping sense of dread, no gut feeling something lurked in the dark. Until I saw my door.

The metal edge gleamed where the latch should've caught. Except it hadn't. The door stood cracked just an inch or two, enough to stop us cold.

I placed my hand on my weapon. "No."

Parks clocked it instantly. "You locked it?"

"Are you really asking me that?" My pulse hammered, not with fear—with anger, hot and fast.

"Stay behind me," he ordered, his voice low but steady.

I didn't argue. He drew his weapon, edged forward, and nudged the door open. The hinges creaked. Inside, the apartment looked untouched. No wreckage. No sign of a break-in. My stomach twisted tighter.

Parks cleared the living room fast, then the kitchen. He moved toward the bedrooms.

But something clawed at me, something tight and unrelenting. I scanned the main room. "Everything's where I left it." Except it didn't feel right. Because every time I walked through that door, Bob greeted me. "Where's Bob? He always greets me at the door." The words slipped out low and sharp.

Parks shot me a glance. "I'll check under the beds. If someone came in, he's probably hiding."

I shook my head. "He can hear my voice. He would come running."

Alyssa's voice echoed in my head. *Mommy, you won't be lonely anymore. Bob will keep you company.* She'd insisted, all five years of her wrapped in stubborn sweetness, until I caved. I didn't know how to breathe in my place without seeing that cat weaving between my legs. I drew my own weapon, ignored Parks's warning glance, and moved. "I'm clearing it again."

"Jenna, let me look—"

"I've got this," I snapped.

I swept Alyssa's bedroom first. Empty. Neat. Just the way I left it. Too perfect.

I moved fast to mine, my heart pounding, not from fear but from the gnawing dread clawing at my ribs. "Bob," I called. My voice cracked. "C'mon, buddy."

Nothing.

I edged toward the closet, bracing for I didn't know what.

Then I heard him. A low, pitiful meow.

I yanked open the door, and there he was, his yellow eyes wide, body low to the ground, and his tail puffed up twice its normal size. I exhaled hard as my knees nearly gave in.

"Found him," I muttered, sinking to a crouch. "Bob, sweet boy, you scared the hell out of me."

He didn't move. Just stared up at me with those sweet eyes.

I reached out and ran a shaking hand down his back. "You good? Huh? You okay?" I checked him for injuries, but he appeared to be fine.

He purred then, a shaky, weak sound, but it was enough.

Parks appeared in the doorway. "I checked the closet."

"Yeah." I stood, scooping Bob into my arms. "But you're not me."

Bob pressed into my chest and trembled. And I knew then, whoever came through the apartment made sure even the cat felt it. And if they scared Bob, they meant to scare me. Too bad it made me angry instead.

Parks and I walked back toward the main living area but stopped short at the kitchen.

I followed his gaze to the kitchen counter. My gut dropped. A photograph sat face up next to the sink. Not framed, not on photo paper. Just a glossy printout.

I acted quickly, snatching it before Parks had a chance. My breath caught for a moment, then fury surged in its place. Whoever left it hadn't just trespassed into my apartment—they were trying to invade my mind. And I had no idea who they were.

The picture told me everything I needed to know.

Alyssa. Standing at practice, hair up in a tight bun, arms raised. Pink tights, black leotard. Mid-pose. Focused. Perfect.

"I didn't take this."

Parks hovered close. Tension radiated off him. "You're sure?"

"It's from last night. I was outside the studio watching through the glass."

His jaw ticked. "Here we go again."

I exhaled. "They're showing us what they see. Where they've been."

"They were there," Parks growled. "Watching her."

"She's not part of this," I bit out.

"We'll make sure of that."

The rage burned hot and steady, burning up my throat. I gritted my teeth. "They're trying to get inside my head."

"They think you're vulnerable." Parks took a step forward. "They're wrong."

I looked at him. "This doesn't scare me." Maybe a little, but mostly it just angered me.

"I know," he said. "I think it pisses you off." He scanned the room again and kept his hand hovering near his weapon. "You and Bob aren't staying here."

I snorted. "Don't start."

"I'm not asking."

"You forget who you're talking to?" I turned toward him and squared my shoulders. "They want me running, and I'm not giving them the satisfaction."

Parks exhaled hard. "This isn't a game, Jenna. They were inside your place. Close enough to breathe your air. If you're not leaving, then I'm staying."

"Again."

He closed the distance between us, standing so close I felt his breath on my forehead, and in a low voice said, "We're better as a team. You're not staying here alone."

I looked up at him, wanting to sound tough, but my voice betrayed me. In a raspy whisper, I said, "I don't need protection, Parks."

His mouth twisted. "Maybe I need to protect you."

6

Leland answered on the first ring. "How's the investigation?"

"Someone got into my apartment and left a picture of Alyssa from ballet last night. I was there, and I didn't notice."

"You can't be in protective mode twenty-four seven. Sometimes, being a mom is good."

"Not when unknown psychos know your kid's schedule and take photos of her."

"What if it was a photo of opportunity?" he asked.

The realization of his point took me by surprise. I hadn't thought of it. "He followed me, and the photo was a bonus for him."

"That sounds like an option to me," he said in his slight Southern drawl.

"Except if they were following me, he knows where she lives."

"True."

I hit the nuclear button on my vocabulary and dropped an f-bomb or three. "Nick and I finally have a decent custody arrangement, and we're talking to each other like humans. I can't tell him. If I have to, I'll never see my daughter again."

"Jenna," he said, "you don't have to tell him, but if you don't and something happens, you're right. You'll never see your kid again. He knows what you do for a living. He knows there's a risk. Be honest, but get Taylor to put security on them. That should come off his dime, not yours."

Nick had hated that option last time, especially when they stuck him, Alyssa, and Heather in a hotel until we caught the person threatening them. I couldn't care about that more than I cared about keeping them safe. "You're right. I'll set it up now and let him know."

"Good idea," he said. "I made a few calls about the gun, but Taylor already has everything you need for it. Did he get it to you?"

"It wasn't in the initial information, but I'm sure he'll send it."

"Knowing him, he's waiting to deliver it when you're home. Call him now."

"Good idea. Thanks, Leland. I appreciate you keeping me centered."

"I'm not just the guy that fired you."

I grinned. "You always have to bring that up, don't you?"

"Not always. Let me know if you need anything." He said goodbye and ended the call.

Parks stretched out on my couch, boots still on, and hands behind his head. "He said the same thing I did, didn't he?"

I gave the faintest curl of my lip, barely there, but enough to make my point. "Are you really lying on my couch with your boots on?"

He sat up and removed each boot, then lay down again. "Nope."

"He must have talked to Taylor, because Leland says Taylor has all the information on the gun."

"We have what's in the police report. Do you want to see the actual gun?"

"I'd like to. I need it in my hands."

He sat up again, then raised his eyebrow. "Because?"

"Sometimes it gives me a sense of the crime."

"Intuition," he said. "I get it. You're calling Taylor tonight, yes?"

"Right now." I hit his name on my cell phone contact list and put it on speaker.

He answered right away. "Ms. Wyatt. Do you have news?"

"Has Riley called you since we talked to her today?"

"She told me the truth," he said, "and assured me she would maintain honest communication from now on."

"I hope," I said. I gave him the details about Alyssa and the photo in my apartment.

"I can get security on her immediately."

"I want Bateman," I said.

"You're aware she's assigned to Riley, correct?"

"I'm aware, but I don't care. I want her on my child."

"I can provide—"

I shut him up with, "Let me be clear. This is a deal-breaker, Taylor. Find someone else for Riley."

"Done," he snapped. "Anything else?"

"I spoke with Leland. He said you have everything on the gun. What you get, we need. That includes all your notes, deposition and interview transcripts, and anything else you have. The first thing your team needs to do is copy it and get us two copies before anything else." That came off a little demanding, but so be it.

"I have it all ready for delivery first thing tomorrow."

"We're not sleeping. Send it over."

"Consider it done."

"Do you have the gun?" I asked.

"Only temporarily. We have to return it by ten a.m. Shall I send that as well?"

"Please." I ended the call.

Parks whistled. "Poor guy has no idea who he's up against."

I couldn't stop my lips from curving into a smile. "He wants his client acquitted. He'll do what we ask."

He grinned. "In what part of that conversation did you ask?"

"I assumed he assumed."

"Yeah." He chuckled. "No."

"Oh well." I plopped onto the couch and called the emergency number for my apartment complex's security and politely asked for a new lock after telling them my home had been entered.

"Is the lock broken?" the man asked.

"No."

"Then how did they get in?"

I closed my eyes and tried to summon the little bit of patience I had left. "My guess is they used a bump key. Do you know what that is?"

"No, ma'am. I've only been on the job a few weeks."

"It's a specially cut key designed to bump the pins in a standard lock, which then allows the door to open."

"Really? Can't we do anything about that?"

"Tell your boss he's cheap and is going to end up in a lawsuit if this happens to anyone else."

"I'll be right over with a new lock, but that's the best I can do."

"I'll take it," I said, knowing it would allow the person entry again if they tried.

Parks yawned after I ended the call. "We should have added some coffee to our order. Do you have any?"

"I thought you hated my coffee?"

"Desperation does things to a man."

"Now I know what that look means." I laughed. "I'll make a pot."

He made the cross over his chest.

"Why'd you do that?" I asked.

"Said a silent prayer to not die from the lead you make."

I tossed a throw pillow at him. "You can go to RaceTrac. They're open twenty-four hours."

"I'm not leaving you."

I stood. "Then lead it is."

An hour later, I had a new lock plus an additional one. If someone wanted in, they'd have to go through two dead bolts to do it.

Waiting for Tiffani and the files tortured me. First, I paced, expecting her to show up any minute, but the time dragged on. I had planned to call Nick in the morning, knowing if I called at the late hour, he'd be on edge from me waking him. But where was she? It had been an hour. "She should be here by now," I said to Parks. He sat on the other end of the couch, swiping through his phone.

"She's in Buckhead. She probably had to get her things together and is on her way."

I agreed, but that didn't mean I liked it. "I'm tired of putting my kid in the line of fire."

"Then get a nine-to-five job."

I blanched. "I can't be around people all day like that, let alone sit for eight hours."

He laughed. "Picturing that is hilarious. The poor people in that office."

"See? I do this to save nine-to-fivers' lives."

"Right." He went back to scrolling.

I grabbed the crime scene photos from the police file and stared at the first one. Bob purred low against my thigh, his steady weight grounding me, but my mind stayed locked on the picture balanced in my lap. The smell of my bad coffee lingered, but my cup had gone cold, forgotten on the table.

I studied that photo over and over. Gregory Hoover, sprawled on the Persian rug of his study. Eyes open, mouth slack, arms splayed wide, lifeless and awkward as if gravity had forgotten him. The neat circle of the bullet wound dead center in his forehead told me everything and nothing.

I stared at the scattered papers, the chair toppled on its side. Chaos, but not the right kind. Not the desperate scramble of a man fighting for his life. The more I looked at the photo, and the more I pictured it in my mind, I knew the scene had been staged to look like a controlled mess. The shooter intended for it to scream crime of passion, but every detail screamed control. Too deliberate.

I closed my eyes and built the scene in my head. Greg at his desk, maybe reviewing contracts, sipping some overpriced scotch. He'd been stressed because of two, possibly three women, a major corporation under his watch, a wife ready to drag him through court. Was his heart built for that kind of strain? Was his ego?

He'd gone down fast, that much was clear. Heart attack, if the autopsy was right, which it should have been. Ischemic damage, pulmonary edema, arteries screaming for mercy. He'd probably clutched his chest, gasped, then crumpled. No time for a final word, no time to call for help. Just gone.

And then the killer walked in. Was that perfect timing or coincidence?

My gut said they'd been waiting. Maybe they watched him fall, or maybe they'd planned it all—pushed him until his heart gave out. Either way, they were ready. Calm. No rush. They planted the shot with surgical precision, knowing the bullet would look like the cause of death. Knowing most people, even some detectives, would stop there.

But dead men don't bleed.

I flipped to the next photo. The entry wound was so clean it could have been done in a lab. Minimal back spatter. That was wrong. A head shot should've painted the wall. Instead, the fibers of the rug were barely stained. I rubbed my temples. "Think, Jenna."

The report said Evelyn Hoover made the 911 call at 10:34 p.m. She found him unresponsive. Not dead, not shot, just unresponsive. That read like shock, but it smelled like calculation. Had she known what she'd find and rehearsed those words? No forced entry. The front door open, but only because Evelyn ran outside, supposedly in a panic. I called BS on that. No city was trauma-free, and I suspected Hoover's house was a fortress with alarms and cameras everywhere. How'd the shooter get in? Through the garage?

I scrolled through the sequence again. Papers, the chair, his body. Hoover looked surprised, even in death. But not afraid. There were no other wounds, no sign he saw it coming. I used my phone to enlarge the photo showing his hand. Nothing to show defense wounds or anything under his nails. That fit the heart attack.

The timing. I couldn't get past it.

My pulse ticked higher. What if Evelyn had been there all along? What if she watched him drop? Maybe she didn't have the guts to pull the trigger while he was alive, but afterward? Easy. All the rage, the betrayal, it would boil over. One clean shot. One message. *You don't leave me.*

Or maybe it wasn't her.

Maybe Riley panicked. She found him dead, realized what it looked like, and tried to stage it. But then why lie about the gun? She lied and said she found it on her counter. The report said only her fingerprints were found on the weapon. The print pattern, full with no smudges, told me she held it steady. Not like someone who picked it up in shock. But holding a gun to someone's head wasn't like aiming at a target. Her hands had to shake, had to move on that gun. Unless, of course, she was a sociopath, which I had once considered to be true.

I leaned back and closed my eyes again. "There's more."

"What?" Parks asked.

I turned my head toward him and opened my eyes. "Sorry. I'm thinking through something."

"Let me know when you're done."

I closed my eyes again. Greg had enemies. Angry clients, bitter employees, a bitter, territorial, manipulative wife, and a mistress-turned-ex. Maybe more of those. If there had been one, there usually had been another. Anyone could've slipped in through the garage and waited him out. The killer might've known his heart was a ticking time bomb.

Because they made it that way.

I grabbed the autopsy report and scanned it again. "There's nothing on here about testing for drugs, legal or illegal. Why not?"

Parks looked at me. "Is that meant for me, or are you talking to yourself?"

"Yes," I said, meaning both.

He grabbed his copy of the autopsy. "Probably no need. It says significant blockage. To the coroner, he was the walking dead."

Leland's voice popped in my head. *Pressure breaks men like that, Jenna.* "But what if the person who shot him gave him something to stop his heart first?"

"Why do that first and then shoot him after he's dead?"

"To watch him suffer. The shot was just an emotional response to their anger." I pictured Greg's final moments. Slumping at his desk, the first pang of pain blooming in his chest. He tried to stand, grabbed the desk for support, sent the papers flying. The chair went over as he fell. By the time his killer stood over him, he was gone. The killer didn't call for help. Didn't panic. Just lined up the shot and pulled the trigger. I shivered. That kind of cold took practice. Bob shifted on my lap. I stared at the last photo. The shell casing gleamed in the soft lamplight like a signature. Not wiped. Not hidden. Just left there like punctuation.

"This wasn't sloppy," I said. "It was a message."

The question was, who was it for?

I called Taylor again. "We need a blood test on everything we can test for. Illegal drugs, abuse of legal drugs, everything."

"Are you always a step behind?" he asked evenly. "There were no drugs in his system."

"Are you always forgetful when it comes to getting us information that can help us prove your client's innocence?"

"Ms. Wyatt, there's a fine line between efficiency and rudeness. Lucky for you, I admire efficiency."

"You're paying for me to do my job, not be polite." I ended the call after that and glanced at Parks, who stared at me. "What?"

"That was cold."

"But correct."

7

Tiffani Bateman brought the additional files with her. "This was my idea," she said as she handed us the boxes. "I thought I'd save the poor soul who arrived with the files from your wrath." She winked at me and acknowledged Parks with a nod. "The weapon is in the first one. He needs it back first thing."

"I'll make sure it gets to him," I said.

"Tell me what happened," she said as I kicked my door closed.

I gave her the 411.

She hit me with a sly but serious smile. "Sugar, they so much as look at your sweet angel wrong, and I'll put them in the ground myself."

I trusted that she would.

"Would you like me to tell Nick and Heather in the morning? I can soften the blow."

"I've got it," I said. "I'll be there around seven. Do you need his address?"

"Is that a test? You know as well as I do details like that stick with us."

"Darlin'," I said, mimicking her strong dialect. "I don't question your skills. I might even fear them if I find myself on your bad side."

"You should." She watched me open the first box. "I'll leave y'all with this. I'm off to protect your little darlin'."

As she opened the door, I said, "Tiffani."

Reading my mind, she turned and winked. "I will."

"Well," Parks said from the couch. "As they say, sleep is overrated." He set the last stack of printed emails on my coffee table with a heavy thud, making the thing groan under the weight. "Two thousand forty-three emails. We're either solving a murder tonight or developing carpal tunnel." He got up and joined me at the kitchen counter. "You sure you're ready to read what Hoover and Riley were really saying to each other?"

"I've read worse." I shrugged, feigning indifference. "And I'd rather see it than have Taylor spin it for me later." I pulled my hair up into a messy knot and rubbed the back of my neck, already feeling the tension digging in. "First, I'm examining the gun."

"Here you go." Parks slid the case onto my kitchen counter and flipped the latches. Nestled inside the foam cutout was the 9mm Glock, tagged and bagged, but still carrying that distinct weight of finality that always came with handling a murder weapon.

He peeled back the evidence bag and glanced at me. "Gloves?"

I pulled a box from under my couch and tossed them to him.

"You keep a box of latex gloves under your couch?"

"Don't you?"

"Normal people don't do things like that, Jenna."

"I don't care what normal people do. It's convenient."

He rolled his eyes, then lifted the weapon and turned it slightly under the light. "Glock 17. Standard 9mm. Polymer frame. No visible modifications."

The slide gleamed in smooth, matte black. Someone had scratched over the serial number on the side until nothing remained. "Magazine?"

He popped it free and checked it. "Empty. Clean, no residue around the mag well, but that could be because it's already been processed."

"Likely. It's a commonly purchased gun, so it's easy to come by legally or illegally." I'd worked with Glocks plenty back at GBI, and there was something coldly efficient about them. No frills, no theatrics. They did their job.

He continued analyzing the weapon. "Threaded barrel's standard on some models, but this one's smooth. Factory issue."

"Good to know," I said. I wrote a note about the gun. "If it was used inside without a silencer, they should have had neighbors reporting a shot, even if the place had decent soundproofing."

"Yep. Unless they didn't want to get involved, which is the case more and more these days."

"Agree," I said.

"This feels clean. Someone wanted it that way."

"They always do," I murmured. "But there's always something." I snapped multiple photos of the gun for our records.

He set the gun back in the foam and resealed the bag, then returned it to its case and shut it. "I'll have someone pick it up in the morning."

"Let's start with the emails flagged for Jessica Moore."

He groaned. "Here we go."

We returned to the couch, and he slid the first email across the table.

Someone had separated the emails into content, date, and then person as they printed. Whoever did this deserved a gold medal. It made our job so much easier.

"I have my own copies. Let's go over them together."

"Works for me," he said, sliding the email back to his side of the table.

From: Jessica Moore

To: Gregory Hoover

CC: Riley Chatsworth

Subject: RE: Experimental Treatment Coverage - Additional Considerations

Greg, as discussed, the experimental trial coverage adds significant cost but offers a 60% higher survival rate for participants. If PAC covers the estimated additional $2 million annually, we maintain control of the provider network and avoid bad press.

I read it twice. "Sixty percent survival rate increase," I murmured. "That's not nothing."

"Yeah, but read Riley's reply," Parks said, tapping the next printout.

. . .

From: Riley Chatsworth
  To: Jessica Moore, Gregory Hoover
  Subject: RE: Experimental Treatment Coverage - Additional Considerations
  Jessica, your passion for the trial is admirable, but I'm not convinced the risk outweighs the benefit. We're already over budget. I'll present it to the board, but no promises.

I clicked my tongue. "She knew they were never going to approve that trial coverage."

"Still, she called it 'admirable,'" Parks said. "That's corporate speak for 'I'm about to screw you, but thanks for playing.'"

I cracked a grin. "You've been to too many budget meetings."

"Too many," he agreed. "And by that, I mean none."

We sifted through more of Jessica's emails—clinical trials, experimental treatments, actuarial tables—each more damning than the last, but none outright criminal. Still, a pattern formed. Moore pushed the trial. Hoover hesitated. Riley shut it down.

"This was personal for Moore," I said. "Maybe she knows about Riley and Hoover?"

"It's possible," he said.

The next email caught my eye.

From: Gregory Hoover
  To: Riley Chatsworth
  Subject: RE: Trial Coverage Decision
  Riley, I get it. Budgets, optics, all that. But we're talking about real people. If we pull the plug, you know what happens? Those families lose hope. Jessica's not going to let this go quietly. We need to talk about PAC and Tellion perhaps splitting the additional costs. Perhaps we can negotiate an arrangement that benefits us all?

The next was another email from Jessica. One sharper and angrier.

. . .

From: Jessica Moore
   To: Riley Chatsworth
   CC: Gregory Hoover
   Subject: You don't get to play God
   I fought for this because it mattered. You get to walk away from the fallout, Riley. I don't. But just wait. Today's world isn't friendly to elite, rich women who get jobs because their daddy has connections. When the first patient dies because we wouldn't cover it, that's on you.

Parks let out a low whistle. "She was pissed."

"Wouldn't you be?" I muttered. "She was trying to save people. Riley was trying to save her bottom line."

Parks shuffled the papers and pulled the next one. "Here's where it turns," he said. "Read the time stamp."

I did. It was dated two weeks before Hoover died.

From: Riley Chatsworth
   To: Gregory Hoover
   Subject: Re: Your Concerns
   Greg, I've reviewed the numbers again. The board isn't going to budge. Off the record—drop it. You're not going to win this one. And frankly, you don't want to be on the wrong side of this when the dust settles. If you want to cover the additional costs, PAC is more than willing to administer that for Tellion, but unfortunately, I can't approve a shared cost plan or discount. I'm sorry.

I blinked. "She wasn't pulling the strings on this."

"I agree," Parks said grimly. "The board wouldn't budge, and they made that clear to her."

We worked in silence for a few minutes, reading email after email until my eyes blurred. Most of them danced around the same issues. Cost, coverage, and potential lawsuits if the trial failed. A few referenced conference calls with legal and "the consultants," but we found nothing sent to them.

Parks pushed a particular email toward me. "This one's different."

From: Jessica Moore
   To: Gregory Hoover
   Subject: Off the record
   I know you're worried. I am too. But I heard something—Phillips said if the trial goes public, it's not just us on the hook. He thinks PAC knows about the undocumented patients. The whole thing could blow. Be careful.

A jolt of ice shot through me. "Phillips," I repeated. "Dr. Lawrence Phillips?"

Parks nodded slowly. "Same one."

"And undocumented patients?" I sat back. "We know what that means."

"They moved forward with the trial without approval," Parks said. "And Hoover knew."

"And Jessica knew." I tapped the paper. "And she warned him."

"And Riley?" Parks asked.

I let out a slow breath. "If she didn't know then, she found out. No way she didn't."

We read on. Another email, this time from Hoover, threw me completely.

From: Gregory Hoover
   To: Riley Chatsworth
   Subject: RE: Trial Concerns
   Riley, I'm not backing down on this. If this goes sideways, I'm taking every-thing—including your ass—down with me. You're just as much a part of this as me, and you know it.

My skin prickled. "'You're just as much a part of this as me.'"

Parks blew out a breath. "That's the smoking gun."

I nodded. "She knew."

"What if that's why he died? Not the affair. Not the rate hike. But this. Hoover threatening to expose PAC's dirty laundry."

"And someone made sure he couldn't."

He ran a hand down his face. "Maybe you were right to not want this case," he said. "Maybe she did it."

I stared at the emails, my gut twisting. "No," I said finally. "I think someone wanted to stop him from going public with the trial."

"And they framed her," Parks finished.

"Yeah. My question is, why? What happened that made Hoover say that?"

"Hopefully," he tapped the pile of emails, "we'll find the answer in one of these."

We kept reading. The last few emails were from Jessica. They read as desperate, almost frantic.

From: Jessica Moore

To: Gregory Hoover

Subject: Please call me

People's lives are on the line. And not only your employees and their family members. If this hits the press, we're all done. You, me, Riley—everyone. Please don't let that happen. Please call me.

"She was angry in the emails we saw to Riley's personal address, but these are different. An act, maybe?"

Parks shook his head. "Not sure, but Hoover's death stops it all, so it's possible that was a warning for PAC."

"Convenient," I muttered. "Almost like someone needed to shut him up before he made that call."

We sat in silence, letting the information settle over us.

Parks finally broke it. "Why didn't Riley tell us any of this?"

"Does she know?" I asked. "Did she even write the emails?"

"Chandra," he said. "She could have handled this *inconvenience* for Riley."

"I'm thinking she did."

"Before we go that route, think Jessica cracks if we push her?"

"She might," I said. "Especially if she thinks we know about the trial."

"She had a personal relationship with Hoover," he said quietly. "You can see it in the way she wrote to him. Not like Riley. Not calculated. Real."

"Chandra wouldn't know the nuance of how Riley and Hoover communicated and would have kept it completely professional, but I'm not sure Riley would have." I sighed. "We need to talk to Moore and Dr. Phillips."

"And what about Riley?"

I exhaled hard. "She's still lying to us about something. But I don't think it's the murder." I glanced at the pile of emails. "We need to dig more. Harder. Find out who stood to lose the most if it came out."

"But it did come out," he said. "To Tellion employees. I don't think that was an accident."

"It's harder to deny the trial if employees know about it," I said.

"This is where the good stuff happens," he said, followed by his natural, slow and easy grin. "We make a good team."

I snorted. "You're just saying that because I didn't make you read all two thousand of these yourself."

He shrugged. "Maybe. But I will because that's what partners do."

The air changed between us—something unspoken, heavy, but not unwelcome, filled it. I cleared my throat and shoved the emails aside. "I'm going to bed. We'll hit this hard in the morning."

———

I woke to the smell of coffee and something filled with sugar. After climbing out of bed and tossing on a pair of sweats and a Harvard sweatshirt, I walked into the kitchen to load up on carbs and caffeine.

Parks stood there holding a cup of coffee and a chocolate-frosted donut from Dunkin'.

"I made you the breakfast of champions."

I rolled my eyes. "That's cereal, not a donut."

He smiled. "I'll take a sugar-laden donut over a bowl of cardboard any day."

I gave him a slow once-over, realizing, with his muscular build, he likely only ate donuts laden with sugar around me.

"What?" he asked.

I looked up at him and noticed the raised eyebrow.

"Are you scanning me for viruses or something?" he asked.

I scoffed but felt heat rising up from my neck. "Why would you think that?"

"I saw you taking inventory." He winked. "Feel free to admire the equipment anytime, Wyatt. I'm here for your pleasure."

I nearly spit out my coffee. "You're disgusting."

"Em-hm." Another smile.

"I just wondered how you can eat sugar like this and look like you do."

He leaned against my kitchen counter. "You mean damn good?"

"Can we just change the subject, please? I don't want to end up with donut coming back up my throat."

8

Vireon Pharmaceuticals sat in the middle of Midtown and close to the Georgia Tech campus. We hadn't called to see if Jessica Moore would be at work, knowing our surprise visit would catch her off guard.

"It's just off the Connector," I told Parks, nodding toward the mid-rise up ahead. "Behind Tech Square and right in the middle of Georgia Tech's playground."

"GT does rank high for innovation schools," he said. "They probably picked this location for that very reason."

"Maybe," I said. "Or maybe it's the cheap rent."

The glass-and-steel building looked exactly like a place where people used words like "synergy" and "vertical integration" unironically. Floor-to-ceiling windows stared out over Fifth Street, probably offering a great view of grad students running late and the occasional overpriced electric scooter faceplant.

"A dream spot for dirty men with violent tendencies," I said, though I hadn't meant to.

Parks laughed. "I just thought the same thing."

Inside, people walked around wearing suits and dresses or lab coats over something more casual. Several of the coat wearers had face masks hanging around their necks.

The receptionist, probably a biology major flunky from GT, greeted us with an uppity air and a rude scowl. "May I help you?"

"We're here to see Jessica Moore," I said.

"Is she expecting you?"

"No."

"Dr. Moore only meets with vendors and suppliers on Fridays between three and five."

Of course, because she wanted to torture them with their drive home in the heat of Atlanta rush hour. "We're not vendors or suppliers," I said. "We're with law enforcement."

She rolled her eyes. "ID?"

I quickly flashed my private investigator ID I had made to look official for such situations. During my career with the GBI, I learned people in her position didn't look closely at the badge; they just wanted to cover their butts.

She let out an annoyed sigh. "I'll let her know you're here."

A lab assistant led us to Moore's office just outside what I thought was the main lab. The area smelled faintly sterile with a hint of whatever chemical compound they used to clean the floors. I stared through the glass walls showcasing rows of scientists hunched over workstations. It wasn't lost on me that I'd dressed like I belonged—black slacks, silk blouse—but Parks looked like a guy two steps away from punching someone, unusual for him.

Dr. Moore met us at the door. She looked around my age. Mid-thirties, with long brown hair in a practical ponytail, and a makeup-free face.

"How may I help you?" she asked.

"We've got a few questions about Greg Hoover's death," I said. "This is my partner, Jack Parks."

She attempted to smile, then closed the door behind us after we walked into her office. "Greg Hoover? The man from Tellion? Why would I have any information about him?"

Why was she acting like she didn't know him?

"We're talking to everyone he interacted with," Parks said.

She motioned for us to sit in front of her desk, then walked behind it and sat in her chair. "Are you with the police?"

"We're investigating for a law firm," I lied. She didn't need to know we worked for the defendant. "A possible wrongful death lawsuit."

"I'm not sure how I can help you."

Parks tapped my foot with his and said, "We're aware of a cancer medicine trial you're working on, and that it might be the reason Mr. Hoover dropped PAC as Tellion's health insurance provider."

Jessica's face shifted. "I can't say for certain why Mr. Hoover dropped PAC, but I do know he was upset with PAC for refusing to cover the additional medical costs for the trial. He had several employees and dependents suffering from various types of cancers, but the additional costs to the benefit plan were through the roof. PAC refused to pay them, so I'm assuming he went elsewhere for coverage."

"Would that coverage include the trial?" I asked.

"Vireon is a PAC-owned company. We funnel many of our trials to other insurance companies, but there are some PAC chooses to keep in-house. I can't speak for other insurance companies and their knowledge of this trial. I don't handle who is approached and who isn't."

I nodded. "Can you speak for PAC?"

"I am employed through their corporation, but not specifically with the carrier, so no, I can't speak for them either."

The corners of Parks's lips curled upward. "Did you speak with Mr. Hoover about the drug and the trial? Or was that left to PAC?"

"I only speak to clients when I'm brought in, which is usually for questions on drugs and their possible impacts on members."

She hadn't answered the question. "And Mr. Hoover? Were you brought in to speak with him?"

"I was not."

I pretended to believe her. "So, you've never spoken to Mr. Hoover?"

She cleared her throat. "I have talked to him, yes, but I wasn't brought in by anyone from Tellion or Vireon. Mr. Hoover came to me himself, multiple times if I remember correctly."

"For?" Parks asked.

"As I said, questions regarding our pharmaceuticals."

"Can you elaborate on that?" I asked.

"I'd have to check my records."

Her evasiveness got on my nerves. "Who do you engage with at PAC regarding trials and possible use with members?"

"My main contact is Dr. Phillips, PAC's chief of medicine, but I do interact with others."

"Their CEO, Riley Chatsworth?"

"At times, yes. I'm assuming you're here about her involvement in Mr. Hoover's murder?"

"Actually, we're investigating the murder, not the suspect," I said through gritted teeth.

"What about Wallace Bennett?" Parks asked. "Would you work with him on this now?"

"Mr. Bennett? I can't say, though I would assume so. As I stated earlier, much of my interaction is with Dr. Phillips. But I can tell you this. Wallace Bennett's priority has always been ensuring clients get the care they need. He stepped up before Riley's arrest, taking a more hands-on role to look good to the board. I think he was ready to move forward or move on. I don't know for sure, but given his first question wasn't about budget reports but rather coverage continuity for affected members, I think he was pushing for Riley's job. That's not something you fake. He was trying to look good, and now he wants to steady the ship."

"How does coverage continuity affect your position?" I asked.

"As you can assume, normally, I focus on the clinical side. I evaluate trial data and make treatment recommendations, for starters. But when a client like Tellion leaves midstream, especially with employees who are being considered for an experimental drug trial, my work shifts. I'm brought in to assist in assessing whether we can justify continuing coverage, even if it means bending policy, and if a trial is officially begun."

"Wouldn't that be something the CMO, Phillips, and his team would do?"

"Of course, but given my area of expertise, Wallace asked my team to prioritize that. He didn't want people caught in the fallout."

"But they hadn't started the trial," Parks said.

"Correct," she said. "I'm talking in generalities and simply using them as an example."

"Tell us about the drug," I asked.

Jessica's lips tugged into a smile, like talking about the science was a relief to her. "It's immunotherapy based and designed to target tumors without the carnage of traditional chemotherapy. Early trials are promising, but expensive, and this is why we've had such an issue with it as an option for PAC members."

"Because PAC wouldn't pay the additional charges."

Jessica huffed a bitter laugh. "You're correct. Ms. Chatsworth wouldn't budge on the numbers. She said it was too expensive and not worth the risk."

"Did she decide that or the board of directors?"

"I can't say for sure, but she's the CEO. One can assume she played a part in the decision."

Not always.

"And she delivered that message to Mr. Hoover?" Parks asked.

"I assume so," she said. "I haven't discussed the financial aspects of the trial with him." Jessica's jaw tensed. "Ms. Chatsworth has often talked about wanting to improve the lives and health of others, but that's not her real goal. It's profits for her and the board. Not people." Her voice cracked, just slightly. "And that decision lost PAC their biggest client. Wallace has been working double-time since then," she added. "He's trying to rebuild trust with other employer groups by offering more transparency, even sitting in on calls with clients himself. Not many execs do that. He believes in the science. We just didn't have the backing we needed at the time."

I raised my brow. "I'm curious how you know this if you work primarily with Dr. Phillips."

"Dr. Phillips keeps me in the loop." She paused. "What is your name again?"

"Jenna Wyatt."

"Ms. Wyatt, PAC owns Vireon. While I'm not involved in the day-to-day activities of the company, their reputation affects my business. It's imperative for me to stay informed."

"Understood," I said. "Are you aware of any personal relationship between Ms. Chatsworth and Mr. Hoover?"

Jessica hesitated, then nodded. "I had my suspicions, but they were never confirmed."

"How did you hear of it?" Parks asked.

"I'm not sure," she said. She glanced at the ceiling. "Chandra must have said something. I often communicated with Riley through her."

"And Mr. Hoover never mentioned it?" I asked.

"It certainly wasn't personal the few times we've spoken."

I stood. "Thank you for your time."

"Of course," she said as she stood. "If I can help any further, please feel free to ask. And for what it's worth," she said, glancing toward the hallway, "Wallace Bennett didn't inherit an easy role. But from what I've seen, he's not dodging responsibility, nor has he ever. He's trying to make things right for the patients and for the company. You should talk to him."

I flipped around and said, "Oh, there is one more thing. Just a technicality, of course."

"Sure. Anything."

"Just for our notes, can you tell us where you were the night of Mr. Hoover's murder?"

She glanced at her desk, then back at me. "What time?"

"Let's say between six and eleven p.m."

"I was here until about eight, then went home."

"Did you leave home that night?" Parks asked.

She bit her bottom lip as if she had to think about it. Then, shaking her head, she said, "Not that I know of. I did have food delivered through Door-Dash. Would you like to see the record of it?"

Parks hesitated, but I said, "Yes."

She showed it to us. "Will that suffice?"

"For now," I said. "Ms. Moore—"

"It's *doctor.*"

"Dr. Moore, in your opinion, is there anyone within the walls of PAC or Vireon who you believe would benefit from Mr. Hoover's death?"

Her bottom lip trembled. Had I hit a nerve?

"Mr. Hoover was a kind, caring man. I can't imagine why anyone would want him dead."

"And you gathered that from your limited, professional-only relationship?"

She nodded. "I have a unique ability to read people. Few people can."

"Right," I said. With a slight smile, I added, "I have that too."

"I could be wrong," Parks said on the way to his vehicle, "but I think Dr. Moore and Wallace Bennett are doing the nasty on the side."

I blanched. "Some women use that as their ladder to a better position."

"That's very anti-women of you to say."

"Not at all. Do men in positions of power take advantage of women? Absolutely. And it's disgusting. But women can also play that card and work the men to move forward. There are many who will admit to that."

"Maybe she thinks he can help her level up to Phillips's job."

"Could be." I yanked open the door to his truck saying, "Have I mentioned how much I hate liars?"

He tapped the button to start the engine. "Hate the lie, not the liar." A smile stretched across his face.

"Right. I'll give that a shot."

A laugh escaped him. "When hell freezes over."

"Aside from the fact that she outright lied about her relationship with Hoover, she changed her story on her communication with him multiple times, and she spoke as if the trial was in progress. Did I miss something?"

"You're not missing anything. She knows something she's not telling us."

"What are the odds we'll figure it out?"

"I'd bet high on that."

"Right," I said.

"I did a little research during our chat with Moore." He tossed his phone into my lap. "Knock yourself out."

I glanced at the screen. A browser tab sat open with a headline blaring, *From the Lab to the Boardroom: Dr. Lawrence Phillips Joins PAC Health.* I shot him a look, but he kept his eyes on the road, one hand gripping the wheel and the other resting casually over the top. "You don't want to talk about the patient and amazing acting CEO?"

"I think Moore did that enough, don't you?"

I shrugged. She had. After a quick scan of the first few sentences of the article, I figured he was headed toward PAC.

I scrolled.

The first article dated back two years, right around the time Phillips joined the company. The image showed him in a white coat, sleeves rolled, arms crossed, standing outside a sleek, glass-walled medical research facility. Its design oozed modern technology and cutting-edge science, but it didn't belong to the PAC family as far as I knew.

Dr. Lawrence Phillips, a renowned infectious disease specialist and former director of clinical research at several prestigious institutions, has joined PAC Health as its chief medical officer. With over two decades of experience in translational medicine and pharmaceutical development, Phillips is expected to lead initiatives aimed at improving disease outcomes and integrating experimental treatment protocols into insurance-based care models.

"Did you know he had a research background?" I asked, skimming the rest.

"Not until I started digging," Parks said. "He's kept a low profile since he came on. No press, no interviews. Unusual for a guy who's published more papers than most academic departments."

I clicked to the next article, one from a medical journal, technical but accessible if you knew what to look for. Phillips had once led a multinational team developing experimental therapies for emerging infectious diseases. His early work with the CDC pre-COVID had been widely praised. Then he pivoted into oncology, focusing on biologics and immunotherapy.

One section highlighted an experimental drug regimen designed to stimulate targeted immune response in pancreatic and esophageal cancers. Early trials showed modest, but promising remission rates.

"Guy's not just a pencil pusher," I muttered. "He's legit."

Parks nodded. "Yeah. But legit doesn't always mean harmless."

I raised an eyebrow and scrolled further.

Another article from a healthcare magazine painted a more strategic picture. Phillips hadn't just joined PAC just to sign off on coverage claims and analyze medical data. He'd brought his clinical trial mindset into the boardroom—pushing for collaboration with pharmaceutical companies to integrate promising new treatments into PAC's coverage models earlier in the approval cycle.

"Interesting that he wanted to work with other big pharma companies, don't you think?"

"Maybe has arrangements with some or felt Dr. Moore couldn't provide the solutions he wanted."

The buzzword-laced language hinted at big-picture thinking. Synergy. Alignment. Scalability, and others specific to the medical and insurance industries. Early adoption of promising therapies, cost-efficiency through treatment success, shifting investment toward long-term health gains. Blah. Blah. Blah.

One line caught my eye. "Dr. Phillips's move to PAC Health represents a strategic alignment of clinical innovation with outcomes-driven insurance modeling."

I leaned back against the seat and let it all sink in. "He's not trying to cut care," I said slowly. "He's trying to change the game by using experimental drugs to reduce long-term costs and improve outcomes."

"Right," Parks replied. "Which sounds great until you realize someone has to green-light the risk."

I frowned. "And someone has to *be* the risk."

"Exactly."

I tapped through a Q&A with Phillips. He spoke confidently about integrating newer, more effective therapies even before they were fully mainstream. Not by denying current treatments, but by pushing alternatives he believed had stronger long-term potential. I read his quotes out loud.

"We don't want patients to suffer unnecessarily," he said. "If there's a therapy that can improve quality of life, reduce long-term cost burdens, and shift the standard of care forward—even if it's not the cheapest up front—we have a responsibility to pursue that. Especially when partnered with the right pharmaceutical allies."

I stared at the screen. "He's playing the long game."

Parks took a left onto Peachtree. "Yeah. But long games have casualties, especially when you're trying to prove something works on a large scale."

"You think Greg Hoover was one of those casualties?"

He didn't answer right away. His jaw flexed, and he drummed his fingers once on the steering wheel. "I think Greg saw something in the data," he said finally. "Something that didn't line up. Maybe patients denied access to standard care because Phillips wanted to steer them toward an experimental protocol. Maybe outcomes were fudged to look better than they were."

"Or maybe someone didn't want word of the trial proceeding without PAC knowledge getting out."

He nodded once. "Or that."

We pulled into the PAC parking deck, a pristine labyrinth of spotless concrete and narrow turns that would challenge anyone driving a pickup. Except for Parks. He navigated his too-big truck like he'd done it a hundred times, backing into a compact spot that made me glad I wasn't the one behind the wheel.

He cut the engine. "You get the vibe now?"

"Yeah," I said, handing back his phone. "He's not a villain. But he might be dangerous."

"Especially if he thinks the ends justify the means."

I looked up at the PAC headquarters, its glass gleaming in the sunlight, towering over the street like some kind of utopia. But I knew the truth. It was just a polished surface hiding a thousand decisions, good and bad, made behind closed doors.

"I sent an email and asked for a meeting," he said.

"And he agreed?"

"I told him we're looking into Tellion's coverage path and treatment history, and I implied that if we didn't get a straight answer, the press might."

"So, persuasion. I like that."

"Light pressure," he said with a half smile.

I shook my head and stepped out of the truck. "What's our play?"

"You're the PI with a personal stake. I'm the guy who used to read people for a living. And Phillips?"

"I can read people better than you can."

Parks ignored that and paused near the building entrance. His gaze narrowed. "Phillips is the guy who might've turned someone's or multiple someones' illness into a proving ground."

"Let's go shake the tree."

We walked toward the doors. If Phillips had tried to build a better system at the expense of the ones who couldn't keep up, someone had to call him on it.

We stepped through the doors of PAC's main building and into a lobby that reminded me of a hotel, not a healthcare conglomerate. Polished marble floors stretched to every corner, and the sleek furniture whispered high-end interior designer. I tucked my purse closer to my side and scanned the space while we headed toward the security desk.

A heavyset man in a navy uniform eyed us over wire-rimmed glasses. His badge read *M. Reynolds.*

"Good morning," I said, offering my most professional smile. "We're here to see Dr. Lawrence Phillips. We have an appointment."

He nodded as he typed something into the system. "Names?"

"Jenna Wyatt. Jack Parks."

He looked between us and then back at the screen. "All right, you're on the list. Dr. Phillips's assistant is on her way down to get you. Please take a seat."

I thanked him and turned toward the seating area. Parks followed with his body, but his eyes continued scrutinizing the space.

"Maybe if PAC spent less on decor, they could lower their rates," he muttered.

I couldn't disagree, noting the expensive-looking photos hanging on the walls. We didn't sit, choosing instead to stand beside each other and watch the people moving about.

"I'd like to take the lead on this interview if you don't mind," Parks said.

I glanced at him and noticed the grin stretched across his face.

He added, "Since we're partners."

I rolled my eyes. "I'll give you a chance, but we both know I'll interrupt and probably take over."

"I'm willing to take that risk."

The elevator dinged behind us. I turned, half expecting Dr. Phillips's assistant. Instead, a man in a charcoal suit stepped off and headed straight for the security desk. He walked like he owned the place.

"Detective Marcus Sullivan," he said, flashing a badge with an air of practiced impatience. "I'm here to see Chandra Martin."

He must have parked in the garage. My chest tightened.

Parks whispered, "Sullivan's on the case. Great." He cleared his throat quietly. "You know him?"

I nodded. "The GBI worked with him on multiple investigations. We're not friendly."

"He thinks he's a real ballbuster."

"Yeah? Well, I know I'm a bigger ballbuster," I said. "I can handle Sullivan."

The security guard nodded and picked up the phone. Sullivan turned, scanned the room, and zeroed in on us. I knew that look. I'd seen and worn it before. Target acquired, annoyance activated. For each of us.

He walked over.

"Jenna Wyatt," he said. "And you." He nodded to Parks and then looked at me again. "Good work on the Steadman investigation." He looked back at Parks. "Heard you helped as well. You two workin' your own version of Remington Steele these days?"

"Isn't that a TV show from the eighties?" I asked. "Your age is showing, Sullivan."

Parks dropped his head and shook it, then added, "You just lack charm all the time, don't you?"

Sullivan didn't flinch. "Let me guess. You're here about the Hoover murder. Did Taylor hire you or something?"

"Or something," I said.

He stuffed his hands into his pants pockets. "Let me give you a little advice. We're working a homicide investigation, and the last thing we need is two wannabe cops mucking it up."

I didn't move. "We're not mucking up anything. Call it a side-by-side investigation."

"Same thing, far as I'm concerned." His eyes narrowed. "Since we worked together in the past, Wyatt, I guess I should tell you we have enough evidence to put Riley Chatsworth away for life."

Parks crossed his arms. "Funny. If that were true, you wouldn't be chasing her executive assistant through a corporate lobby."

Sullivan's mouth flattened.

I pressed. "You came here to see Chandra, which means you don't have as much as you want us to believe."

He glanced over his shoulder, then stepped in a little closer. "I don't care what you think you know. This is my case, and I'm kindly requesting you stay out of it."

Parks moved closer to Sullivan. Not aggressive or confrontational, but commanding. "Your case doesn't give you a monopoly on the truth, Detective, but don't worry. We're not trying to steal your thunder. But we're not backing off either."

Sullivan turned to me. "You want to gamble with your license, Wyatt? Be my guest. Just know the house always wins."

I stepped forward until we stood toe-to-toe. "If I were you, I'd spend less time playing poker metaphors and more time finding real evidence. Like you said, we've worked together in the past, so you should know threats don't work on me."

"I don't threaten people."

"Call it what you want. Either way, we're not backing off."

The elevator dinged again before he could answer. A young woman in a PAC blazer stepped out and scanned the room until her eyes landed on us.

"Ms. Wyatt? Mr. Parks? Dr. Phillips will see you now."

I smiled. "Perfect timing."

We walked past Sullivan without bothering to look back. Let him stew. He hadn't come to intimidate. He'd come to find something he didn't have.

Which meant we were getting closer.

9

Dr. Phillips stood outside his office as we came off the elevator.

"Ms. Wyatt," he said, offering me his hand. He turned toward Parks and did the same.

"Please, come in and have a seat."

I wasn't the jealous type, but if I were, Phillips's office would bring it out. Two massive windows that framed the Atlanta skyline like a mural, not a city full of people trying to survive. The light pouring in caught on the sleek lines of his walnut desk and the absurdly overpriced leather chairs. Everything in the room screamed curated. Designer-looking medical books, abstract art, and a sculptural lamp that had to have been something. I just wasn't classy enough to determine what. My office, on the other hand? Wayfair for the win.

There wasn't a single thing out of place. No clutter. No personal photos. Just perfectly arranged success.

He showed us to those two leather chairs and then sat at his own. "I'm assuming you're here because of the unfortunate news and not what you mentioned in your email."

"If you mean Greg Hoover's murder, then yes," Parks said.

"And the subsequent arrest of the PAC CEO," I added.

He looked straight at Parks. "You should have mentioned that instead of threatening me with something. I would still have been happy to meet with you."

"You never know in our line of work," Parks said.

"I'm not sure how I can help, but I'll do my best."

"We understand Vireon Pharmaceuticals is working on a cancer treatment trial," Parks said. "Can you tell us about that?"

"Have you spoken to Dr. Moore? I've overseen the development, but she would have more details on the specifics."

"We have," Parks said. "She explained that it's immunotherapy based and designed to target tumors without the risks of chemotherapy."

"That's correct," he said.

"It sounds like a worthy trial," I said. "And something you would be interested in."

"It most certainly is," he said. "I've worked hard for many years to create new therapies to improve quality of life for the chronically and terminally ill."

"I think I read that," I said. I closed my eyes and let my photographic memory do its thing. "I believe you were also quoted as saying something about reducing long-term cost burdens and shifting the standard of care forward even if it wasn't the cheapest up front. You said you have a responsibility to pursue that. Especially when partnered with the right pharmaceutical allies."

He tilted his head to the side. "Photographic memory?"

I smiled. "Yes."

"That must have been beneficial at Harvard Law." After a moment, he added, "I read about the Steadman investigation. Ms. Chatsworth said she went to law school with you."

Riley had talked about me while I had done my best to forget about her.

"Are you aware of the costs associated with this specific trial?" Parks asked.

Of course he was, but we needed to ask all the questions to determine what he chose to tell us in relation to what we knew.

He turned toward me, that easy smile still on his face. "Of course. I pushed for the trial because I believe in it. I read the recommendation memo and attended the review meeting. After the cost analysis, the board didn't see enough return for the level of investment required. I disagreed, but my opinion didn't swing the room."

Parks scribbled something down. "Was it voted on?"

"Yes, and I didn't have the power to override it. I advocated for further discussion, even presented alternatives. But the financial side won out."

He didn't flinch, didn't hedge. If he lied, he was excellent at it, which meant my truth radar kicked into high gear.

"Did you discuss this with Riley Chatsworth?" Parks asked.

Phillips's face softened. "Riley? Of course. She wanted the trial and to get the medicine on the market, but I think she knew from the start PAC wouldn't support it financially."

"And she signed off on the decision not to fund it," I said.

"Technically, the medical research and development had been funded already, by PAC. Additional funding was to cover the added claims resulting from Tellion accessing the trial."

"So, to make sure I understand, the trial was complete, but you needed an additional company to what? Verify the results?" Parks asked.

"No. The trial was not complete. I said the medical research and development was, at least the portion required prior to running a full trial. While we had access to preliminary data from sample tests, we hadn't used the protocol enough to determine its success or failure rate. That's where the trial came in, or would have if we could have followed through with it."

"Did Ms. Chatsworth push for the trial?" I asked.

"I believe I already answered that," he said. "Riley never made decisions like that lightly. I know she took it personally. She didn't want to deny Tellion, but she couldn't go against the board and keep her job at the same time."

"Do you know if Greg Hoover wanted the trial?"

"I believe he did, yes."

"Was he upset that it wasn't approved?"

Phillips shook his head. "I believe he kept his grievances away from me and tried to work with Dr. Moore. Their meetings were tense at times, at least the ones I was privy to."

That contradicted Moore's statements, but I had already known she hadn't been honest. "His meetings with Dr. Moore?" I straightened in the chair. "How tense?"

"He visited her office at least three times in the two weeks before his death. More as the medical research progressed over the past year or so. Voices were raised, and she always looked rattled afterward as well."

"You visited the lab often, then?"

"I spend a lot of time there when we're working on something important, and given the trial was in the planning phase, or, shall I say, the preliminary phase, since the medicine was already formulated, I had to be there often."

"Did you hear what they said?" Parks asked.

"At times. The doors were closed, but one didn't need a transcript. Hoover carried a storm with him when someone or something upset him, and it was obvious."

"Do you think their disagreements were personal or professional?"

Phillips hesitated. Not long. Just long enough to signal he chose his words carefully. "Both, I suspect. It wasn't common knowledge they were involved romantically, but I believe they were. I couldn't say how serious it was, but there was something there."

Riley had claimed Evelyn Hoover told her Jessica and Greg slept together the one time, but I believed it happened more than that. "What made you think they were involved?"

"As I said, I've made multiple trips to the lab's location. I've run into Mr. Hoover when there. When I saw them together, their body language stated something different than how they spoke, though I must admit emotions often look different when someone desperately wants to help their employees, like Mr. Hoover."

"What do you mean?"

"Emotions take a front seat when lives are at stake, Ms. Wyatt. I suspect you understand that."

"So, are you saying he reacted on an emotional level to the arguments regarding the trial?"

"He was upset on a personal level, yes, but when he must have thought no one was looking, his body language around Dr. Moore in general appeared emotional, not professional."

"So just to be clear, you assume they had a personal relationship, but you believe it was kept quiet."

"That is correct."

"Is it possible something happened between the two personally?" I asked.

"Such as?"

"Maybe you're right about them having a relationship, but Mr. Hoover ended it."

"Are you asking if it's possible Jessica Moore murdered Mr. Hoover?"

"Yes."

"I don't have an answer for that, but I would urge you to investigate their relationship before you make assumptions."

Parks asked, "Do you think Ms. Chatsworth knew about their relationship?"

"I never asked her, but if I noticed their connection, it's likely she has as well." He showed no emotion. "Riley doesn't miss details."

"Do you believe Mr. Hoover wanted the trial for his employees and their families?" Parks asked.

"Mr. Hoover wanted it to move forward. Unfortunately, it didn't work out. PAC determined it wasn't advantageous financially. We are all disappointed. The results could have proved incredible."

Not enough for Tellion to cover the costs. "Are you aware if he ever considered having Tellion fund the additional medical costs?"

Phillips tapped a single finger against the arm of his chair. A subtle tell he knew more than he'd admitted. "I can't answer that, but given the cost increase we had implemented into his healthcare plan upon renewal, I would assume not."

I nodded. "Are you talking about the additional medical claims from the catastrophic illnesses?"

"Yes. His subscriber premiums increased dramatically to cover the cost of those claims. Are you familiar with how health insurance works, Ms. Wyatt?"

"Yes, but please elaborate."

"The rate increases based on usage and doesn't just affect the individual member, it impacts the entire plan. I can't speak to Tellion's ability to carry the weight of that additional premium, let alone the additional costs from the trial."

"This trial means a lot to you," Parks said. "And to Dr. Moore."

"Of course it does. We want to heal the sick."

"Enough to provide the treatment off the books?" I asked.

His Adam's apple bobbed. "Undocumented trials are not only unethical, but they wouldn't garner our treatments any approval. Look," he said. "I didn't agree to meet with you to be accused of dishonorable medical practices."

His change in behavior hadn't surprised me. Guilty people did that, and he knew the trial had moved forward under the table.

"Understood," Parks said. "Do you think Ms. Chatsworth is involved in Mr. Hoover's murder?"

He stared at the wall behind us. "I don't like to throw anyone under the bus, but I have worked with Riley Chatsworth for some time. She is a respectable, honorable person."

Parks looked at Dr. Phillips. "Is it possible someone murdered him because of his refusal to pay for the trial?"

"I think we all know how high the stakes are when lives and billions of dollars hang in the balance."

"Where were you the night Greg Hoover was killed?" Parks asked, not bothering to soften the tone.

Phillips blinked. "I was home. I'd just finished a call with our West Coast team—around eight thirty—and stayed up late reviewing the draft protocols for Trial 7-C."

"Alone?" I asked.

"Yes. I live alone. I uploaded the trial protocol summary to PAC's server that night. Around 9:45, I think." He lifted a brow. "Our emails are all time-stamped."

Parks scribbled something in his notebook. "Any communications with Hoover that night?"

Phillips hesitated, though not enough to scream guilty, enough that I noticed. "Yes. I sent him the protocols for the trial. I think he was reconsidering funding the additional claims because he requested them earlier in the day, which is why I reviewed them when I had the chance. I didn't want to send something that could be detrimental to PAC or sway him in the wrong direction. Obviously, I'd like the trial to move forward, whether with Tellion or another company."

"Did he respond?"

"Yes, with a thank-you."

"Did you send them to anyone else?"

"Dr. Moore, but that's to be expected. Oh, I did see that he sent Jessica Moore a follow-up email regarding the lab results."

I frowned. "You saw it?"

"Yes," he said quickly. "It was in the project logs I reviewed the next morning. I'm copied on most of Jessica's work. Greg was meticulous like that. Always looping people in. I attribute part of his success to working after hours as well as his genius IQ."

Parks closed his notebook and stood. "Thank you for your time, Dr. Phillips."

Phillips rose and extended a hand. "I hope you find who did it." He escorted us to the elevator. "If you have additional questions, please call."

We stood silent in the elevator, not wanting to discuss anything without knowing who could be listening.

Once in the main lobby, I said, "Should we wait for Sullivan?"

"You're kidding, right?"

I smiled. "Absolutely."

We pushed through the main entrance doors and out into daylight.

Parks asked, "If someone wanted the trial buried, and Hoover was the one keeping it alive, that makes him a target."

"Especially since it was under the table and funded by PAC without the board's knowledge."

Tiffani called on our way to Riley's place. "Darlin'," she said over speaker. "I've done a little research and located the person responsible for that photo of your daughter."

Parks and I shared a look.

"Is he still alive?" I asked.

She chuckled. "I don't shoot to kill unless someone gives me reason."

"Where is he?"

"We're at Harris's office. I think you should come by. His story is interesting."

"Do you believe him?" I asked.

"I do."

Harris Taylor's office sat at the top of a glass tower downtown. His security was so tight they practically stripped us before allowing us inside.

"That guy could have at least bought us dinner before violating us like that," Parks said as we waited for Harris's assistant.

I turned away from him and cracked a smile but didn't dare laugh at his joke. He didn't need the ego boost, though I appreciated the distraction from thinking the worst even though Tiffani hadn't sounded concerned at all.

"Hey," he said, clearly sensing my worry. "If Tiffani has him, Alyssa's going to be fine."

"I know." Logic and rational thought never stopped a mother from worrying about her kid.

An attractive woman wearing a black pencil skirt, a white blouse, and heels higher than my knees walked through the door from the offices.

Parks whispered, "Damn, why couldn't she have been the one to frisk me?"

I quietly called him something my grandmother would have smacked me for as the woman approached.

"I'm Mr. Harris's executive assistant. If you'll follow me."

"Anywhere," Parks said.

She sidestepped his attempt at flirting like dodging a pothole.

Harris's conference room was just another ritzy room in an expensive building with another stellar view. But in that moment, the view meant nothing. I could only focus on the kid sitting across the table. His shaggy blond hair needed a cut. His hoodie, which was two sizes too big, needed a wash, and he needed something to calm the twitch in his left knee that hadn't stopped since we walked in. He didn't look old enough to vote.

Tiffani sat beside him with her arms crossed and her jaw tight. Parks sat next to me, silent, his body angled just slightly forward. And Harris stood at the head of the table, a neutral expression stretched too tightly across his face to be real.

I folded my hands in front of me. Tight. Controlled, or at least pretending to be. "You took the photo of my daughter." My voice didn't shake, which was a miracle.

The boy's head bobbed once. "Yeah."

"This is Jason Henderson," Tiffani said.

"Why?" I asked him. "Why did you take a photo of my kid?"

He swallowed. His eyes flicked to Tiffani and then to Harris.

"She wants to hear it from you," Harris said. "Not us."

The kid looked back at me. "I didn't know why. I swear. This dude came up to me at the gym near the ballet studio. Said he'd pay me five hundred bucks if I got a picture of you with your kid."

I blinked. "When? Who?"

"The day I took it. I didn't get his name."

"Did he say why he wanted it?" Parks asked.

"No, bruh, and I didn't ask."

"He showed me a picture of you," Henderson said quickly. "Just you. Said he needed a photo of you with your daughter and told me to sit and wait until you showed, even if it was the next day."

"That doesn't make any sense." My voice cracked at the edge as fury began bleeding through. "How would he know when I'd be there?" That wasn't a coincidence.

"I don't know!" Henderson's knee jerked against the table. "I swear, I didn't know who you were. I didn't even know your name. He just said you'd be there, and to wait. That's what I did."

"How long?" Parks asked, his voice low but firm.

Henderson looked at him. "Three hours. I felt like some perv standing out there, I swear. I was about to give up when she...when your daughter and you walked up. But I couldn't get both of you in the shot. So, I went in after you and just took the picture of her."

My stomach flipped. I pressed my hands flat against the table to keep from launching across it. "You took a photo of a child you don't know. For money. And you don't see how that's a problem?"

"I do. I do now. Bruh, I wasn't thinking. I'm not a perv. He said it was just a one-time thing, and I needed the money."

"Did you follow me home?" I asked. "Did you break into my house?"

He shook his head so fast his hair flopped into his eyes. "No. I didn't go anywhere near your house. I swear. I don't even know where you live. He said to leave the photo in locker thirty-four at the gym, lock it, and walk away."

"When did he pay you?" Parks asked.

"The next morning, there was cash in an envelope at the gym's front desk. You can ask them. I haven't seen the dude since."

I turned to Parks. He watched the kid closely, but something had shifted in his expression. Less edge. More calculation.

"Can you describe the man who gave you the money?" he asked.

"I mean, yeah, but he looked like every other dude. Not tall, but not short. Old. Like a dad."

"Eye color?" I asked. "Age?"

He shrugged. "I don't know, man. I didn't pay attention. He just said he'd know if I followed the instructions, and I'd get paid. I figured maybe he was a stalker or something, but five hundred bucks is a lot of cash."

Parks tapped his knee against mine. I twisted and looked at him. "You believe this kid?"

He didn't answer right away. Just rubbed the back of his neck, then studied Henderson. "I think he's scared out of his mind."

I snapped at the kid. "And you didn't think it was weird that some random guy wanted a picture of a woman and her kid? You didn't think to ask why?"

"I said I thought he was a stalker or something." He flushed red. "I didn't mean to freak anyone out. I mean, I thought he was a perv or maybe a dude checking on his wife, but five hundred bucks is a lot of cash for a picture," he said. His voice cracked. "And it's not like I followed you or tried to hurt anyone. I just needed the money."

"And you didn't report this to anyone," Parks said.

"I thought I was doing something shady but harmless. And then the cops showed up at my mom's house. You think I'm not afraid now?"

I stared at him. At the slouched shoulders, the twitchy hands, the way he couldn't meet my eyes. He didn't look like someone trained to lie. He looked like a dumb teenager who got caught doing something awful because someone promised him cash. "You're damn lucky it wasn't worse. If I'd caught you outside that studio myself, it would've been a very different conversation."

"I believe you," he said. "And I'm sorry." He looked at Taylor. "Can my mom come in now?"

"I'll have my assistant take you to her," Taylor said. He turned toward me. "We'll make sure his statement is recorded officially, and that he cooperates fully with the investigation. Tiffani will get him home."

I clenched my hands. "If I find out he lied—"

"You won't," Henderson said quickly. "I told you everything."

After he left, I asked Tiffani how she found out.

"I didn't personally. I just directed part of the team to the ballet studio and asked them to check video cameras. He showed up on the ballet studio's and the gym's, both inside and out."

"Did you get the guy who asked him?" Parks asked.

"We did, but he's unidentifiable. He knew where the cameras were and made sure not to look at them."

I chided myself for not thinking to check their cameras. "I should have done that right away."

Parks placed his hand on my knee. I didn't jerk away from the touch. "Whoever did this banked on you getting emotional. He knew you'd act like a mom, not an investigator."

"Which is my mistake."

Taylor broke in and asked if I wanted to press charges.

I shook my head.

He nodded once, said, "If you'll excuse me, then," and left the room.

"This wasn't your fault, darlin'," Tiffani said. "And I can tell you that no one's been by Nick's place or yours. You made the news because of the Steadman investigation, and now with Riley's. This person wanted to intimidate you. They got the photo, but they're not goin' after your baby."

"Are you sure?"

"More sure than a hooker in a bar, sweetheart, but I'll have someone keep an eye on things if that will make you feel better."

A tear slid down my cheek. I wiped it off and looked at the table. I hated getting emotional in front of my peers. "I'd appreciate that."

"Consider it done," she said and left the room.

I leaned back in the chair and let out a shaky breath, one that rattled in my chest like it didn't know whether to collapse or scream.

"You okay?" Parks asked.

"I'm going to beat the hell out of whoever did this."

"Not without me."

10

Riley wore a pair of black leggings and a Harvard sweatshirt three sizes too big. We'd always bought sweatshirts like that, and neither of us stopped. I sat on one side of her couch while she sat on the other.

"Do you have news?" she asked.

I exhaled to stall while formulating how to approach everything. "Hoover's murder is growing tentacles."

She pulled up her knees and wrapped her arms around them. "That's good, then, right?"

"It could be." I decided to drop the bomb. I knew how Riley had felt about the victim, and dropping it would get an honest reaction. "Had you heard anything about a possible affair between Hoover and Dr. Moore?"

"Not again." She tipped her chin toward the ceiling and rolled her eyes. "Did she tell you that? They didn't have an affair. Jessica had feelings for him, but Greg didn't look at her that way."

"How do you know?" A woman handed me a glass of water. I smiled and said thank you.

"Because he told me."

"He also told you he was going to divorce Evelyn, and that hadn't happened."

I caught the quick rush of anger darkening her cheeks. "Greg founded Tellion. He's worth a lot of money. Divorce wouldn't be a quick process."

"It's never a quick process. Do you have the attorney's name?"

"I know his business attorney, but not who he contacted for the divorce. Why does that matter, anyway?"

"Just clarifying." I sipped the water.

"Why did you ask about Jessica and Greg? Please, did she say something?"

"No. I'm just checking off boxes, Riley."

"So, no one's said anything about it, then?"

I lied, knowing we would eventually know more, and I would tell her. "No one."

She nodded as if I had satisfied her. "Did you drive here? Where's Jack?"

"I do have a car, if that's what you're asking. He dropped me off at the office earlier, then went to meet with the detective in charge of the investigation."

"Detective Sullivan? Why? That man thinks I'm guilty."

"They usually do when they arrest someone."

She shook her head. "You know what I mean."

"Parks just wants to have a discussion," I said. "It's how things work." Private investigations didn't have specific procedures to follow, but some things, like introductions of investigators from different teams, aligned with law enforcement practices.

"He's obviously not going to be unbiased."

"Doesn't matter," I said. "We just want to know what's not in the reports. Can you recall your conversations with the victim about his relationship with Jessica Moore?"

"As I said, she wanted something, but he wasn't interested, and can you call him Greg, please?" she asked. Her eyes pooled with tears. "It sounds so impersonal when you say 'victim.'"

It was meant to be that way to help keep my emotions out of it. "Can you recall your conversations with Greg about Jessica?"

"Not word for word, but he said she was very flirtatious with him when he came to the lab."

I set my water on the table and got comfortable, leaning my side into the couch and hiking my legs underneath me, like I did when Riley and I had stayed up talking at night years before. Some things fell in line with us, whether I wanted it or not. "How many times did he go to the lab?"

"I can't say. I was only there for a few of them, and those were at my encouragement."

"Did she flirt with him then?"

"Yes."

"Because she didn't know about you two."

"I don't know if she did, and I didn't care. We kept it as private as possible, but I can't imagine someone didn't know, especially when he told Evelyn."

"How did seeing her flirt with him make you feel?"

"I felt bad for her for acting that way, even though it stung, but given the reality that was my relationship, calling her out would've felt like throwing stones inside a glass house."

"Why would you have?"

"Because her behavior was unprofessional."

I grinned. "More so than you sleeping with him?"

She blew out a sigh. "I always hated when you called me out like that."

The laugh that escaped me was real and unexpected.

She laughed as well. "We kept our personal relationship separate from our professional relationship."

"Is that all?"

"I guess I thought I was different because he loved me." She rubbed her eyes. "God, I sound like an elitest, don't I?"

I held up my fingers, leaving just a sliver of space between them. "Little bit."

She dropped her head to her knees with a groan, then popped back up a few seconds later. "Smack me if I ever sound like that again."

I raised a brow. "Well, if you *insist*."

"I take that back. You know how to fight."

She had no idea how true that was. "Why would he go to the lab without you? Is that normal?"

"It depends on the company and the person. He mentioned once or twice that he had gone to make sure things were moving along as they said. Before PAC decided not to move forward with Tellion and the trial. He also emailed with them as well. Greg wanted the trial. He cared about his employees. He once told me he considered them his extended family."

"Yet he wouldn't allow Tellion to cover the additional medical expenses."

"He had his reasons."

"Which were?" I asked.

"I don't know. He didn't tell me."

"And that didn't concern you?"

"Of course it concerned me. Tellion was our largest client. I fought for us to take the hit on the additional expenses, but the risk was too big. I'm sure that was Greg's reason as well."

"Did he still have controlling interest in the business?"

"Yes. As the brains of it, he steered the ship. Strategic decisions, partnerships, funding, it all went through him. But he wasn't the only owner."

"So, they could have voted against it?"

"I guess, but I can't say how much ownership they have or if it was solely his decision."

"Riley, I want you to really think about this again, okay? Is it possible Greg and Moore developed something a little less professional? Think about it from an attorney's point of view. He's already cheating on his wife with you. He kept it private for years, then he suddenly breaks up with you. If he cheated with you, what are the odds he did it with others?"

She considered it for a moment and said, "As an attorney, yes, it's possible, but personally, I never saw anything that alluded to that."

"I want you to think about that for a while, and don't look at it through the eyes of a woman involved with him. Use that law degree."

She nodded. "Jenna, tell me the truth. Did she tell you they were involved?"

"Let's table this part of the conversation for now. I want you to come by your thoughts without the bias."

"I'm telling you, if she thought there was something between them, she didn't get that from him."

"Okay. Noted."

"Good. I know Greg. He wouldn't do that to me."

"Riley, he was doing it to the mother of his children with you. Why wouldn't he do it to you?"

Her face reddened. "I'm not talking about this anymore. I have a question for you."

I attempted to lighten the mood. "Is this going to make me mad?"

"That's always possible with you, Jenna."

"Good point. Go ahead."

Her gaze sharpened. "You're sleeping with Jack, aren't you?"

I blinked. I straightened, met her eyes, and answered without hesitation. "No."

She studied me for a long beat. "But you want to."

I opened my mouth, then closed it.

She gave a quiet, knowing laugh. "You still get that look. The one when you liked someone but hadn't figured out what to do about it yet. The last time I saw it was when you were getting to know Nick."

"I don't have a look, and I was too busy in college to care about relationships."

"No, you were too busy avoiding relationships and using college as an excuse. And you still went out with men."

"Never anything serious. But fine, what's the look?"

"Eyebrows tight, lips pressed like you're trying not to smile. Same exact face you made over that bartender in Boston. What was his name? Jared?"

I rolled my eyes, but the heat blooming in my cheeks betrayed me.

She grinned just a little. "You were always so bad at hiding things from me."

Parks and I met back at my office, where I watched him roll around in my chair like a middle school troublemaker, half mockery, half distraction, but all Parks. I leaned against the window and crossed my arms. "You were the rebel, weren't you?"

He flattened his feet to stop, then whirled the chair in my direction.

"Busted."

He popped off the seat and rolled it back to my desk. "It's all yours."

I walked over and sat. "How did you make it to NCIS?"

"I got my ass kicked in high school and decided the thug life wasn't for me."

A sly smile tugged at my lips. "Did you deserve the ass-kicking?"

"Absolutely." He grabbed his things. "How 'bout we grab dinner?"

"I want to know what happened with Sullivan and tell you about my conversation with Riley."

"Which we can do at dinner."

My stomach growled in agreement. "What are you thinking?"

"Mexican."

I organized my things. "You're buying."

The Mexican restaurant had a wait longer than our collective patience tolerated, so we placed a to-go order and brought it back to my house.

Parks opened and organized the containers on the coffee table, then collapsed onto the couch. He leaned forward and grabbed a spoonful of refried beans and plopped it onto his plate. "I've got my bag in the car."

I had just bitten into a crunchy taco. "Bag for what?" I asked with a mouth full of food.

"I've always got a bag with clothes and shower necessities just in case."

"In case what? You pick up a chick in a bar?"

"Yes, that's what the Navy taught us. Just in case we wanted to get laid but needed an extra shirt."

I laughed. "How kind of them, but I'm fine. Everything's fine. You don't need to stay here again."

"Someone got into your home and put that photo on the counter."

"I know that, but Alyssa's okay. You even told me I have nothing to worry about."

"Except for the fact that someone got into your home and placed that photo on the counter." He kicked off his shoes and heaved his feet onto the couch. "Besides, I like this thing. It's comfortable."

"It's from La-Z-Boy. Steadman paid us well. I'm sure you can afford one."

He smirked. "Maybe I like it because it's yours."

I had two options. Let him stay or pull his chain hard enough to make him leave. I chose the latter, not just to drive him out, but because I was genuinely worried about him. "Tell me about Nash."

"Nice try."

"No, seriously. Tell me about him."

He exhaled. "Nash was a good guy. Tough boss who would kick you in the balls just to make a point, but he always had my back. Always."

"Sounds like Leland, minus the ball-kicking."

"I hate that he's gone." He set his plate on the table. "But he'd struggled for a long time. At least he's with his wife now." He leaned forward and grabbed his drink. "That enough for you?"

"Is that all I'm going to get?"

"Can we talk about the investigation?"

I stretched toward the table, grabbed a chip, and dunked it into the container of salsa. "Definitely."

An hour later, Mexican takeout containers covered my coffee table like forensic evidence from a case neither of us wanted to touch yet. The scent of spicy salsa and charred carnitas hung in the air, comforting and exhausting all at once. I knew the smell would linger for days, but I wasn't sure I cared. What smelled better than Mexican food? Certainly not Parks's socks, the ones he'd dragged across my furniture for over an hour. Truth be told, his feet didn't smell, but the threat of them stinking up my small apartment panicked me.

He sat sideways on my couch, one leg draped over the arm, a half-eaten burrito in one hand and my favorite throw pillow jammed under his elbow.

I kicked his foot off the corner cushion and dropped down next to him with my notepad. "I don't even know where to start," I said, reaching for the cold queso. "Everything we've been told leads to more unanswered questions."

"That's the problem with intelligent suspects," he said. "They know just enough truth to make the lies hard to catch."

"Right? And I'm a pro at reading people."

"You've said that many times." He nudged me with his elbow. "We usually deal with drug dealers and murderers. Maybe they're easier to read than doctors and lawyers."

"Nope." I stared at the food on the table. "I think they're all readable. We're just missing something." I took a bite, chewed, and grabbed my pen. "Okay. Let's break it down. Start with Phillips."

"Yes, ma'am." He grabbed his notes and scanned through them. "Dr. Lawrence Phillips. Head of PAC's clinical division, longtime champion of experimental medical treatments, and poster boy for plausible deniability."

"Exactly," I said. "He never denied the program existed," I air quoted with one hand. "But he never outright said Tellion used it under the table."

"He didn't lie. He just sidestepped." He set down his burrito. "He used that phrase—'preliminary data access.' Like they weren't actually treating patients yet."

"But they were," I said. "We know from Moore's notes and the internal emails. Off-record. Off-budget. Possibly off-consent."

Parks grabbed the printout from Jessica Moore's interview. "Moore's the emotional one. Passionate, borderline frantic. She wanted Hoover to push PAC into funding that trial—no matter what. And she admitted she went around Riley to do it."

"She said Riley killed the trial," I reminded him. "But Chandra confirmed Riley shut it down because neither PAC nor Tellion would pay the additional cost. She had no control over what the board decided."

"Which begs the question," Parks said, "if Riley already said no, why did Moore keep pushing Hoover?"

"Because she knew a work-around. Phillips and Moore both want the trial pushed forward, but Riley says no officially. But someone's moved forward with it under the table. Who?"

"Wallace Bennett?" Parks asked.

"Maybe, but he'd have to do it behind Riley's back."

"Or get her out of the picture."

Parks stretched his arms above his head. "So, if Wallace green-lit it off the books, and Hoover found out, it gives him leverage. He could've been planning to blow it wide open or wanted it on the books in case one of his employees or their family members died. Bing, bang, Wallace murders Hoover to keep him quiet and frames Riley."

"Or," I said, "he was in on it."

He arched a brow. "I think Hoover agreed to the back-door deal and changed his mind."

"The emails allude to that. Or someone thought he was going to. And that made him dangerous."

"He knew." He flipped to the next page. "Let's talk about Riley. Her time-line is shaky. We know she touched the gun. She lied about where she found it. Everything she's told us could be a lie. We haven't verified any of it, and Taylor can't get videos from anywhere she went that night. Nothing strange about that to you?"

I rubbed my temples.

"Right. But she also had motive," I said. "A ten-year affair with Hoover ended abruptly, no explanation. She thinks Evelyn made him end it. He cuts off all contact, and then he's dead."

"Doesn't scream innocence," Parks said.

"But she hired us," I countered. "And she's not stupid. If she did it, why involve me?"

"Because she thinks you'll believe her. Or because she's desperate."

I didn't respond. Both were possible. And neither made her innocent.

Parks flipped through the notes again. "Chandra's interview didn't help much. She's loyal. Maybe too loyal. She could have easily covered for Riley. Even Riley admits she could see her killing someone for her."

"Maybe she did it to protect Riley?" I asked. "Maybe she has feelings for her boss?"

"I don't get that vibe from her," he said. "But if she's involved, it defi-nitely could be a protective thing. She knows where the bodies are buried. Figuratively. Maybe literally."

We sat quietly for a moment, listening to Bob's faint snoring from the back of the La-Z-Boy.

"There's one more angle," I said. "What if Hoover was never going to expose anything? What if he faked it, and someone thought he was going to and acted preemptively?"

"It's possible," he said.

"Or his murder had nothing to do with the trial." I picked up my pen again. "We need to talk to Wallace Bennett."

"Definitely," Parks said. "If PAC was already providing treatment off the books, he'll know."

"And Riley's ex," I said. "If anyone saw changes in her behavior or knows something she didn't tell us, it's him."

"I think Evelyn Hoover's the wild card. If she found out about the affair and confronted Riley like she claims, that's motive."

The possibilities spread out before us like broken puzzle pieces, none quite fitting yet.

"You still think Riley's innocent?" he finally asked.

I looked at him. "I think she's hiding something. But I don't think it's murder."

"What's your gut say?"

I stared at the notepad in my lap, the chaos of scribbles and arrows and names underlined three times. "My gut says Hoover was caught between two sides of something bigger. Something corporate, messy, and dangerous."

"And someone cleaned it up the old-fashioned way."

I nodded.

He stood and began clearing the takeout containers. "Then after the funeral tomorrow, we start with Wallace."

I chewed my bottom lip. "I need to call Riley."

He checked his watch. "It's pretty late. May I ask why?"

"I want to know if she's going to the funeral too."

"That would be a mistake on her part."

"Probably, but I'll put ten on her going."

He shook his head. "You know her. I can't take that bet."

I texted her instead. She replied immediately. "She'll be there but in the background."

"This will be fun," he said with a hint of sarcasm.

"Or a murder scene. You brave enough to handle it?"

"I'll wear Kevlar," he said, and disappeared into the kitchen.

I stared at the notes. Riley's name circled, the word "HOLES?" written in all caps beside it.

She'd said she didn't kill him. She'd said she loved him. But something still didn't track, and until we found something that did, we had no idea who pulled the trigger.

11

Parks had slept on my couch that night after all. The shower in Alyssa's bathroom woke me the next morning. I shuffled barefoot across my apartment's cold hardwood floors, hair in a tragic state of bedhead rebellion and my tank top clinging to one side like sweat had glued it there. I didn't care. Comfort first, vanity never, at least not before caffeine. I made a pot of a decently flavored dark roast I'd ordered from Amazon and scrolled through Apple News, waiting for the coffee to finish brewing. My sweats hung just below my hips, and I was vaguely aware that my sleepwear screamed *divorced woman who owned one too many cat mugs*. I could run and change, but I wasn't there to impress Parks, and again, coffee. Priorities. Besides, Parks was too busy making himself pretty to get a shot of me like that.

After what felt like hours, the pot finished. I poured myself a cup and placed another cup on the counter for him. I cradled my mug and turned the corner toward the bedrooms, only to almost slam headfirst into a wall of warm, wet muscle.

I froze.

Parks stood in the narrow hallway outside the bathroom with steam still trailing from the cracked door behind him. A towel hung well below his belly button, and water dripped in slow, dramatic trails down a torso that had no business existing outside a firefighter calendar, and one I hadn't even considered being on someone like him.

I blinked at the sight of his cut abs, then again, two more times.

"Morning, sunshine."

"Oh," I said, because my brain short-circuited.

He arched an eyebrow, clearly not in any rush to move. His dark hair was damp and messy, and part of me wanted to slap him for being so obviously cocky while the other wondered why the hell I couldn't stop looking at him.

He smirked. "See something you like?" His eyes scanned from mine to my baggy sweatpants. "You always look this cute when you wake up?"

My coffee sloshed dangerously close to the rim. "Can't you get dressed or something?" I gestured wildly to the hallway like I blamed it for the towel situation.

He looked at his towel. "Uh, I was just planning to do that in Alyssa's room. In case you can't tell, I just took a shower. You have great water pressure, by the way."

I stared at the bathroom door because I couldn't look at him, but it hit me then that I had fallen asleep on the couch because I remembered getting up and going to bed. "Did you sleep in Alyssa's room?"

"I did," he said, smiling. He casually leaned a shoulder against the wall like he wasn't half naked in my hallway and I wasn't ready to climb out the window and hide in my Bronco. "You fell asleep on the couch mid–case file, so I covered you with the blanket and borrowed Alyssa's bed. Should I have borrowed yours instead?"

"What? No." I shook my head as if the thought of that made me physically ill.

"You were cute there," he said. "You drooled a little. Thought I'd let you get some sleep."

I groaned and tried to cover my mouth. "I *do not* drool."

"You do, and it was kind of adorable. I'm glad you feel safe enough with me around to do that."

"Whatever," I muttered as I squeezed past him and accidentally bumped my elbow against his towel-clad hip.

He chuckled as I squeaked—*squeaked*—and nearly dumped my coffee everywhere.

"I didn't see anything," I said too loudly, though I was certain my pupils had fully dilated from the brief exposure.

"Didn't say you did," he replied, folding his arms across his chest. "But I appreciate the intense forensic sweep your eyes gave the crime scene."

I barked, "You're impossible," as I hurried to my bedroom.

"I'm charming. You're just not used to being impressed before eight a.m."

I slammed my door and locked it, then spent the next hour getting ready for Greg Hoover's funeral and building the strength to not feel like an absolute idiot after our embarrassing run-in, but the clock ticked, and I had to show my face, ready or not.

"Sorry I took so long," I said as I walked into the main area of my apartment. I grabbed my weapon and placed it in my bag without looking in his direction.

"Wow," Parks said. "You clean up nice. I had no idea you even owned a dress."

I tossed my bag over my shoulder. "Let's go."

He handed me my raincoat and umbrella from the closet. "You're going to need these."

The rain came down in sharp, slanted lines, soaking the tent where the funeral had already begun by the time Parks and I arrived. We parked on the street behind a long string of luxury cars, Range Rovers and BMWs lined up like VIP seating at a funeral no one wanted to attend.

Except the press. Hoover's murder had made national news, and understandably so. His tech company had played a large part in the development of AI, created electronic prosthetics which he then donated to thousands of military vets, and had advanced the country far enough in technology to top China. Sure, he had employees, but Hoover had been the brains to get it moving, and the world felt his loss.

News vans with satellite dishes perched like vultures on their roofs lined the far end of the cemetery. Reporters huddled under clear umbrellas, whispering dramatically into microphones as if their words weren't being drowned out by the downpour. A ring of protesters circled the outer edge of the service, holding signs like "Corporate Greed Kills" and "Blood Money CEO."

I rolled my eyes and tightened the hood of my rain jacket. "They're not even protesting the right person."

"Accuracy is a dying art," Parks muttered. "Just let them be wrong in peace."

The crowd gathered close under the tent, forced together by the weather and the shared discomfort of public grief. Evelyn Hoover sat at the front, flanked by her two kids. Her face, pale and strained, held the vacant expression of someone going through the motions—until she spotted Riley. Then, her persona changed, going from the devastated, grieving wife to the angry, hateful one who'd been cheated on by her husband.

Parks pointed to a man standing alone next to the side of the second row of chairs. "That's Bennett."

I recognized him. "He doesn't appear upset."

"He's probably here for his image. If he wants that CEO spot permanently, he's got to project the right image while keeping the company from tanking any further than it already has."

"True," I said, "but he might want to work on his compassionate face."

Parks grinned. "He reminds me of you."

"Nice, Parks. Real nice." I felt his smile without having to look at him.

"Dr. Phillips is sitting there," he said as he pointed to the back row on the far right. "Hasn't spoken with anyone that I can tell."

I crossed my arms and studied him carefully. "He's had his eyes on Dr. Moore since we arrived."

"Looks like someone might have a crush."

"That was my thought as well. Phillips spends more time at the lab because he's got a thing for Moore, realizes she's only got eyes for Hoover, so he kills him."

"Valid theory," Parks said. "He told us he thought she and Hoover had a relationship. Maybe to make himself look innocent?"

"Or distract us from the truth."

"I don't see it, though," he said. "Phillips tracks as a workaholic. The trial probably consumed him more than he's letting on, and if that's the case, Hoover either backing out or threatening is a better match for Phillips as the killer."

"I agree."

Riley stood a few rows back from the crowd with Harris Taylor, Tiffani, and two stone-faced bodyguards. Most people wearing ankle monitors couldn't go outside a mile of their home, but Taylor's name, and his promise to the court to be by her side, allowed her special privileges. She wore black, of course, sleek and flawless, with her hair pinned tight in a bun. Taylor kept a respectful distance, but Riley wasn't hiding. I watched as she met Evelyn's stare head on.

Bad move.

I nudged Parks's shoulder with mine. When he looked at me, I pointed to Evelyn Hoover. "Are you watching this?"

"Yep. It's going to get ugly fast."

He was right.

Evelyn whispered something to the woman sitting beside her, then pushed herself from the chair, lifted her chin, and stormed through the crowd like Moses parting the Red Sea. The entire crowd stopped and watched her, dead silent, as if no one could breathe.

"You've got a lot of nerve showing up here," Evelyn seethed. "You murdered my husband."

Taylor stepped between them, but Evelyn shot past him, her voice rising over the rain. "You killed him. You killed my husband!"

"I didn't," Riley said, her tone cool but her posture coiled. "I loved him."

"You don't get to say that!" Evelyn's voice cracked. "You destroyed him, and now you're here to what? Grieve publicly? Build your image? You should be in jail! Why should you have your freedom when my husband is lying there in a casket?"

Taylor reached out and placed a hand on Riley's arm to signal a retreat, but Riley didn't move. She stood there, with her shoulders back, ready to cat fight.

"This isn't the place," Taylor said.

"You're right," Evelyn said. "It's not the place my children should be.

They shouldn't be watching their father's coffin being covered in dirt." Tears streamed down her face. "I don't care what you think you had with my husband," she said. "You'll never be part of his family. Never."

The bodyguards flanked Riley instinctively, not touching her, just creating a wall. Someone who looked a lot like Evelyn hurried the children away.

"Tell me," Evelyn hissed. She sidestepped Taylor and forced herself closer to Riley. "Did you plan it together? You and whoever helped you?"

"Ma'am," Tiffani said. "This isn't the time or place for this."

Evelyn shot her a look so fierce I thought Tiffani might take her down right there. "Shut up. This is my husband's funeral. I can say whatever the hell I want. So, back off."

"Oh my," I said.

"You might want to take off those stilettos," Parks whispered. "We may need them as a weapon."

I covered my smile with my hand.

"Enough," Taylor said, more forcefully that time.

"It'll never be enough." Her eyes locked on Riley. "Even when you're rotting in a jail cell, it won't be enough. If you make it to one."

"Mrs. Hoover," Taylor said, "threatening my client is cause for arrest. I suggest you stop now."

"You." She jabbed her finger at his chest. "Are pathetic. Defending a murderer." She spat on the ground. "It's disgusting."

"She is presumed innocent unless proven guilty by a jury of her peers."

"Don't you dare talk to me about innocent!" She glared at Riley. "I know the truth. He died because of you, and you'll live to regret it." She turned and marched back through the crowd. Tears raced down her cheeks.

I understood that level of anger. Not only had I seen it multiple times, but I experienced it when I learned who murdered my sister. Anger fueled the souls of the people the deceased left behind.

Taylor and Tiffani attempted to leave with Riley, but she refused, instead stepping a few feet back, in the pouring rain, to stay for the funeral.

Parks stood beside me with his hands jammed into his coat pockets and his shoulders tensed. "Yikes."

"Right?" I asked. "That went well."

"It could've been worse."

"A lot worse. Have you seen Chandra?"

He pointed ahead. "Second row. The one with her head down and crying."

"Crying?"

He arched an eyebrow. "Not the mascara-drip kind. The quiet, tight kind. Like she lost someone who meant something to her."

I scanned the crowd again and spotted Jessica Moore standing off to the side. Her shoulders shook as she cried into a tissue, real tears, ugly sobs. I turned to Parks. "She's a wreck."

"I noticed. No one cries like that at a business associate's funeral."

"God," I muttered. "How many women was this guy sleeping with?"

Parks murmured, "Probably enough to keep Maury Povich employed for a decade."

Sullivan moved along the edge of the crowd, hands clasped behind his back, glaring at us like he tried to bore holes through our foreheads. We ignored him.

Everyone acted as if Evelyn Hoover hadn't just given her husband's accused killer a verbal bitch slap.

Tellion employees packed the right side in corporate solidarity, every one of them in black, looking like they'd just lost stock options. The only person who didn't fit was a man in a black suit standing off near the flower display. He didn't look like he belonged anywhere.

Parks shifted beside me. "You see that guy?"

"Yep."

The man turned just slightly, revealing sharp cheekbones and mirrored sunglasses despite the rain. He stepped away from the display. Then he walked, calmly and calculated, toward the street. Parks and I broke off without a word and trailed him at a distance. He climbed into the driver's seat of a black SUV parked three blocks away. The engine started. He pulled into traffic and left.

Parks raised his phone and tried to zoom in on the license plate. "Too far," he muttered.

"Too clean," I added. "That guy just made his drop."

We turned to head back, but Sullivan stepped in front of us.

"Not so fast," he said. Rain dripped off his trench coat.

Parks's voice turned to gravel. "You need something, sir?"

Sullivan's smile didn't reach his eyes. "Yeah. Like I told you before. I need you to back the hell off."

I sidestepped, intending to go around him, but Sullivan blocked me. "Excuse you," I said. "You going to arrest us for walking?"

"I'm going to arrest you for interfering with an active investigation if you don't get the hell out of here."

"You mean the investigation you're running in circles?" Parks asked. "The one where the lead suspect might be innocent, and half the people here have something to hide?"

Sullivan didn't flinch. "You're not cops anymore. You're vultures in trench coats playing pretend."

"Didn't know private investigators came with so much intimidation value," I said, keeping my tone light.

He leaned closer and breathed into my face, his breath sour with coffee. "Stay out of my way, Wyatt. You too, Parks. Or next time I won't be this polite."

"That was polite?" Parks asked. "I've seen more charm in a bear trap."

Sullivan stepped back just enough to let us pass.

I leaned toward him as we walked past. "You're welcome to arrest us. I'd love to see the press run that story."

"You're not worthy of the press," he growled.

"No," I said, not bothering to look back. "We're worse."

That shut him up.

"I don't like him," Parks said.

"I could be wrong, but I think the feeling's mutual."

"Think he noticed the guy in the suit?"

"If he did, he didn't show it."

"Which means he either didn't see him," Parks said, unlocking his truck, "or he's playing blind for a reason."

"He's got a weapon with Riley's prints and a pissed-off widow. That's not enough for murder." I wiped my wet hands on my dress. "You ever notice that funerals bring out the worst kind of truths?"

"Not always. Sometimes people act respectably." He pulled ahead and parked his car far enough away from the funeral for Sullivan not to notice, but close enough to know when it all ended.

I replayed it all in my head. The mystery man, the SUV, the appearance of a drop. It wasn't just strange. It was planned.

The service ended, and the crowd thinned. Umbrellas dipped and dodged along the path to the parking area. A few reporters lingered, fishing for quotes from anyone dumb enough to open their mouths.

"Loop back around?" Parks asked, glancing toward Hoover's final resting place. "They're all leaving."

I nodded. "Let's see what he left."

He cut across and took a different route through the cemetery so we wouldn't be in the way of cars leaving. We parked and slipped back into the tent area like we belonged. The flower arrangements still stood tall, drenched in rain but intact. The spot the man had hovered near remained untouched—or almost.

Parks stepped to the left of the main wreath and knelt beside the small table holding a velvet guestbook. "Here," he said, nodding at the ground.

A single black envelope rested beneath the edge of the table leg. Tucked just far enough in to stay dry.

He picked it up carefully. "No label."

"Doesn't mean nothing's inside."

He handed it to me. "Your turn."

I popped the seal and tilted the envelope. A single Polaroid slid out and landed in my palm. The photo showed Evelyn Hoover standing in front of a building. Midday, sunny, not Atlanta. Somewhere out of state. With a red X drawn over her chest.

Charming.

I flipped the photo over. One line had been scrawled in thick black marker.

Next time, I don't miss.

We exchanged a glance because we didn't need to say it.

"We need to get this to Taylor and to tell Sullivan," I said.

"We will. But not before we make copies and have your buddy Drew look at the prints."

"That's not a good idea. I'll call Taylor, and he can decide what to do with it." I tucked the photo and envelope into an evidence sleeve and sealed it while Parks kept an eye out, scanning the road for the SUV.

"Gone," he said. "Whoever he is, he knows how to vanish."

We climbed back into Parks's truck. My phone buzzed before I closed the door. Unknown number again. I shot Parks a look. "I think it's our buddy."

He grabbed his cell and hit record. I answered on speaker. "Wyatt."

Static, then breathing.

Parks tensed.

A voice, distorted again: "Didn't I say walk away?"

I gripped the phone. "You did. We just don't listen well."

"Too bad. You're not going to like what happens next."

"It was you," I said. "You left the photo."

The call cut out.

12

Although Greg Hoover was laid to rest at Arlington Memorial Park near Buckhead, Evelyn hosted the repast at their home in Milton.

"You ever seen the Hoover estate?" Parks asked.

"Nope. You?"

"I've been around it, just never inside. But it's about twice the size of the Steadman home."

"Seriously? I thought the Steadmans were the ones with all the money?"

"At that level of net worth, nothing's off the table." He pointed to an iron gate on the far right of the road. "And here we are."

The Hoover estate sat behind a wrought-iron gate at the end of a winding, tree-lined drive, nestled on ten private acres of rolling North Georgia land. The house itself, if you could call it that, looked more like a boutique resort. A modern Southern manor with a brick-and-stone façade, its grand entry boasted towering white columns and a wraparound veranda framed by meticulously manicured boxwoods.

Massive arched windows stretched two stories high, flooding the interior with light and revealing glimpses of vaulted ceilings and iron-railed balconies.

I gawked at the place. "Wow."

"I warned you."

I had called Taylor on the way and told him about the photo and the calls. He said he knew the Hoovers' personal attorney and would notify him, but that we needed to get the photo to the police ASAP, which meant we couldn't get my forensics guy at the GBI, Drew, to pull prints.

"There's an unmarked here," Parks said. He pointed to the black SUV parked at the end of the driveway.

"It's Sullivan."

"We'll have to pull him aside and give him the photo."

"Maybe we'll win some points with him."

"Would you have in his position?" he asked.

"Good point."

Inside, we made a beeline for Sullivan, who'd stationed himself next to the bar like he owned the place, his eyes scanning the crowd with practiced detachment.

"Detective," I said, keeping my tone even, "we need a word. Outside."

He didn't even look at me. "Busy."

I crossed my arms and tilted my head. "Cool. We'll just keep the threat against Greg Hoover's widow to ourselves, then. Good luck with your... scotch."

That got his attention. He grabbed my arm as I turned to leave.

Big mistake.

I yanked free and stepped in close. "Touch me again and I'll make sure your badge is mailed back in pieces."

Parks didn't miss a beat. "Pretty sure that counts as assault, Detective. Want us to call it in, or would you prefer to do the honors?"

Sullivan's glare bounced between the two of us like he was debating which one to strangle first. Then he jerked his head toward the exit. "Outside. Now."

I hated being told what to do, especially by a detective that thought too much of himself, but I walked outside anyway. I handed him the photo. "We found this after the funeral ended."

He glanced at it, then back to me and Parks, and asked, "You went back?"

"Of course we went back. That's what an investigator does when they see someone acting strange."

Parks said, "Had you not been so interested in us, you might have seen the guy."

"Did you recognize him?"

"No," I said, "but someone here might have."

"You want to ask people about a strange man at the funeral in the victim's house, while his wife is feeding them?" He rolled his eyes. "That's bold."

"And it's exactly why you're here, to ask questions for the investigation, so don't give us that BS," Parks said. "We just don't have the badges to make us look better doing it."

He ignored the slam, but we all knew Parks spoke the truth.

"I'm going to need to keep the photo," he said.

"Understood," Parks said. "But we'd like to talk to Mrs. Hoover with you."

Sullivan dragged his hand down his five o'clock shadow, and a scowl appeared after. "Fine, but I'm leading this, not either of you." He strutted off, expecting us to follow, which we did.

The tone shifted when we stepped into the office. Out there, everything screamed funeral brunch. Flowers, polite voices, and the sadness of mourning the dead. The air turned heavier in the office. More personal. Greg Hoover had built the room to impress, and a piece of him still lingered with his books, his pen collection, and the rest of his things. Like he'd meant to come back.

The room oozed masculine power. Paneled walnut walls, floor-to-ceiling bookshelves with expensive hardbacks, and a massive desk carved from what looked like mahogany.

Evelyn Hoover gestured to the seating area in front of the desk, a pair of leather chairs facing a low table.

"I'd prefer to stand," I said.

Evelyn carried herself in a way that said she had adjusted to being watched and judged and still managed to stay perfectly composed. Had I not seen her screaming at Riley at the funeral, I wouldn't have believed it.

Her eyes slid past Sullivan and landed squarely on Parks and me with narrowed suspicion. She spoke low, but sharply. "Detective Sullivan, I was told you'd be stopping by. But no one mentioned you'd be bringing along Riley Chatsworth's mouthpieces."

Parks didn't flinch. I kept my tone calm. "We're not here on behalf of her legal defense, Mrs. Hoover. But we are investigating leads related to Mr. Hoover's murder."

She crossed her arms. "I have nothing to say to someone working for that woman."

"I understand your anger," I said, "but we've come across something that suggests *you* might be in danger. We thought you'd want to see it."

Sullivan held the photo for her to see. She took one glance and went still.

Her hand shook. "Where did this come from?"

"Ms. Wyatt and Mr. Parks found it after the funeral. Can you tell us where it was taken?"

"It's me in Savannah a few months ago." Her voice shook slightly. She blinked fast, the first visible sign of any emotional crack. "How was—who took that?"

"We're not sure," I said. "We think whoever did might believe you know something about Greg's death or something he was involved in that led to his murder."

She looked up sharply. "I don't. I didn't. Why would anyone think that? We all know Riley Chatsworth murdered Greg. Her fingerprints are all over the weapon." She glared at Sullivan. "Why is this happening?"

"That's what we're trying to find out," Parks said.

Her eyes flicked back to the photo, then back to me. "Riley must have taken this and had someone drop it off. She's trying to make herself look innocent."

"We can't confirm that yet, but we will talk to her about it," I said.

"Then why bother me with this? Especially on the day I've buried my husband. That woman has caused me and my children enough pain."

"Again, we're trying to determine who took the photo," I said. "I have received multiple calls from someone strongly suggesting we stay out of this investigation, which leads us to believe Riley might be wrongly accused."

"Of course." She shook her head softly and added, "You're trying to prove she didn't murder my husband, but you're wrong. She had motive, and she has no shame. She showed up today like she belonged there. Like she wasn't responsible for this. Ask her about it. She must have been following me since my husband dumped her and is paying someone to scare me, but it's not going to work. Regardless of the fact that my husband died of a heart attack, she was there. She let it happen and didn't get him help, then shot him in cold blood like he meant nothing to the world." Her calm demeanor began to shatter.

"Mrs. Hoover, we know emotions are high right now. But this"—I gestured to the photo—"is more than just grief or anger. It's a threat."

Parks leaned casually against the bookshelf. Sullivan sat, taking up more space than necessary. Evelyn remained behind the desk.

I gave her a moment, then spoke carefully. "We're not here to tell you Ms. Chatsworth didn't murder your husband. We're here to find out if you know anything about why someone murdered him, and if he had said anything to you, anything that might cause the killer to threaten your life as well. Specifically his work, his relationships, and any tension he might have had with clients or partners before he died."

"I don't know anything about his work," she said quickly. "That wasn't something he brought home."

Too quick. She said that too quickly.

"But you knew about Riley."

She tensed. "Eventually, but he had sworn multiple times he had ended it. At first, I didn't take it seriously. It wasn't the first time or the last time he cheated. I didn't realize at the time how long she had been a part of his life. I told him to end it, and when he didn't do it fast enough, I handled it."

"You confronted her?"

"I told her to leave him alone. She didn't like that." Evelyn's mouth twisted slightly. "But she got the message."

"Did you consider that the end of it?"

"Yes," she said, but her voice lacked conviction.

"Did he end it because he wanted to," I asked, "or because you gave him an ultimatum?"

Her nostrils flared. "Greg chose me."

Parks tossed out a ball that should have been a home run. "That's not what Riley says."

Sullivan cleared his throat. "They're here to find out what you know about his work environment and people who might think you know something about his murder. Mrs. Hoover, they brought the photo to me, but they didn't have to do that."

She ignored him and spoke directly to Parks. "Of course it isn't. That woman doesn't accept rejection."

"She said the affair lasted ten years," I said. "He transferred his benefits plan to her company. That means something."

"Not to me, it doesn't. She said a lot of things, but so did the rest."

I paused, then shifted gears. "Can you tell us more about the other women?"

"Why?" She pushed back the chair and stood. "Why does that matter now?" That hit. Her mouth opened, then closed, then she folded her arms. "There were others. Greg wasn't perfect. What man is?"

"No man is expected to be. But husbands are expected to be faithful." I felt for the woman. Heather was enough of a hit, but if Nick had cheated with multiple women, I wasn't sure they could have survived me. "Was one of them Jessica Moore?"

Something flickered in her expression—just for a second.

"Yes," she said finally. "But that was short-lived. And it meant nothing."

"But it happened?"

"Briefly. I put a stop to it."

"How did you find out?" Parks asked.

I wondered if he wanted to know in case he found himself in a similar situation, like he had with Jessica Steadman. Sleeping with her wasn't one of his brightest ideas, not that I knew many of those.

"I saw an email he'd left open on his tablet."

That answer came a little too easily.

She had moved to the opposite side of the room and stared at a large photo of her with Hoover and their children. I took advantage of the opportunity and wandered toward the desk, careful not to appear too interested. I had spotted a scattering of printed emails on the corner. Most had the subject line *RE: Patient Case—Private.* But a few were personal.

Jessica Moore. Gregory Hoover. Riley Chatsworth. I made mental notes of the limited words I caught. *Trials. Fraud. Money. Dying. Love. Cancer.* All key words in a murder investigation. If I remembered right—and I always did— the crime scene photos had shown that desk nearly bare, which meant someone had printed those emails. Once we left, I'd pull the emails from my photographic memory and see what they said. In the meantime, I didn't react. I just kept walking around the office.

"I know what you're thinking," Evelyn said suddenly, as if she'd seen me glance that way. "But I didn't know anything about his business dealings. I didn't ask."

"Did he ever mention concerns about anyone at PAC? Maybe some internal conflicts? Fraud?"

"No," she said, but her fingers tapped the table across the room nervously.

I let the silence stretch a beat too long, then turned back to her.

"Did you know about the cancer treatment trial? The one Tellion fought with PAC over? It's my understanding the trial is the reason Tellion dropped PAC."

She stiffened. "No, and that wouldn't have been the reason. He dropped them to get away from Riley."

She had just lied about it all.

Which meant those papers had been added *after* Greg died.

And Evelyn was pretending not to know a damn thing about them.

I meandered slowly toward the bookshelves and let my fingers brush the spines of titles, like *The Future of Fintech* and *Medical Liability in the Modern Age.* Impressive reading, if Greg actually read them. Evelyn, on the other hand? I doubted she had touched any of them.

"You said you don't know anything about Greg's business," I said, not looking at her. "But I see email printouts on the desk. That one looks like it's between him and Riley. Another from Jessica Moore."

"I didn't read them," she said. "They're private."

"Were they on the desk when he died?"

Silence.

Sullivan finally perked up. "Excuse me?"

I ignored him and looked at Evelyn. "Were they on the desk when he died? It's a simple question. The crime scene photos showed the desk. They showed scattered papers on the floor, an office in some disarray. I could be wrong, but I believe there were papers on the desk as well." With another glance at Sullivan, I added, "You should have noticed this, Detective."

She walked over to the desk and let her gaze drop to its edge as her nails tapped rhythmically against the wood. "They were in a drawer," she said. "I pulled them out when I was going through his things."

"Before or after the police left?" I asked.

She didn't answer.

Sullivan cleared his throat. "Mrs. Hoover, anything found after the fact needs to be turned over to us. You know that, right?"

"I didn't think they mattered," she said. "They're personal. Not work related."

But that wasn't true either. I'd caught enough of the subject lines to know that.

One of the printed emails had read, *We need to talk. Someone's been stealing from the accounts, and I think Greg knows who.* I didn't say that aloud. I wanted to check with Parks first, compare notes, make sure I wasn't reading too much into it too soon. But Evelyn had officially joined the list of people holding back.

"I need to ask you something uncomfortable," I said. "And I'd appreciate a straight answer."

"Okay."

"I know you've said that Greg ended things with Riley because you told him to, but is it possible he had other reasons? Maybe something going on between their companies?"

Her expression darkened. "That woman threw herself at him for years. He made mistakes, but he came home to me."

"That's not what I'm asking," I said.

"Of course, I knew there was tension between the two companies. Yes, Greg had mentioned their rates increasing, but I wasn't aware of why, and I'll be honest, that was when I decided to force the issue. I thought it was perfect timing."

Parks cocked his head to the side. "I thought he didn't discuss business with you?"

"In general terms, sometimes, but I had heard him discussing it with Wallace Bennett at an event several months back. Greg wasn't happy, so I asked him about it. He told me that and nothing else."

I called that a backpedal. She knew we'd busted her, and she needed to figure out how to come back from it. Except for me, she hadn't. I knew the answer to the next question, but I asked anyway. "And the night he died? Were you here?"

"No. I mean, yes," she said quickly. Again, too quickly. She hesitated. "I mean I arrived home and found him unconscious, but I wasn't here when it happened. The nanny was here. She had just put the kids to bed."

"Name?"

"Deliah Marks."

Parks leaned into me and whispered, loud enough for her to hear, and intentionally from the tone of his voice, "We'll need to talk to her."

"You're not seriously—" Evelyn scoffed. "This is ridiculous. The killer has already been arrested." She glared at Sullivan. "Why are you letting them talk to me like this?"

He didn't get a chance to respond.

"No, what's ridiculous," I said, "is you insisting Riley killed him when the evidence suggests someone wanted to make it *look* like she did."

"She had the motive!" Evelyn snapped. "She ruined my marriage! She manipulated Greg for years, and when he finally saw through her—when he chose me—she couldn't take it."

"You really think she would kill the man she wanted to marry?" I asked.

"Don't you? She had an affair with my husband. She's not innocent."

"She might not be," I said, "but neither is Greg."

She glared at me. "Excuse me?"

"He cheated," I said plainly. "More than once. And you knew it. You stayed anyway. Why?"

The room chilled.

"Because I believed he would stop."

"And when he didn't?"

"I reminded him what he had to lose."

There it was. The edge. The steel under the silk.

"Evelyn," I said, my voice softer, "did Greg ever tell you he feared her?"

"No."

"Did he ever say he feared *anyone*?" Parks asked.

She shook her head. "Never."

"What about at PAC?" I asked.

"I already told you I don't know anything about his work."

I watched her carefully. She curled her fingers into fists. Her gaze darted toward the emails again.

She knew something. Maybe about Greg's work. Maybe about who was really behind what was happening. But for whatever reason, she chose silence. Maybe because she was scared.

Or maybe because she was involved.

I turned to Sullivan. "We'll need copies of those printouts."

Evelyn stiffened. "No."

"Then you'll need to turn them over through your attorney," Sullivan said.

Her lips pressed into a hard line.

"I'm not accusing you of anything, Mrs. Hoover," I said. "But if you're not honest with us now, it will come back to bite you. The truth's coming out either way. Help us get there sooner."

She didn't speak.

I looked to Parks, who nodded toward the door. Time to go.

"Thank you for your time," I said.

"I didn't do anything wrong," she said. She stormed out before us, slamming the door hard enough it almost smacked Parks in the face.

"I hope not," I replied through the thick wooden door.

Parks leaned close and muttered under his breath, "She's lying through her damn teeth."

I agreed. But the question wasn't whether Evelyn was hiding something. It was whether it was about Greg's affair, his work, the cancer treatment trial, or his murder.

Sullivan chastised us for being hard on a murder victim's widow after Evelyn Hoover stormed out. He had a point, but someone had to ask the questions.

"You made her feel guilty for her husband's murder," he said.

Parks shrugged. "She might be."

"We've got our killer already." His jaw clenched so tight a muscle twitched near his temple. "This was supposed to be about the photo of her!"

"Detective Sullivan," I said, "if you think this photo is something separate from her husband's murder, you don't need to be a detective. We can't know who's threatening her without asking what she knows. It's simple math."

"There's a better way to go about it," he said.

"Agreed," I said. "And I apologize if we came off too hard on her."

"There's also no silencer noted in the initial report either," Parks said. "Will that be mentioned in the additional report as well?"

"The gun didn't have a silencer."

"Yet no one heard the shot?" I asked.

"Or the kids?" Parks asked.

"We've been over this. The nanny was off for the night. She was in her room with her headphones on, watching a movie."

Sullivan yanked the door open and barreled out of the room.

Parks grabbed my shoulder and squeezed. "That went well."

13

A woman serving food directed us to the private kitchen where Deliah Marks poured hot water over a tea bag.

"Deliah Marks?" Parks asked.

She flinched at the sound of her name, then slowly pivoted, eyes glassy and rimmed in red, the trail of a single tear catching the light. "Yes?"

"I'm Jack Parks, and this is my partner, Jenna Wyatt. We'd like to ask you a few questions from the night of the murder."

Her eyes cut to me, then Parks. Her expression tightened. "Are you the police? I've already given a statement."

"We're private investigators," he said.

"Hired by Mrs. Hoover?" She blinked. "She didn't tell me."

"No, ma'am." Parks drew in a breath and let it out before adding, "We're working with Harris Taylor."

The confusion that flickered across her face quickly give way to annoyance, and I knew we'd lost her. "I'm sorry. I'm not allowed to talk to anyone working for Ms. Chatsworth. I don't want to lose my job."

"We could have you subpoenaed," I said.

Behind us, Evelyn Hoover said, "Then do it."

Deliah Marks dropped her head, stirred her tea, then picked up the cup and scurried out.

Mrs. Hoover crossed her arms and looked at me like I'd broken one of the sacred laws. I almost told her I was raised Southern Baptist—we didn't do cardinal sins, just casseroles and passive-aggressive prayer circles, but that wouldn't have gotten me far.

Instead, we left without an apology and with an unspoken agreement to get that subpoena request to Taylor.

Outside, I filled Parks in on the emails. I wiped a bead of sweat off my temple and said, "I didn't read every word, but I saw enough."

He lifted a brow. "You're sure?"

I gave him a look. "Photographic memory, remember?"

He waited, though I didn't need more prompting.

"Jessica Moore wrote that it was imperative the trial continue—even though PAC denied paying the extra claims associated with it. She said they'll put the employees and dependents in the trial without notifying PAC management, and the additional claims will be processed like regular ones, so it would be paid through both companies."

Parks shifted his stance. "How? Won't the doctors have to note the trial information on the claim? And wouldn't it be obvious the additional claims are a result of the trial?"

"She promised Hoover that Phillips would talk to the doctors directly involved in the trial and make sure they follow the designated protocol."

He whistled low. "Meaning the trial's running behind PAC's back like we thought."

"Looks like it. I saw another from Dr. Phillips—he confirmed the doctors assigned to Tellion's trial patients. Gave the list, and Hoover agreed to it all. Based on what I read, it sounds like he initiated the idea."

"Phillips?"

I nodded.

Parks muttered something under his breath and opened his notes app. "Holy shit. This could blow open the investigation, Jenna."

"I know."

"Did you get the names of the doctors?"

I rattled them off as I pulled my hair into a knot to keep it off my neck. "Riley also emailed Hoover, and I don't think it came from Chandra."

"About the trial?"

"Nope. Something about their breakup. She didn't threaten him, but the tone was heated."

"Emotional doesn't mean guilty," he said.

"I didn't say it did, but if Evelyn got these emails, her lawyers will get them as well."

"Understood," he said. "Any others?"

I nodded. "One from Hoover to Wallace Bennett. He accused Bennett of embezzling from Tellion. He said he had proof."

"Embezzlement?" Parks straightened and pushed off his truck. "That's a new one."

"Right," I said. "And now Hoover's dead."

"Let's go," he said.

"Hold on. I need to get out of this dress. It's so tight I feel like I can't breathe."

He grinned while giving me a once-over. "The tight part is what makes it look so good on you."

"Parks, give it up. We might be partners in business, but we'll never be partners in bed. I couldn't get involved with someone who's slept with most of the state. Not that I even considered anything like that in the first place."

"Right," he said with a smile. "Me neither."

I rolled my eyes. "Just find the first place I can change into something that doesn't feel like someone glued it on me."

"Just change in the back," he said as we climbed into the vehicle.

"In the back of what? Your truck?"

He nodded. "I won't look. I promise."

"There is no way I'm going to change in the bed of your pickup."

"The back seat, Jenna."

"Still not happening."

"Fine. I'll take you over to the gas station." He whipped the truck around and kicked it into high gear. A few minutes later, he pulled into the grimiest armpit of a gas station.

"You picked this one on purpose."

"Yes, because it's the closest one around, and God forbid that glued-on dress suffocate you."

I exhaled, then grabbed my bag and jumped out of the truck.

I needed a key to access the outdoor bathrooms, so I headed inside.

"The bathrooms aren't working, ma'am," the attendant said.

"I just need to change my clothes."

"I'm sorry, but I can't let you in them."

"Do you have one in here I can use?"

"It ain't public."

"Like I said, I'm just changing my clothes."

He shrugged. "I don't make the rules, ma'am, I just follow them."

"Thank you, then, for your help." I might have said that with a sarcastic clip, but I didn't care. I whipped around and hurried back to the truck and yanked the back door open. "Move your mirror so you can't see, and put your suit jacket over your head."

That sly smirk he got when he wanted to laugh appeared again. "You want me to put a jacket over my head so I don't watch you changing? Do you think I'm that kind of guy?"

"Listen, Parks. I like you, and I'd like to keep on liking you, so I really don't want to take that chance and not like what happens."

He nodded once, then moved his mirror and draped his jacket over his head.

A few minutes later, I returned to the front seat, and we headed straight for Riley's place. I called Taylor and asked him to meet us there.

Even though Riley's place looked like a page ripped from an *Architectural Digest*, none of it could gloss over the tension crawling up the walls.

She stood by the floor-to-ceiling windows, arms folded, her back straight but her mouth set too tight to be casual. Taylor perched on the edge of the sectional like he belonged there, like men like him always belonged somewhere they hadn't earned. Though from what I knew about him, his hard work earned him spots no one else could sit.

Parks leaned against the bar, his expression unreadable. I sat on the opposite end of the sectional with one ankle slung over my knee, pretending I didn't feel like I'd walked into a war room. We were about to uncover the truth and shift the entire investigation—or walk straight into the trap Riley laid from the start.

I cleared my throat and pulled out my notepad. "We need to talk to you about some emails I saw on Hoover's desk today, and I need you to be completely honest with us, Riley. Can you do that?"

She turned toward me, her face pale under layers of makeup. "Emails? Yes. Of course. I've told you, Jenna. I've been honest from the start."

"Don't act surprised," I said, flipping the notepad open. "They're not written by you. I'm hoping you had nothing to do with them. But Greg, Jessica Moore, and Dr. Phillips? They did."

Taylor's eyes narrowed. "What kind of emails?"

"Ones that suggest PAC was continuing a cancer treatment trial without board approval and mention the funneling of claims through standard channels so they wouldn't get flagged."

Riley's composure cracked just enough for me to notice. Her voice didn't shake, but it stiffened. "That can't be right. We don't push trials through without formal review. We can't."

"You didn't," I said. "But Jessica Moore and Dr. Phillips did, along with Greg. And Riley, to do it, they had to go around the PAC board, and around you."

She dropped into the armchair across from me. "I don't know what to say."

"I do." I listed the emails. Jessica Moore's—passionate, idealistic, desperate to keep the trial alive even if it meant skirting procedure. Dr. Phillips, calm and complicit, confirming which physicians were prepped to ignore trial codes on insurance claims. And Greg, who orchestrated the whole thing.

She rubbed a hand across her face. "If what you're saying is true, PAC is screwed. Jessica doesn't have the authority to green-light anything on her own. And Phillips—he's on the ethics committee, for God's sake."

I nodded. "Which makes it all the worse. They knew what they were doing."

"What about the claims?" she asked. "If they were filed as standard— PAC and Tellion split those. That means we'd eat a portion of the cost without ever knowing."

"Exactly."

Taylor tapped his pen against the table. "That's fraud. Not on her part," he said quickly, nodding toward Riley. "But if it's true, that opens the door to litigation from multiple directions. You'll be facing lawsuits from every insured patient who didn't know they were part of a trial. That's informed consent law."

Riley looked like she'd been slapped. "It's more than that. They're partially self-funded. Tellion handles primary claims until a ceiling, then PAC steps in. If the claims were processed without the trial tags, our system would've flagged none of it. Which means—"

"Means the extra cost hit your bottom line."

She stared at the floor, blinking fast. "Greg was willing to jeopardize everything—his company, ours—for that trial. How did I not know this? Why didn't he come to me?"

"Because you couldn't get approval for the additional funds to pay the doctors," I said.

"You think he did it out of the goodness of his heart?" Parks asked.

She looked up sharply. "He believed in the drug. In the trial. It was personal for him. One of his engineers had a kid on the treatment. I knew that much."

That tracked with the Greg Hoover I'd heard about—more heart than most corporate suits. But that didn't mean he hadn't made enemies in the process. "Then maybe he was desperate."

"He should have come to me. I could have tried to help."

"You did try," Taylor said. "It was the board that said no."

"And you knew nothing about the emails?" I asked.

"Nothing." Her voice cracked then. Just barely. But I believed her.

Taylor exhaled through his nose. "We'll need copies of those emails."

"Too late," I said. "Evelyn has them. You'll have to subpoena them. They're not the only emails. There was one from Greg to Wallace Bennett."

Riley's brows lifted. "Wallace? What about?"

"He accused him of embezzlement and claimed he had proof."

Her face went slack. "That's not possible."

"Apparently it was," I said.

She sat very still for a beat, then reached for her phone. "We need Chandra."

Taylor placed a hand over hers. "I already called her. She's on her way."

The elevator chimed before I could reply. Chandra Martin stepped inside dressed in head-to-toe navy, a laptop case slung over one shoulder, and not an ounce of makeup. Just clean lines and a calm expression that said, *I know something.*

"Ms. Wyatt. Mr. Parks," she said, offering each of us a polite nod. "Riley? Is everything okay?"

I briefed her quickly on the emails.

"Chandra," Riley said, visibly shaken. "Do you know anything about this?"

Chandra didn't answer. Instead, she turned to Taylor. "Can I speak with them privately?"

Taylor frowned. "Why?"

"I have something to show them before I discuss it with Riley."

Riley's brow furrowed. "What? Why?"

"Because I need you to believe me," Chandra said. Her voice stayed soft, but it carried.

Taylor looked to Riley, who nodded after a long pause. "Go ahead."

Chandra led us down the hall into Riley's home office. Once the door clicked shut behind us, she dropped the bag and pulled out a stack of printed files.

"I copied these from the shared executive drive in Riley's office," she said, placing them on the desk. "I wasn't supposed to, but I knew they'd disappear, eventually."

Parks flipped the top page and said, "Damn." He scanned the rest of them. "Shell company charts. Bank transfers. Wire-routing instructions. All with Wallace Bennett's name on them. That's bold."

"It was bold, and it's still happening," Chandra said. "Wallace has been diverting client payments into accounts he controls. Money from PAC. Money from Tellion. He spread it across holding companies. I think he's even used some of it to buy property, because I saw him meet with brokers."

"You knew?" I asked. "That he was embezzling money? And you didn't say anything?"

"I suspected. I couldn't prove it at first, but Riley doesn't know. She doesn't dig into the operations like I do. That's my job. She manages the strategy. I've always filtered the day-to-day for her. It's how our relationship works."

"And you didn't tell her?"

Chandra exhaled. "I was afraid."

"Of what?" Parks asked.

"Of Wallace. You don't understand what he's like behind closed doors. He smiles in meetings, but he's cruel. He threatens employees and undermines them. Once I confronted him about something small, just a ledger discrepancy, and the next week I was written up for insubordination. HR sent me a file with doctored emails supposedly from me. I knew he was behind it."

"And what happened with it?" I asked.

"Riley handled it. She said she was the one that asked me to go to him."

"And did she confront him about it?"

"She was going to," Chandra said. "But I asked her not to. I just wanted to drop it."

"Why not go to the board about him?"

"Same reason everyone doesn't. He's careful. Leaves nothing obvious. But this," she tapped the documents, "this is different. These are copies of emails and financials from an old version of the server before the update last quarter. He or someone he's got working with him, because I don't think he knows how, forgot to wipe the backup." She took a moment before continuing. "Wallace is ambitious. He wanted the CEO role. If Riley got pushed out over the trial, over Greg's death—"

"He'd slide into her chair," I finished for her.

Chandra nodded once. "And he did."

I looked at Parks. He was already staring back.

"This changes everything," he said.

"Can we have these?" I asked, referring to the stacks of documents.

"Absolutely. I brought copies for Mr. Taylor as well."

We spent about thirty minutes reading through some of the documents as Chandra summarized what she believed Bennett had done. When we finished, we walked back into the main room.

Riley straightened from the couch the second she saw our faces. "What? What is it?"

I dropped the folder onto the coffee table, pages fanned wide like a crime scene display. "Tell me you didn't know about this."

She reached for the first page, but Taylor stopped her with a hand on her arm.

"Wait," he said, scanning the top sheet. His mouth went tight.

Chandra didn't say a word—just stood at the edge of the room, stiff as stone.

"What am I looking at?" Riley asked.

"Wallace Bennett has been stealing from PAC," I said. "Diversion of client payments. Multiple shell corporations. Unregistered holding companies. And at least two of them trace back to Tellion's reimbursements."

Riley blinked. "No. That can't be right."

"You said Tellion's coverage was self-funded up to a cap," Parks said. "Once they hit that, PAC takes over?"

She nodded, slowly. "Correct."

"Wallace siphoned off the difference," I said. "The part no one at PAC would've scrutinized because it looked like overflow. He buried it across different accounts. Greg found it and emailed Wallace directly. He said he had proof."

Riley's hands shook. "Greg never said a word. He wouldn't have kept something like that from me."

"Maybe not at first," I said, softer than I expected. "But after he broke up with you? Maybe he wanted to protect you from the fallout."

"That's what I think," Chandra said. "He was trying to protect you."

"Or maybe he didn't trust you anymore," Taylor said. His voice wasn't cruel, just blunt.

Riley sat down slowly, her knees buckling beneath her. "He should've told me. I could've fixed this."

"No," Chandra said quietly. "You couldn't. Not without being dragged down with him."

Riley's eyes flicked to her. "You knew?"

"I suspected. I started pulling files after you and Greg split. I figured maybe it was personal. Maybe Wallace wanted to create enough chaos to get you ousted."

Riley's mouth parted, but she didn't speak. Her gaze drifted to the files again, like they might rearrange themselves into a different story if she stared long enough.

"I was going to come to you," Chandra continued. "But I was scared. I've seen what Wallace does to people who cross him, and you know how he reported me to HR."

"What has he done to people who've crossed him?" Parks asked.

She hesitated, then said, "Our head of compliance filed a concern about a misreported vendor contract six months ago. Nothing criminal. Just a flag. Two weeks later, his wife's private medical history was leaked to a third-party insurer, and she lost her job over it."

"Jesus," I muttered. "That's illegal. Did she fight it?"

"It was her therapist's notes. She said things about people at work she shouldn't have said, so no."

"That wouldn't have mattered. HIPAA was designed for things like this."

"I understand, but you'd have to talk to the head of compliance."

"Who quit three days before my arrest," Riley said. "Now I think I know why."

"There's no proof it was Wallace," Chandra added, but the tone said otherwise. "He has people. He keeps his hands clean."

"And Hoover confronted him about the embezzlement." Parks and I made eye contact. "That's a big enough reason to want Hoover out of the picture."

"Agreed," Parks said.

"That email was sent two weeks before Greg died," Chandra said. "I think he gave Wallace an ultimatum. Come clean, or he'd take it to the board. Greg believed PAC could survive it, but I really do think he wanted you out of it, Riley." Her voice cracked.

I looked at Riley. She had pressed her hands together so tightly her knuckles had turned white.

"I would have survived it," she said quietly. "But not like this."

"And now Greg's dead," I added.

Parks crossed to the bar cart and poured himself a glass of water he didn't drink. "This puts Wallace right at the center. He had motive. Means. Access."

"You'll see in the emails that Wallace didn't want the trial," Chandra said. "He opposed Tellion's experimental involvement. Publicly, he said it was about liability, but off the record? He said it would expose our financial gaps and that we couldn't survive a class action."

"She's right," Riley said. "Wallace was adamant we didn't move forward with the trial. We argued about it."

"Did Greg know that?" I asked.

"He knew Wallace was blocking it," Chandra said. "And when the board refused to fund it, that's when he worked around them. When Dr. Moore and Dr. Phillips helped him push it through off the books."

Taylor rubbed a hand down his face. "This is a disaster."

"That's putting it mildly," I said.

"But it clears Riley, right?" Chandra asked. "She didn't know. I swear to you, Jenna. She's been in the dark the entire time."

I turned back to Riley, realizing then that while I had said, multiple times, I believed her, I truly hadn't. But I finally took the jump. "You really didn't know." It wasn't a question, but a realization.

She looked up at me, eyes glassy, voice hoarse. "Not a damn word. I thought he left me because of Evelyn. Or because I was too much. Too public. Too messy. I never imagined it had anything to do with this, and I would never murder the man I love. Or anyone. You know me, Jenna. The real me."

Parks stepped closer to her. "If he was trying to take down Wallace, wouldn't he want you on his side?"

She shook her head. "I don't know. I swear to God, I don't know."

"Maybe Chandra's right. It was about protecting you," I said. "If Wallace thought you were in on it—"

"He could've discredited me," Riley whispered. "Used Greg to do it. Made it look like I was part of the trial cover-up or the embezzlement. He's smart and ruthless enough."

"And now Greg's out of the way," Taylor said. "And Riley's on trial for murder."

I looked at the papers again. Evidence of corporate theft, fraud, manipulation. But what stood out most wasn't the numbers. It was the timing. The urgency.

Greg had found the truth.

And someone had made sure he'd never get the chance to reveal it.

Riley stared down at her hands. "He was trying to do the right thing. And now he's dead."

I nodded. "And if we're right, Wallace made it happen."

She looked up, eyes locked on mine, pain tightening every muscle in her face. "So, what do we do?"

"We prove it," I said. "And we build the case that should've been built from the start."

For a moment, no one moved.

Parks stood at the edge of the room, arms crossed, gaze pinned to the stack of documents. Taylor sat back on the couch, suddenly silent, his usual commanding presence gone quiet beneath the magnitude of what we'd just uncovered. Riley looked fragile in a way I hadn't seen before—less like a lawyer, a CEO, more like the woman I used to pull all-nighters with in Harvard dorm rooms, back when we still believed the world could be cracked open with ambition and caffeine. It hit me then how much I had missed that girl, and I knew I had to make sure she didn't go down for a murder she didn't commit. I owed that to my friend, regardless of what had happened between us.

I broke the silence. "We need to be careful. This is bigger than murder. If Wallace has been cooking the books this long, and if Hoover was about to expose him, what will he do to Riley?"

"She's already gone to jail because of him," Chandra said.

"Right," I said.

"And now," Parks added, "she's bait."

That landed hard. Riley blinked slowly. "Excuse me?"

"He framed you," I said. "Maybe not with his own hands. But if Wallace orchestrated this, then he wanted you blamed. And from the looks of it, he succeeded."

Taylor shifted forward. "Then we flip it."

"How?" Riley asked. "With what? Some half-buried files from a forgotten backup server? No jury is going to bite unless we connect it to Greg's murder."

"We don't need a jury," I said. "Not yet. We need to attach his motive to this, and a trail of evidence. Witnesses. People Wallace has scared. People who might talk now that he's no longer hiding in the shadows."

Chandra crossed her arms. "That's not a small list."

"Even better," Parks said. "The more pressure, the better chance one of them cracks."

I turned to Taylor. "You have access we don't. You know the executive team. Can you get us their internal personnel files?"

"That depends. You want official or unofficial?"

I gave him a hard look. "What do you think?"

He nodded. "I'll see what I can do."

I looked at Riley. "You said you thought Greg broke things off because of Evelyn."

"That's what I assumed."

"But he didn't tell you that."

Her jaw clenched. "He never gave me a reason."

"Then we need to find out what he learned between the night he said he loved you and the day he ended things."

Chandra sat down on the armrest beside the files. "That was the week he emailed Wallace."

"Exactly," I said. "Something spooked him. Maybe Wallace threatened him. Maybe Evelyn did."

"Evelyn?" Parks asked.

"Don't look so surprised," I said. "She had motive. Pride, family, reputation. If she found out Greg was leaving her for Riley, that's a trigger. And if she found out about the fraud—"

"She might've wanted it buried," he finished.

"But Greg wouldn't have told her," Riley said. "He barely told me anything."

"Maybe not directly," I said. "But she's not stupid. She might've seen something. A name. A file. She could've gone through his laptop. How do you think these emails appeared on his desk? They weren't in the crime scene pictures."

"I can't believe any of this is happening," she said. "What do we do?"

"We go back through Greg's calendar. Phone records. Every conversation in the last three weeks of his life. We find out who he talked to, who he met with. If Wallace shows up anywhere in that timeline, we dig."

"Chandra can help with that," Riley said.

"I'm assuming she already is," I replied.

Riley gave a small nod. "She's the only person I trust right now."

That sat heavy between us. Because once, a long time ago, that sentence had belonged to me.

I pushed the thought away and pulled my notebook from my bag. "I'll get in touch with my contact at the GBI. He can get what Chandra can't."

"Will it be above board?" Taylor asked.

"How quickly do you want your client acquitted?"

"I'll find a way to make the information admissible."

I smiled. "That's what I thought. We'll create a timeline. Map out who knew what and when."

Taylor stood. "And what about the police?"

"What about them?" I asked. "Right now, Riley's their cleanest suspect. They've got motive, opportunity, the gun, and a media narrative. Until we have something stronger, we keep this close. For Riley's safety."

"But you'll go to them eventually?" he asked.

"When we're ready," I said. "And when the case points somewhere else. Right now, it just points at her."

Riley stood and brushed her hands against the sides of her pants. "And what do I do in the meantime?"

"Lie low," Parks said. "And don't talk to anyone. Don't take interviews. Don't respond to press. Don't go to any more funerals."

"I—"

He cut her off. "Just let Taylor speak for you."

"And you?" she asked me.

"I dig," I said. "It's what I do, but I'll need a backup of that drive for my contact. It'll be easier for him to get what he needs if he's got it all digital."

For the first time since we'd walked in, she looked straight at me—no mask of bravery or indignation, just that raw, vulnerable girl from our past. "Thank you, Jenna. I mean it."

I held her gaze a beat longer than I meant to, then said, "Don't thank me yet."

Chandra escorted us to the elevator, saying she'd send the full backup drive by courier and make sure nothing else went missing. As Parks and I stepped inside, the tension in my shoulders finally began to uncoil.

"You believe her," he said. "You said you did before, but now? It's different. Something in you shifted."

I didn't answer right away. Just watched the penthouse floor disappear behind us like the lid closing on a bomb we'd only just defused.

"Yeah," I said at last. "I did before, but I think I still might have doubted it or something, because now I know she's innocent."

"Good. Because I do too, and if we're wrong, we're helping a murderer."

I met his eyes as the elevator settled into a glide. "Then let's make damn sure we're not wrong."

He nodded and pulled out his phone. "You want to take the upstairs angle or the financials?"

"Let's both do both," I said.

His brow lifted. "You sure?"

I gave him a half smile. "We need to make sure we've got what we think we've got, and two sets of eyes trump one."

"And then?"

"And then we have a little talk with Bennett."

"What about Sullivan?" he asked.

"I hope you know the answer to that."

He let out an amused hum while nodding.

The doors opened, and we stepped into the quiet lobby armed with nothing but paper, instincts, and a growing pile of secrets no one wanted found.

And we were just getting started.

14

We stopped at the GBI office to drop off the digital files for Drew Holland, the forensic guru at my former employer, but only after getting Leland's approval.

Leland wrapped me into a tight hug when I walked into his office. I missed seeing his face every day, but I didn't miss the constraints of working for law enforcement.

"Are you here to hand over the Hoover investigation?" He said that in his deadpan, monotone way, and I knew he didn't mean it.

"Yes," I said. "It's too much for us. We need your expert team to do the hard stuff. We just can't figure it out on our own."

That got a laugh out of him. "How're things going with Sullivan?"

"Just peachy. He's a real sweetheart, that one."

"Give him a break. He's had it tough since his wife died a few months back."

I let out a heavy breath and dropped my chin to my chest. "His wife just died?"

"Uterine cancer."

I rubbed my forehead. "You could have told me this before, you know."

A smile stretched across his face. "You're the one that reads people like some kind of psychic." He walked back to his desk and sat. "Just don't do your usual Jenna thing. He's not too bad to work with."

I sat in one of the chairs in front of his desk. Parks sat in the other.

I raised my eyebrow. "My usual Jenna thing?"

Both of his brows shot up. "You know what I mean."

I had a feeling, but I wanted to hear him try to figure out how to say it. "Actually, I don't."

He looked at Parks. "See what she does? She knows what I'm talking about but wants me to throw myself in front of a train by telling her."

"Yep," he said. "I learned that lesson the first day I met her."

"I'm right here, you know, and I treat people the way they treat me."

They both blurted out, "Right."

I tried not to smile but failed miserably.

Parks explained our situation.

"Wallace Bennett is stealing money from PAC and Tellion." He nodded like he completely expected it, but as far as I knew, he'd never met the guy. "If he's doing it with one client, odds are it's not the only one."

"I know," I said. "We have a copy of the files and are hoping Drew can take a look."

"He can, but I'm not sure he'll find anything different than the assistant did. Now, if you had access to a laptop that can get into the company's systems, he could do a lot for you."

I hadn't considered that. I tapped Parks on the knee. "Why didn't you think of that?"

"You're the attorney. That should have come naturally to you."

Leland chuckled. "As wonderful as she is, she's not perfect."

"I think we can get a laptop for him. Does he have time to do it?"

"He adores you. He'll make time."

"Respects," I said.

"The kid has had a crush on you since the day he started. If you didn't see that, maybe we should reconsider your investigative skills."

"Too late." I plucked my phone from my back pocket and called Chandra to ask about a laptop. She said she would drop one off at the GBI office in the next hour, but she would need it back the next afternoon at the latest.

"Thank you, Leland. I appreciate you."

He stood and met me halfway for another hug. "Come over for dinner soon, sweetheart. We miss you."

"After we clear Riley's name, I'm there."

He glanced at Parks. "And bring him along." He winked at me, but I didn't have a clue why.

Parks and I returned to my office to review the load of intel from Chandra. It took us several hours to go through.

"This is a lot," I said. "But I think Leland's right. The emails are damning enough, though the DA's going to want hard proof."

"You think Drew can get that?"

"Drew can get anything."

We spent four hours going through the files and were just leaving my office to grab some dinner when Evelyn Hoover called. She spoke softly, almost as if she was afraid someone else might hear. "I have to talk to you and your partner, please, but I don't want to say anything over the phone."

I put the call on speaker and asked, "Are you okay? Do you need medical attention or the police?"

"No. I'm fine, but can you come now?"

"Are you alone?" Parks asked.

"Deliah and the kids are upstairs. None of them will come down again, unless it's to the private kitchen, and they can't see or hear me from there."

She didn't explain further, and we didn't press. I looked to Parks for confirmation. He nodded and said, "We're on our way."

Thirty minutes later, we pulled up in front of the same house we'd been to earlier that day.

"She's scared," I said. "We need to be kind."

He laughed. "You're telling me to be kind? That's the definition of ironic."

I climbed out of the truck and headed to the door, shaking my head at what he had said even though I agreed.

Evelyn Hoover opened the door before we knocked. Her appearance hit me hard—eyes swollen, face pale, her hair pulled back with no care for how it looked. She was barefoot and wearing a pair of leggings and an oversized sweatshirt. Either the loss of her husband had finally sunk in or something was very wrong.

"Come in," she said, stepping aside. Her voice cracked. "Thank you for coming."

Parks and I followed her into the living room. The same space that had been filled with people felt cold and empty. She hadn't turned on many lights, only one lamp in the corner glowing yellow over the room.

Evelyn sat on the edge of a chair, hands clenched in her lap, her shoulders hunched. She didn't speak right away.

"What's going on?" I asked. "Is it the photo? Is your security team sending extra people?"

"Detective Sullivan is handling it."

"Then what can we do for you?" Parks asked. "You have to know this is a major conflict of interest for all of us. Do you have an attorney coming?"

"I don't need an attorney here. I just didn't know what else to do," she said finally. Her eyes darted between the two of us. "That photo. It stirred something in me."

Parks stood near the fireplace with his arms crossed, but his face softened.

"You need protection, Mrs. Hoover. We can call Detective Sullivan or your security company, if you'd like."

She shook her head quickly. "I can't. Not yet. This isn't about my safety. It's about doing the right thing, and I should have done that before. It can change everything."

Parks and I made eye contact.

"Okay," I said.

"If something happens to me, I need someone to know the truth. That's why you're here."

Was she telling us she knew something was going to happen, and she didn't care? Or maybe she planned to take her own life? Nothing she said sat well with me. I positioned myself across from her and asked her if she was planning to take her life.

"What?" Her eyes widened. "God, no. I would never do that to my children."

"Then tell us what's happening."

She took a deep breath and then exhaled. "I don't think Riley killed Greg."

The words were soft, but they filled the room.

"I did think it," she went on. "For days I was sure of it. I hated her. I still do, if I'm being honest. But I started going through Greg's things, and I found the key to his office drawer, then the code to the safe behind the bookshelf. I don't know what I expected to find. Maybe something that would prove she murdered Greg, but I found something else."

She reached down and pulled a folder from beside the chair. Her hand trembled as she passed it to me. "Those are copies. But they're not just about what people think I know. They're every email my husband wrote or received over the past six months. I didn't want to risk someone taking the originals."

I opened the folder. Inside were printed emails, bank statements, a few spreadsheets we would need time to study, and the emails I saw on the desk earlier.

"That's proof," she said. "That Wallace Bennett—PAC's acting CEO—was stealing. Claim inflation. Billing manipulation. Money routed to shell accounts. Greg knew. He found out and confronted Wallace. There are emails to prove it. It's all there."

"We're aware of this," Parks said.

"Did you know Greg was going to expose him?" She wiped a tear from her eye. "He was planning to take it to the board and to the press. He even met with a lawyer—I found the name in his notes."

"And now he's dead," Parks said quietly. "Is that why you think Riley is innocent?"

Evelyn nodded. Her eyes filled with tears. "I think she was either framed, or she knows who did it and didn't say anything. I don't know. But I don't think she pulled the trigger."

I glanced at Parks. He watched her carefully, and I knew his mind raced with information and theories.

"There's more in the safe," Evelyn said. "And it connects Wallace to every part of this."

"You haven't told the police?" I asked.

"No."

"Why?"

Her eyes locked on mine. "I just found them, and honestly, I wanted Riley in prison. I wanted her to suffer the way I did. She didn't have to murder my husband to break my family. She's already done that. I blamed her for everything, so I kept it to myself. I didn't want anything coming out that might clear her name."

"Then why now?" Parks asked. "Because of the photo from the funeral?"

"That and..." Her voice cracked again. She looked away. "I was wrong. I still blame her—she's not innocent—but like I said, I don't think she pulled the trigger. And I believe someone else knows I know what Wallace Bennett's done."

"You're afraid," I said.

"Yes." She rubbed her arms. "For me. For my kids. I keep checking the doors. That photo was a warning."

"You need security," Parks said. "Call Sullivan. He can put someone outside tonight."

"I know. I will, but I wanted you to know first."

"Why?" I asked. I looked back down at the papers. Everything pointed to a pattern—payments tied to claim approvals, discrepancies in trial fund allocations, patient lists altered. Greg had found the smoking gun, and he died because of it. But how? How did he get the information? Had someone leaked it to him? "Why tell us this tonight?"

She looked up at me. "Because it's not just about Riley anymore. It's not even about Greg. It's about whoever thinks I know too much. And if something happens to me, I wanted someone outside that world to know the truth. Someone I could trust."

Silence stretched for a moment.

Evelyn took a breath. "I didn't want to admit it at the time, but I knew he loved Riley, not me. I told him to end it. I threatened to take the kids, to ruin him. It was ugly. I was angry. I was hurt. But deep down, I knew it was over." She rubbed her forehead. "I don't know if it was the affair, the threats, or the fraud that finally made him pull away from her. All I know is it happened around the same time I told him to end it."

"Do you think he tried to protect her?" I asked.

Her mouth tightened. "Yes. And I hate him for that." It came out in a whisper, barely audible. She looked down at her hands again. "He died protecting a woman who wasn't his wife. And I spent the last few days trying to make her pay for it." Tears fell then, but she didn't wipe them away.

Parks and I stayed with her another fifteen minutes, urging her again to call Sullivan before the night ended. She nodded, but I wasn't sure she would.

As we left, she said, "I'm sorry. I'm not ready to let Riley off the hook. Even if she didn't kill him, she still destroyed my family."

I didn't try to argue. There was nothing to say.

Back in the car, Parks stared straight ahead.

"That was real," he said. "She's not faking any of it."

"I know."

"She's in danger."

"I know that too."

I looked back at the house. The porch light was still on, but Evelyn hadn't moved.

"We've got to call Sullivan. She knows too much."

"And now," Parks added, "so do we."

It was after nine by the time we finished talking with Evelyn. I had sunk into my couch a little too much, thinking I might just sleep there because the day had exhausted me. We had learned a lot, but instead of getting us the answers we needed, we landed with more questions, and we both needed a break. Sometimes a few hours of normalcy brought clarity to an investigation, and those few hours had to include sleep.

We'd grabbed Thai food from a place off 141 and took it to my apartment, where we briefly talked through what we could without pulling out files. After agreeing to cut the work talk, Parks grabbed the remote from the coffee table and turned on Hulu.

He lounged at the opposite end of the couch, long legs stretched out, his arm resting across the back like he lived there. Even though he didn't, and we *both* knew that, the way he occupied space, one would think he had a spare key.

"True crime or Hallmark?" he asked.

I raised an eyebrow. "Those are my only choices?"

"It's after eleven. I'm not even sure Hallmark's still on."

I wasn't too embarrassed to tell him it was and probably playing *Golden Girls*.

"You watch Hallmark?"

"In our line of work, sometimes I need a guaranteed happy ending. Besides, the *Golden Girls* is hilarious." I regretted using that phrase immediately after it left my lips.

Surprisingly, Parks ignored it. "Okay, Grandma." His eyes trailed over me, slowly. I wanted to crawl under a blanket and hide. "You look like a Hallmark watcher right now." He hit a button, and a romance came to life on the TV.

I blanched. "What does that even mean?"

"The sweats and hair up in a messy bun."

"The fact that you know the term 'messy bun' scares me."

"I know a lot more than you think I do."

"And I'm fine never knowing what that might be." I ignored the sly grin taking over his face.

"How's this, then? We've done a lot today and gotten nowhere, and mindless, feel-good TV will lift our spirits."

"I agree," I said. "Hallmark it is." I glanced at the screen and smiled. I may have watched ten romance movies in my lifetime, and I secretly laughed when Alyssa told me Nick watched them with Heather, but I saw their value after dealing with corporate crime and murder. "Plus, I like this guy. He's attractive. Too bad it's almost over."

He studied the actor for a second. "That guy?" He shook his head. "Not even close to your type."

"How would you know anything about my type?"

"I met Nick, remember?"

"And?"

"You're more into the preppy, straitlaced, tech nerd than this guy."

"First of all, no one says the word 'preppy' anymore, and that's not at all my type."

"Then why'd you marry him?"

I closed my eyes, knowing whatever answer I gave would spark even more discussion about my type. "Can we just watch the show?" I tugged the throw blanket across my lap.

"Yes, ma'am. I'm sorry you missed your time with Alyssa."

"It's part of the job. At least Nick and I have finally come to an understanding about it."

He looked over at me. The corners of his eyes crinkled. "She would have talked you into dancing too, wouldn't she?"

"She wouldn't have to talk me into anything. She'd just give me that look, the one where I'm suddenly a terrible parent if I don't participate, and next thing I know, I'm doing pirouettes in fuzzy socks and nearly busting my knee on the coffee table, all in front of the home-wrecker."

Parks laughed, full-out. "I wish I could see that. I bet the home-wrecker would hate you for it."

The way he said "home-wrecker" with an intentional accent on the words made me smile. "I'm sure she would, but trust me, you'll never see me pirouetting in fuzzy socks." I paused and watched the way his smile lingered. "But it's always fun, despite the audience, doing things like that with her. I consider it a win in my mom world."

"It's more than a win," he said, his voice softer. "It says a lot about how you feel about her, and she can sense it."

I wasn't great at taking compliments, especially ones that went below the surface. I shifted a little and tried to act like his words didn't hit somewhere deep. "She's five. A cheeseburger from McDonald's makes me an okay mom."

"You're much more than that."

He said it like it was just a fact. No fluff. No performance. Just a steady truth he saw and figured I should too.

I didn't know how to respond to that, so I did what I usually did when my emotions got too close to the surface—I deflected. "You get any sleep lately?"

"Not much." He stretched slightly, and his shirt rode up just enough to flash a line of skin before settling back down. "But this is nice. Low-key. No interrogations. No surveillance footage. No takeout containers full of regret. Well," he smiled, "maybe one."

"You didn't like the pad see ew?"

"I liked it fine, but all this takeout is going to kill me. And you. One day you'll come home, and I'll have a home-cooked dinner waiting. Fair warning."

I snorted. "Come home? Isn't home your place? The one where all your stuff is?"

"I consider it my second home now." He winked.

I rolled my eyes, but there was a smile behind it.

I pulled the blanket a little tighter around me. "I should probably get to bed soon. It's been a day."

He didn't say anything right away. Just leaned slightly toward me and rested one hand along the back of the couch. His fingers brushed against my shoulder, just the lightest touch, like he was checking if I'd flinch or freeze.

I didn't do either.

He leaned in just a little more. His face was close—closer than it had any right to be.

I swallowed. My brain hadn't caught up to my body, which had decided, on its own, apparently, that leaning in was the correct response.

His eyes flicked to mine once. He was going to kiss me, and I couldn't move.

And then my phone rang. Loud. Shrill. Jarring.

Parks pulled back instantly while muttering something that might've been a curse word, or just a long, slow exhale of frustration.

I blinked like I'd just snapped out of a spell. I glanced at the phone. "It's Taylor." I answered and hit speaker. "This is Jenna."

"Ms. Wyatt, is Mr. Parks with you?"

"Why would you ask me that?"

Parks eyed me and raised his brow. "I'm here. What's up?"

Taylor's voice came through like a wrecking ball. "Sorry for the late call, but I've just received a call from Detective Sullivan. Evelyn Hoover is dead."

15

Detective Sullivan sauntered over and scowled at us. "How did I know you two would be here?"

"You're a smart guy," I said. "And it's an easy assumption to make."

An officer called for him to come back inside. He pointed at me. "You can come inside when I tell you, understand?"

Wow. Being nice worked. "Yes."

As he walked away, Parks said, "You're supposed to be easy on the guy, remember?"

"I was. I told him he's a smart guy."

"And then retracted it by saying it was obvious we'd be here."

"That wasn't mean," I said. "It's just true."

"Sometimes it's okay to leave out the obvious, Wyatt." He turned and headed toward the front door of the Hoover residence.

I trailed behind him and threw my palms up, still completely confused. "I was being nice!"

He stopped beside an officer near the front door. I stood by his side.

"Law enforcement only," the officer said. He didn't bother acknowledging us with his eyes.

"Understood," Parks said. "We're waiting for Detective Sullivan."

Without looking at us again, he said, "Please wait behind the yellow tape."

As we walked away, me cussing him out under my breath, an officer from inside hollered, "Are you two Parks and Wyatt?"

We turned around. "Yes."

"Detective Sullivan said to come on in."

I gave the rude officer my prettiest smile and batted my eyelashes at him as we walked past. I knew procedure, though he didn't know I knew that, but either way, he didn't have to be an ass.

"See," I said to Parks. "I was very nice to him even though he's an ass."

Sullivan met us in the kitchen. "She's in the office. No sign of forced entry, and the nanny didn't hear a thing. She came downstairs and saw the lights on in the office. Went to turn them off and found her."

"Shot?"

He nodded. I noticed the guilt washing over his face. "I should have put men on her after the photo, but she insisted her security could handle it."

"What security?" I asked. "No one was here a few hours ago, and they weren't when we were here before that, either."

"Wait," he said. "You were here again?"

Parks explained that Evelyn had called us and why.

His face reddened. "Why didn't you call me?"

"She wanted to handle this, and we respected that," he said.

Sullivan's jaw tightened so much I thought he might break off teeth. He dropped his head and rubbed the balding spot with his hand. "These kids just lost their parents." He straightened and turned in a circle. "Their lives are ruined." He glared at Parks and then at me. "You should have called me. You know that. However you feel about me, you should have called."

He was right. We should have, and that regret would haunt me the rest of my life. "You're right, Detective. We should have. This is no excuse, but she assured us her security team would keep her safe."

"She doesn't have security. Damn it! Those poor kids. I need to get someone on Bennett."

"No," Parks said. "Let us do it. Please. We'll keep you in the loop one hundred percent."

"No way. You're out completely. You let someone leave those kids without a mother."

I took the deserved gut punch. "Yes, we did, and we want to make up for it. We have studied those documents. We've got a contact at the GBI going through their system to gather damning evidence. We need to take this guy down."

He looked at me and then Parks. "I want continuous updates. If I find out you've hidden anything from me, I'll throw your asses in jail for obstruction. Do you understand?"

"Yes," I said through gritted teeth.

"Yes, sir," Parks said.

We followed him to the office, took a quick look around, and then left Sullivan and his team to do their job.

In Parks's truck, I said, "We should have called him."

"I know."

I leaned my head against the seat. "How is this person getting into their home?"

"I think they know the passcode for the lock."

"Would Bennett know that?"

"It's possible," he said. "If he has any knowledge of technology, he can create a work-around."

"If Bennett did this to shut her up—"

He cut me off. "He's going down hard."

"Wait a minute," I said. "Who else has the passcode?"

Parks turned toward me as the realization slapped him in the face. "The nanny." He whipped the truck around and screamed back up the driveway and jumped out of the car immediately after killing the engine. I raced after him.

He barked at an officer, "We need to see Sullivan again."

"Go on in," the officer said in a resigned tone.

As we climbed the stairs two at a time, I heard him say, "Damn PIs think they know what they're doing."

Sullivan stood outside a child's room staring at a woman gathering clothes and toys into a suitcase. He flipped around and eyed us with a raised eyebrow. "What now? I've got a murder scene to handle."

"We need five minutes," Parks said. "In private."

He pinched the bridge of his nose. "Follow me." He walked us to another bedroom, one decorated for a guest. "What now?"

"The nanny," Parks said. "We think she's letting the killer inside."

"It makes sense," I said, before he could push back. "She hasn't heard anything. There wasn't a silencer on the gun left at Riley's place. Then tonight she comes down and miraculously finds Evelyn dead in the office?"

"She either called the killer, or she did it herself. Did you question her?"

"Of course I questioned her. I'm not an idiot. Her story made sense. The kids clung to her, and it was clear she cared for them."

"Doesn't mean she wouldn't do something for the right amount of money."

I waited for him to disagree, but he didn't. He let loose a string of words sharp enough to peel paint. "How the hell did I miss that?"

"Sullivan," I said, "you're going through a lot right now."

His expression softened. "You know about that?"

"We do, and no one expects you to be one hundred percent right now."

He pointed toward the kids' rooms. "They do. And Evelyn Hoover did."

———

The next morning, I met Parks at the Georgia Bureau of Investigation. We walked into the tech lab where the faint scent of burnt coffee greeted me like an old friend. A brief flash of nostalgia washed over me, then faded even faster. I missed working with the team, but I didn't miss the constraints of the law.

Drew sat hunched over a battered laptop as his fingers flew across the keyboard faster than my brain could keep up.

"You look like you haven't slept in a week," Parks said, pulling out a chair.

"It feels like it," Drew said without looking up. "Not since I got this thing." He patted the company-issued laptop from PAC.

I settled into the seat across from him. "Tell me it's worth it."

Drew cracked a grin, all teeth and exhaustion. "Oh, it's worth it. You ready for the good stuff?"

"Hit us."

He spun the laptop around so we could see the screen. Rows of spreadsheets and system diagrams blurred in front of me. Drew tapped a few keys and pulled up a series of client billing summaries.

"Okay, here's the simple version. Every client of PAC Health—Tellion included—pays premiums based on projected claims and fees," he said. "Nothing shocking there. But it looks like Bennett, or someone working with him, built a secondary billing stream inside the claims system."

"Can you explain it in layman's terms?" Parks asked.

"I thought I was."

I chuckled. Drew, a Gen Z kid, had no problem speaking in high-tech tongue, but he always tried to dumb it down for us old people. "Go on," I said. "We'll stop you if we don't understand."

He nodded. "He set it up so that after claims were processed through underwriting, an automated script would trigger. It quietly increased the charges billed to client companies by an additional five to ten percent, depending on the service category." He pulled up a visual map. "See this? Every time a doctor submitted a bill for, say, an MRI, the amount PAC paid the doctor stayed the same. But it inflated the amount billed to the client."

"Wouldn't accounting spot the mismatch?" I asked.

"Not if you're smart about it," Drew said. "The script inserted new billing codes into the system, making it look like legitimate administrative fees. To anyone not digging into the raw claims files, it would just look like normal overhead."

Parks grunted. "That's ballsy."

"Ballsy and brilliant. Especially because he didn't hit every claim. He targeted a random ten percent each month, spreading it out across hundreds of client companies." Drew tapped a folder labeled "Red Flags." "And he made sure no client got hit hard enough to notice. A few bucks here, a few bucks there. For the largest insurance company in the country and thousands of claims daily, it adds up."

"How much are we talking?" I asked.

He clicked open a spreadsheet so big my eyes hurt looking at it. "Conservatively? Ten million over the last three years."

Parks let out a low whistle. "Jesus."

"And here's the kicker." Drew flipped to another file. "He had help. He couldn't have moved the money without someone inside the accounts billing and receiving department."

"I wouldn't think so," I said. "Can you tell who?"

"I'll get to that. When PAC invoices their corporate clients," Drew said, "those invoices are generated by the claims management system, but the money comes into a separate system for accounts billing and receiving. Someone in that department had to manually approve the inflated amounts before they got rolled into the client-facing invoices."

"Without that insider, the system would have flagged the differences?" Parks asked

"Exactly. And even better?" Drew smirked. "I found manual overrides logged into the system. Someone went in after hours, approved the invoices, and rerouted the excess funds into a shell account. Not a PAC account. One set up to look like a vendor."

I felt my stomach tighten. "Who owns the shell account?"

"Still tracking that. It's layered through three dummy corporations, but I'm getting close. What I can tell you is that it doesn't belong to PAC, and it sure as hell doesn't belong to any real vendor." He pointed to the time stamps. "And whoever was doing the manual approvals? Same log-in ID every time."

"Whose?" Parks asked.

Drew paused, his smile turning grim. "A woman named Meredith Cole. Senior billing specialist."

"She high enough to get away with this?" I asked.

"High enough to access and override billing records without triggering automatic audits," Drew said. "And smart enough to work odd hours so her changes blended into system maintenance windows."

"So Wallace inflated the claims," Parks said slowly, "and Meredith made sure the fake invoices passed, then funneled the difference into a shell account."

"Well, I can tell you that whoever inflated the claims did it with a log-in attributed to Wallace. Whether he did it or had someone do it for him, it traces back to him."

I leaned back in my chair, processing. "And nobody caught this for three years?"

"PAC has internal audits," Drew said. "But Wallace somehow kept the auditors focused on different areas. And Meredith was careful. She kept the numbers low, the clients happy, and the payouts regular."

Parks tapped the table. "If you were the auditor, what would tip you off?"

"Without direct access to the raw claims data? Nothing," Drew said. "But with this?" He pointed at the laptop. "The trail's all over the place."

"Could clients like Tellion sue PAC over this?" I asked.

"Oh, absolutely. Once this blows up, it'll be a feeding frenzy." Drew rubbed his face. "PAC will go down. Their stock will plummet. But if we don't move fast, Bennett's going to bury whatever's left of the evidence."

I glanced at Parks. "We need to find Meredith Cole."

"Already flagged her address," Drew said. "You want it?"

"Send it," Parks said.

The chair scraped against the floor as I stood. My heart thudded hard against my ribs, the weight of the conspiracy pressing down like a heavy fog. "One more thing, Drew. Is there a way to prove Wallace orchestrated the whole thing?"

Drew hesitated, then nodded. "Maybe. Someone had to set up the shell account and authorize it. I pulled metadata from the account's creation. The IP address traces back to a device registered under Wallace Bennett's name."

Parks barked a laugh. "Guy's a genius with fraud and an idiot with tech."

"Most criminals are," Drew said. "They think they're smarter than everyone else."

"Until they're not," I said.

"I created a flowchart of what I explained and provided real-time examples if you have questions."

"Of course you did," I said. "I appreciate it."

"If you can get me the laptop again, I might be able to find more intel, but I can't make any promises."

"We'll do our best," I said. "Thanks, Drew. You're the golden ticket we needed."

He blushed. "I try."

Parks and I asked Sullivan, Taylor, and Chandra to meet us at Riley's place and headed straight there.

He drove again, of course, weaving in and out of traffic down 400. I gripped the *oh shit* handle above the door with both hands. "We're not on the Autobahn."

He'd locked his mind on the case. "I'm assuming Drew made sure no one could tell he went into the system, yes?"

"Yes, and I'm going to throw up all over this fancy truck of yours if you don't stop dodging in and out of traffic."

He glanced at me. "Seriously?"

"Seriously."

He dropped his speed and stayed in the far-left lane long enough for me to release my death grip on the handle.

"We don't have much time," he said. "We need this Meredith Cole woman and the nanny to talk."

"They'll talk," I said. "But we've got the evidence whether they do or not. What we need to do is make sure no one else dies."

He nodded. "Like one of them."

"Right."

16

Tiffani opened the door. She smiled, but it faded quickly. "Sugar, you two look like you've been to a prayer meeting and back without findin' the Lord."

"Add hit by a Mack truck there and back, and you're close," I said.

"I'll make sure you've got fresh coffee, stat." She closed the door behind us and snapped her fingers at the housekeeper. "Darlin', we need two strong coffees and maybe a bagel or two for some energy. Do you have any lox?"

The woman nodded once. "Yes, ma'am."

"Thank you," Tiffani said. "That should help get your blood moving. After this," she said to me, "we're hitting a day spa. There's nothing a mud bath and a massage can't fix."

I smiled, though I doubted I'd ever take a mud bath, and the thought of a stranger rubbing their hands all over my body made me feel more like throwing up than Parks's driving.

Riley hurried into the room. "Hey. Is everything okay?"

I nodded. "I spoke to Harris. We want you all here to go over what we discussed earlier about Wallace. He said he's asked the ADA to come as well."

Her eyes brightened. "It's going to clear me, isn't it?"

"It's very possible."

She threw her arms around me and squeezed so tight it hurt. "Jenna, thank God. I knew you could do this!"

"We're not done," I said. "And it's not just me." I eyed Parks. "Go try and break his ribs now."

She smiled and hopped toward him. "I have no problem with that." He hugged her back, but she pulled away quickly. "I feel awful about Evelyn. Those poor children."

"We do too," I said. "But what matters now is making sure we catch her killer."

"Do you know who it might be?"

"We have a theory, but we need the evidence to back it up. Something to connect them to the murders specifically."

Chandra walked in. "I only have two hours. I can't keep missing work like this, or I'll end up taking unemployment."

"Let's hope that doesn't happen," Parks said.

Taylor arrived and headed straight to the office for a call. Shortly after, Sullivan and the ADA, Zach Christopher, arrived. I knew Christopher and liked and respected him even though we no longer worked for the same team.

"I hope this is strong," he said. "I don't have a lot of time for theories."

"Define theories," I said. "Because we have one, and it's big."

"Big enough for an arrest?"

"Bigger," Parks said. "Multiple arrests."

"Then let's do this."

The housekeeper gathered everyone together and served pastries. We weren't there for a book club meeting, but I doubted she viewed it as something different. A gathering was a gathering, regardless of the reason.

"We believe," Parks said, "we've got enough evidence to acquit Riley."

"Then why am I here?" Christopher asked. "I'll see it in discovery."

"Wouldn't you rather drop the charges than waste taxpayers' money for a trial?" I asked.

"This better be good."

"Wallace Bennett," I said. "We've found reasonable doubt that can clear Riley."

"It's more than reasonable doubt," Riley said. "Right? It sounded like it before."

"That's not up to us," I said. Christopher waited for me to continue. "He's embezzled millions from PAC and their clients for the past three years, and Greg Hoover figured it out. Evelyn Hoover found multiple emails and information in Greg's files, both digital and hard copy, and now she's dead."

"Continue," Christopher said.

"Every client of PAC Health, including Tellion, pays premiums based on projected claims and administrative fees. My contact at the GBI accessed the system through a laptop Chandra provided and found that Wallace Bennett, or someone working under him, built a secondary billing stream inside the claims system. After claims were processed normally, an automated script triggered, inflating the charges billed to the client companies by an extra five to ten percent. PAC still paid the doctors the correct amount. The difference was hidden under made-up adminis-trative fees, so unless you dug into the raw claims data, it looked legitimate."

Parks continued. "He targeted a random ten percent of claims each month, spread across hundreds of companies. Not enough for anyone to notice individually, but at scale, over three years, it added up to about ten million dollars."

"That's crazy," Riley said. "I would have never guessed Bennett was stealing from PAC."

"He did," I said. "And we know the money didn't stay inside PAC. Someone rerouted through accounts billing and receiving. A senior billing specialist named Meredith Cole manually approved the inflated amounts after hours. She used her system access to override normal checks, then redirected the excess into a shell account disguised as a vendor."

Parks added, "Right. The shell account doesn't belong to PAC or any actual vendor. It's layered through three dummy corporations. Drew's still untangling it, but the creation metadata for the shell traces back to an IP address registered to Wallace Bennett's personal device."

"Let me see if I have this right," Riley said. "Bennett's log-in inflated the claims. Meredith Cole manually approved the fraudulent invoices. The money was funneled out into a fake vendor account. That doesn't make sense. How did the auditors not catch it?"

"I think," Chandra said, "because Wallace kept them chasing different issues, and the amounts were small enough not to raise suspicion on client audits."

I let out a slow breath. "We have hard digital evidence linking both Wallace and Meredith." I tapped the file from Drew. "He also created a flowchart with a full breakdown if you want the visual. And if we can get access to Wallace's laptop, Drew might be able to pull even more evidence."

"How does this prove Bennett murdered the Hoovers?" Christopher asked.

"We have an email exchange between Bennett and Hoover. Hoover knew, and he was about to call out Bennett, but he didn't get the chance."

"And the wife?"

"Like Jenna said, she found the emails," Parks said.

"And we think Mr. Bennett believed she knew because of this," Sullivan said. He showed Christopher the photo from the funeral.

Christopher rubbed his eyes. "We need to connect him to the weapon, and this has to be on the down-low. The media will have a field day if this gets out and we're wrong."

"We'll connect him," Parks said. "I can promise you that."

"We still don't know how he, or whoever killed the Hoovers, got into the home."

"We think we do," Parks said. "The nanny."

Christopher drew in a breath and let it out slowly. Looking at Sullivan, he said, "I want you on that nanny. If they're right, she's the only witness we have to talk."

We left then and were headed toward the office when Nick called.

"Hey," I said. "Is Alyssa all right?"

"She's fine. She's got early release today, and Heather said when she dropped her off at school, Alyssa asked if she could spend the day with you."

"Uh..." I paused for a moment. "Absolutely. What time is release?"

"Twelve forty-five."

I checked my watch. I had just over an hour to get her. "And you're just calling me?"

"I've been in a meeting. I would have had Heather call, but you're not her biggest fan."

"That's a nice way of saying it."

He did that almost laugh thing he did when I said something he despised.

"I'll have her home by six," I said.

"Have fun." He ended the call.

Parks asked, "You want me to talk to Bennett?"

"Without me?"

"We could drag Alyssa along if you'd like, but I don't think that's a good idea."

I exhaled. "How about you use that charm of yours on Jessica Moore?"

He turned toward me and smiled. "You think I'm charming?"

"I think you can charm vulnerable women."

"So, you?"

"I'm not vulnerable."

He laughed. "I'll come by your place around seven. Mexican or Italian?"

"I'll never turn down either."

I pulled into the carpool lane a few minutes early, an accomplishment that felt like a win on the rare occasions I did it. Alyssa's kindergarten class hadn't quite spilled out yet, but I could see the line of minivans and SUVs had already backed up down the street. I cracked the window and let the spring air roll in and watched the ice cream truck that always parked just far enough away to avoid school zone rules. Ice cream trucks were no longer for kids but for the potential abduction of them. One day the guy driving it would end up on a mug shot, and I hoped I was the one to put him there.

Alyssa climbed into the back seat a few minutes later with a pink sequined backpack bouncing on her shoulders and a big grin plastered across her face.

"Hey, peanut. How was school?"

"Great! Miss Tilly read us a book about a bear who got lost at the grocery store, and I drew a dinosaur with a birthday hat. And guess what?"

"What?"

"Maggie and Zoey and Harper are going to Adventure Land now. Can we go? Please? Pleasepleaseplease?"

She stretched out the last word like it held the power to sway the universe. Which it did.

I glanced at the dashboard clock. "Adventure Land it is!"

"Yay!" She kicked her feet and shrieked. "You're the best mom ever!"

"I hope you remember that when you're a teenager."

Adventure Land was a converted warehouse with every adult and child-sized distraction known to man crammed under one roof. Massive climbing structures, obstacle courses, bounce houses, and equipment someone could break a leg on, plus too many neon signs blinking at irregular intervals. The smell was a potent blend of pizza grease, feet, and industrial-strength disinfectant.

I checked Alyssa in, fastened the security wristband around her arm, and gave her the standard instructions: stay where you can see the grown-ups, no wrestling, and for the love of everything sacred, no licking anything. She nodded in that distracted, half-listening way kids did when their friends were already shrieking their names across the foam pit.

"Love you, Mommy!"

And just like that, she was gone, darting across the padded floor and disappearing into a maze of bright plastic.

I found the other moms near the cafe area, parked in metal chairs that wobbled every time someone shifted their weight. They greeted me with polite enthusiasm, all fresh manicures and oversized tote bags, sipping iced lattes and pretending not to compete over whose child had the most enrichment activities.

"Jenna, right?"

"Yes. Alyssa's mom."

"I'm Callie," one of them said. "That's Erica, and that's Bree. We were just talking about you."

I raised an eyebrow. "Oh?"

Callie spoke softly. "You caught the person that murdered that poor Jessica Steadman's husband and daughter."

I wouldn't have described Jessica in that victim-like way, even though she had lost her family. "I was a part of it, yes."

"Girl, you cracked it wide open. That story was insane."

Bree sipped from her plastic cup. "I still can't believe what happened. Crazy world we live in, but I imagine you see a lot worse than we do."

I watched Alyssa jumping in the ball pit and wondered what disgusting things hid under the balls. "You could say that."

"Private investigators are the best. I had a friend hire one to follow her husband because he kept working late but rarely answered his phone. The PI found out his working late was screwing his administrative assistant at the Windward Marriott. I swear, if I ever suspect Ray of cheating, I'm calling you." She popped a breath mint into her mouth. "In fact, do you have a business card, or are you on the class list?"

"Unfortunately, that does happen," I said. "And yes, I'm on the class list."

"Have you ever been hired to do that? Follow cheating husbands?" Bree asked.

Alyssa climbed out of the ball pit and ran to the fun house.

"Sometimes."

"And do they always cheat?" Bree asked. "Or is the wife sometimes wrong?"

"Not always, but when someone hires a PI, it usually means trust has already left the building, and the marriage is in trouble."

"Thank God Derek and I have a good relationship." She smiled at me. "We're best friends."

"That's good."

She blinked. "Oh, my gosh. I'm sorry! I didn't mean to—I forgot that you and Alyssa's dad are getting divorced."

"We're already divorced," I said. "And it's okay. No offense taken." I watched Alyssa leap into a pile of foam blocks, laughing as Harper and Maggie followed. The joy in her face anchored me.

Clearly in a tone meant to change the subject, Erica asked, "So, like, do you carry a gun?"

"Not on the job," I lied. "I'm licensed, but that's not usually necessary."

"Okay, but tell us, off the record," Callie said. "Was the Steadman deal as intense as they made it sound on the news? You know, all that sensationalism and such, it's hard to know what's real."

"I really can't share case details," I said, trying to keep my tone gentle but firm. "Confidentiality matters."

"Of course," Bree said quickly. "We get it. We're just fascinated. You don't seem like someone who would chase criminals for a living."

I arched a brow. "Why not?"

"I don't know. You're composed. Not rough around the edges like I pictured."

I bit the inside of my cheek. "I'll take that as a compliment."

They laughed, and I let myself relax. A little. Alyssa had climbed to the top of the play structure and was waving proudly at me through a smudged plexiglass window.

"How's she doing?" Callie asked, following my gaze.

"She loves it here. I think she'd live inside the climbing tower if they let her."

"She seems really happy," Bree said. "And she's such a sweet kid. Polite. Confident."

"Thank you. That means a lot."

Erica crossed her legs. "So, what do you think about Heather?"

The shift in tone was immediate. I blinked. "Alyssa loves her, and that's all that matters."

Callie rolled her eyes. "I don't like her. She keeps trying to make herself the center of every conversation and has to be involved in everything, like she's Alyssa's mom or something, and she's not even married to your ex yet."

"I'm glad she's taking a part in Alyssa's life." I had a sudden urge to grab Alyssa and run out of the place. I didn't fit in with the school moms and didn't think I ever would.

Erica leaned toward me. "Can I ask you one more thing? I know you can't tell us anything official, but do you think people really get away with murder? Like, all the time?"

"More than anyone would like to admit. But sometimes we get them."

They nodded solemnly, as if I'd told them ghosts were real.

Alyssa came running up, cheeks flushed, socks filthy. "Mom!" She beamed. "I'm having so much fun!"

"I can see that."

She gave me a quick hug, sticky and sweaty, then bolted back toward the climbing tower. My cell phone rang. Parks. "Excuse me," I said to the women. "I have to take this." I stood and walked toward the far end of the sitting area and answered the call. "Thank God."

"That's what most women say when they answer my call."

I tipped my head back. "I just meant—never mind. Did you get with Jessica?"

"I did."

His voice echoed behind me. I whipped around to him standing there with a smirk plastered on his face. "What are you doing here?" I stuffed my phone into my pocket and glanced at the women. They all stared and smiled, then Erica waved.

Parks caught me looking at them and turned. "Oh," he said in what I suspected he thought was a seductive voice. "I think they're cheering you on. Should we give them a show?"

"Absolutely. Would you prefer I kick you in the groin or punch you in the gut?"

"Ouch."

I smiled. "Is that a yes to both?"

He stuffed his phone into his pocket. "We have a date tonight."

I pursed my lips. "No, we don't."

He smirked, something he did more often than I liked. "Not us. Me and Jessica."

I furrowed my brow. "What? A date? You're kidding, right?"

"Are you jealous?"

"Parks, it's taken a lot of effort for me to call you my partner. Don't screw it up by thinking I'm interested in something more."

"Got it, partner, and yes, I do have a date. She didn't say much, so I changed my technique. We're having dinner tonight. I'm confident I can get her to loosen up and talk."

"So much for her grieving."

"I'm not sure she considered Hoover much of a loss."

I glanced at Erica and the other women, caught them gawking at us, then pulled Parks behind a half wall with a better view of Alyssa. "Really?"

"Did she care for him? Seems like it, but not to the degree we thought. At least she's acting that way. I did catch something interesting, though."

"What?"

"Dr. Phillips showed up about ten minutes after me. It was almost like he knew I was there."

"How so?" I asked.

"He didn't act surprised to see me."

"Did you talk to him?"

"A little, but he wasn't as kind as he was when we interviewed him. He walked in, said hello in an aggravated tone, then asked to speak with Jessica privately."

"Was it about the trial?"

"I'm not sure. He was irritated and wanted to know why she was talking to me."

"How did she respond to that?"

"She told him he had no authority over whom she spoke to, and she was sick of him acting like he did."

"Oh my. That's interesting."

"My thought too." He smiled at Alyssa when she looked at us.

She ran over to us. "Mommy! Is this your boyfriend? Heather says you wouldn't have such a big stick up your bum if you had a boyfriend."

Parks and I made eye contact. He suppressed a laugh, then squatted and introduced himself to my daughter. "Alyssa, I'm Mr. Parks. It's nice to meet you."

"Are you my mommy's boyfriend?"

"No, ma'am. I'm your mom's business partner."

"Oh, okay." She whipped around and ran back to her friends.

He chuckled. "Heather seems like a real prize."

"Is it wrong that sometimes the thought of running into Heather in an alley one day brings me joy?"

"Only if you act on that thought." He checked his watch. "I'm heading home to change, then off to my date. I'll come by your place on my way home."

"You're not going to sleep with her, are you?"

"Would that bother you?"

"Yes, it would bother me. It could screw up our investigation."

"That's all?"

"Get out of here, Parks."

He leaned toward me and whispered in my ear, "I'm only doing this to make it look good to your friends."

"They're not my friends."

Heather opened the door and smiled down at Alyssa, completely ignoring me. "Hey, sweet girl! Did you have a good day?"

"I did. I played with my friends at Adventure Land. We could take the baby there. I could hold him going down the slide. It's so much fun!"

Him?

"Maybe when he's older," Heather said. She looked up at me. "Thanks for watching her today."

I gritted my teeth and forced myself to not be a bitch. It wasn't easy. "She's my daughter. I don't watch her."

"You know what I mean."

She had just begun to show, and since I'd signed the divorce papers, I wondered if they'd get married before or after the baby was born.

"Nick said you're working that Greg Hoover murder because you're friends with the woman that killed him."

"I'm working an investigation of the woman accused of killing him. We were friends, but we lost touch after law school."

"That's what I meant." She paused, then added, "Is she innocent?"

"According to the law, she is until proven otherwise."

Alyssa hugged me. "I gotta go potty, Mommy."

I crouched down and hugged her. "Love you, baby. See you in a few days."

"Okay," she said and darted off inside.

"Well, good luck," Heather said.

As she pushed the door closed, I said, "Heather?"

She slowly opened the door again. "Yeah?"

I sucked in a breath, realizing what I wanted to say wasn't kind, and even though I couldn't stand the woman, I had promised myself I'd at least be kind, for Alyssa's sake. "I hope your pregnancy goes well."

Her eyes widened just a bit, but enough for me to catch it. "Thank you."

I nodded once, then turned around and left before I had a chance to say something I would regret.

I needed sustenance, so I pulled into Publix to grab one of their precooked meals. The automatic doors whooshed open, and the cool rush of refrigerated air hit me hard. Something about the quiet hum of the store, the slowing down and nearly empty aisles later in the evening, gave me peace.

The smell of rotisserie chicken and buttered cornbread called my name, and I made a beeline for the deli. I was reaching for one of the chicken dinners on the top shelf when I caught a glimpse of someone a few feet away. I checked out of the corner of my eye and noticed the black hoodie. It was always a black hoodie. He turned away when I looked at him.

My fingers hovered over the plastic container as I side-eyed him. No cart. No basket. Just standing there, motionless. I shifted my body, blocking his line of sight. He had disappeared when I glanced back.

I shook it off, not wanting to travel down the paranoia road again. Instead, I kept moving—deli chicken, green beans, and mac and cheese into the basket. I turned down the next aisle toward bottled tea. Halfway down, I slowed. A subtle shift in air pressure made the hairs on the back of my neck stand. I casually turned, pretending to give the shelves behind me a second look but really checking for someone too close for comfort. But the aisle was empty.

I told myself to chill but picked up the pace and made it to the self-checkout to scan everything and pay. My heart beat harder than it should have, but I couldn't shake that uncomfortable feeling, paranoia or not. I scanned the store's front, but nothing struck me as out of the ordinary. Just a mom wrangling a toddler, and a teenage cashier flirting with a girl in yoga pants. Nobody dangerous.

Outside, I opened my driver's-side door and leaned in to drop my purse on the passenger seat. My fingers brushed the cool leather as something pressed against my shoulder—quick, firm, and cold.

A sharp sting followed. High on the back of my right arm.

I gasped and spun and hit my head on the top of the doorframe, but the parking lot behind me was empty—nothing but cars and elongated shadows. The sting pulsed once, then settled into a slow burn.

My hand flew to the spot. My breath caught. Nothing visible. No mark. No blood. Just the lingering echo of the pain.

I scanned the rows, looking for someone, anyone, and saw him, the man in the hoodie from earlier. I moved to grab my weapon, but a sudden dizziness fell over me. The air shifted.

The edges of my vision wavered. I knew exactly what had happened. I watched the man turn and look at me, but I couldn't make out his face. My hands lost their grip on the car.

Panic surged. My legs buckled, barely catching me as I reached for the frame of the car door. My breaths came short and staggered. Too fast.

The asphalt tilted.

My chest constricted like my body had disconnected from itself. My heartbeat slowed and sounded distant, muffled, like it was happening to someone else, but I knew it wasn't.

I tried to call for help, but I couldn't form the breath, couldn't shape the sound. I looked across the lot again, and there he was. Watching me. Calm. Unhurried. As if he'd just finished shopping. He didn't run. He knew I couldn't catch him no matter how hard I tried.

What did he give me?

I opened my mouth again and tried to scream for help one more time. I tried to yell, but the words stuck halfway between a whisper and a choke. The shadows lengthened. The cars blurred. The sounds of the parking lot warped into echoes.

I stumbled sideways. My knees gave out, folding like paper beneath me. Then my hip.

The weight of gravity pulled me down in increments, not one fluid fall but a series of failing parts, every one of them slower than the last. I reached for the ground, thinking I could control my landing. I felt no pain when I met the pavement, just the dull knowledge of contact.

The warmth of the ground seeped into me as the world rocked sideways. I stared into the sky as it cracked open with stars not there seconds before. Falling. It felt as though I was still falling. Inside myself. Into silence.

I whispered, "Help," hoping someone walking by could hear it, but I wasn't even sure the word left my lips.

Everything blurred at the edges. My mind tried to cling to what was happening, to stay awake. I attempted to scream, to stand, to remember how to form words, but all I could do was watch the man staring at me.

"Parks."

And then everything went black.

17

I woke to the sterile brightness of fluorescent lights and the rhythmic beeping of a monitor beside my head and immediately recognized the antiseptic and lemon scent.

A hospital.

A desert settled in my mouth, the dryness stretching across my tongue feeling thick and immobile, while my skull pulsed with a heavy and pervasive pressure. I groaned and tried hard to open my eyes, but feeling so, so tired. Finally, I did, just barely, and saw a blurry figure hovering above me.

"It's about time you woke up," a familiar voice said. Low, gruff. Concern buried beneath sarcasm.

"Parks." I could barely whisper. I blinked. Twice. Then again until the figure sharpened into him. His hair stuck out in unruly tufts, his shirt deeply creased, and though his expression didn't register immediately, something about the set of his jaw and the intensity in his eyes suggested I wasn't waking up from a bad dream, but into something real, something serious I hadn't yet remembered. "What happened?"

"You tell me," he said. "Did you plan this just to ruin my date?"

My dry, cracked lips curled. "Water, please."

He held a large water bottle with a straw at my lips. I took a slow, refreshing sip, thinking it was the greatest thing I'd ever tasted. "Your date good?" I muttered. My throat hurt, though I wasn't sure why.

"A lot better than your night." He set the water bottle back on the tray beside the bed. "Do you remember anything?"

"I was at Publix."

He exhaled. "Yes. Someone found you unconscious on the ground next to your Bronco. They called 911, and the paramedics got there just in time."

"For what?"

"To give you Narcan so you wouldn't die."

My eyes widened, which made my head pound. Still barely able to whisper, I said, "What? I don't understand."

"It'll probably come back to you, but it looked like an accidental overdose."

I blinked at him. "I don't do drugs."

He smirked without humor. "I know. I told them that. I figured unless you'd decided to spice up your night with a fentanyl cocktail, someone else had done it for you."

The room tilted slightly. Had I just heard him correctly? "Fentanyl?"

"Tiny dose. But enough to drop you like a rock. Jenna, you got lucky. A paramedic was pulling into the lot when he got the call. He hit you with Narcan before it was too late."

I tried to push myself up, but the room swam. Parks pressed a hand gently to my shoulder.

"Easy. You're still processing it. You've been out for hours."

Images flickered. The man. The sting. "He stuck me," I whispered. "In the arm. I felt it."

He leaned closer and pushed up my hospital gown sleeve. A moment later, he spotted the mark.

"Got it," he muttered. "It's tiny, but it's there. Hold on." He turned toward the hallway and called out for the doctor.

I closed my eyes for a moment. I'd only felt that tired once before, after thirty-six hours of labor with Alyssa and no epidural. "How did you know to come?"

His expression faltered. Then he looked away, almost sheepish. "I changed your emergency contact in your phone after your house was broken into. I wanted it to be my number, not Nick's."

My throat closed, but not from drugs. I swallowed. Hard. "I hadn't changed it."

"No, you hadn't, and before you get on me about it, I'm not apologizing for doing it."

"How did you know my passcode?"

A smirk formed on his lips. "Really?"

A faint smile tugged at the corners of my mouth, fragile but genuine, the best I could manage.

The door swung open, and a tall, wiry doctor stepped in. Young, maybe mid-thirties, with dark-rimmed glasses and efficient movements. "Ms. Wyatt, I'm Dr. Hatcher. You had a close call tonight. The fentanyl dose was small, but the reaction hit fast. Without that paramedic nearby, this could've gone a lot differently. We'd like to keep you until later in the day today for observation."

"What time is it?" I asked.

"Four a.m.," Parks said.

"I want to go home." I cleared my throat. "I'll be fine."

Parks folded his arms. "She's staying."

I started to argue, but he shot me a look, so I shut my mouth. Dr. Hatcher continued, explaining how they'd monitor my oxygen levels and watch for respiratory dips. He left after giving instructions to the nurse. Eventually, they moved me to a room. Parks followed. Didn't ask. Just took the chair in the corner, dragged it beside the bed, and sat down like he owned the place.

"You're not leaving?"

"Not a chance."

I exhaled. Closed my eyes for a second. Let the noise of the machines and the steady presence of him anchor me. I didn't want him to go. Not really. I wasn't sure I trusted my own instincts anymore. "Thank you."

He pushed my hair from my cheek. "You'd do the same for me."

"Would not."

He chuckled.

A knock at the door jolted us both. Leland stepped in, his face drawn tight with worry. "Jesus, Jenna. What the hell happened? Are you okay?"

I nodded slowly. "I'm fine, though I've been better."

He stepped closer and let his gaze rake over me. "I wish you'd stop putting yourself in these situations."

"I was buying dinner, not tracking a cartel. Nourishing my body isn't usually dangerous."

He gave a sharp exhale, something between a laugh and frustration.

Parks didn't move, but asked, "Anyone see anything?"

"We're working on it," Leland said. "I had them pull the Publix security footage. We should have it by later this morning."

I pressed a hand to my head. "I saw him. I remember that. But I don't remember his face."

Parks tucked the thin white sheet under my arms. "We'll find him."

I closed my eyes again. Not to sleep. Just to shut out the world.

A nurse walked in. "She needs to rest."

Leland leaned down and kissed my forehead. "I'm glad you're okay, Jen. I don't think I could handle losing you."

I opened my eyes. "That's not how tough guys talk, boss."

"I've never been tough around you." He smiled. "I'll be in touch later today."

I closed my eyes again, but I still felt Parks there. Solid. Unmoving. Safe. "Thanks for staying with me," I said.

"My pleasure."

———

No one ever truly rested in a hospital. Between the endless beeping machines that sound more ominous than helpful, the fluorescent lights that refused to dim, and the steady stream of nurses coming in to poke, prod, or check vitals, sleep felt more like a suggestion than a reality. Just as I drifted near the edge of unconsciousness, someone else would walk in and remind me I wasn't going anywhere.

Parks shifted in the chair beside me and groaned softly. "I haven't slept this badly since I got shot."

"You got shot?"

"You sound way too excited about that."

I nudged his arm with my fingers. "Maybe a little." I smiled. "Tell me. I want to hear it."

He sighed and rubbed a hand over his face. "An NCIS case in Virginia. We were tracking a lieutenant commander who'd gone off the rails after returning from Afghanistan."

"PTSD?"

He nodded. "It was tragic, really. He took a woman hostage at a rental cabin near Quantico. Said she was a spy trying to kill his family." He showed no emotion as he spoke.

"That does sound tragic. What happened?"

"We surrounded the place. Negotiators tried to talk him down, but they couldn't. He fired two warning shots out the window, then he dragged the woman out onto the porch with a gun to her head. He didn't leave us much choice. I was closest to him. I took the shot."

I swallowed.

"It was one of those once-in-a-lifetime situations where he fired at the same time and hit me in the shoulder. He went down, and I didn't even realize I'd been hit until I was on the ground. Hurts like hell, by the way."

I winced. "You think?"

"I bled all over a pair of brand-new boots."

"I'm sorry for that."

He smiled. "They were great boots."

"I'm not talking about that."

"I know."

The nurse arrived, checked my vitals, and when she saw everything at normal levels, told us the doctor would be in soon to sign my release papers.

I thanked her. When she left, I asked Parks if they'd towed my Bronco.

"Nope. Leland had an agent drop it at your place."

GBI didn't typically handle incidents like mine, but given my relationship with Leland, I knew he wouldn't let anyone else take the reins.

I swung my legs over the edge of the bed and tried to stand. The cold tile bit into my bare feet. I swayed. My head throbbed behind my eyes, a dull pressure that pulsed in rhythm with the heart monitor beside me. My muscles didn't ache so much as they refused to cooperate, like someone had unplugged them and their charge died. I reached for the chair where my clothes were folded, but my fingers trembled too hard to grip the fabric. Even breathing felt like too much effort.

Parks stood up so fast his chair scraped against the floor. "What the hell are you doing?"

"Getting dressed," I muttered, even though it sounded like a lie. "Can you give me some privacy, please?"

He caught me by the elbow before I pitched forward. "You're barely vertical. Sit down before you face-plant."

I tried to wave him off, but the wave turned into a sag. My knees buckled.

He caught me, steady and firm, and eased me back onto the edge of the bed. "You're not doing this alone. Let me help."

"I can—"

"You can't. And it's fine. I've seen you tackle suspects and outrun serial killers. You can let me help you into your clothes."

"Fine, but if you ever bring this up again, I'll shoot you in your good shoulder."

"I don't doubt that one bit."

He helped me out of the wheelchair and loaded me into his truck.

"Let's go to my office," I said.

"Uh, no. I'm taking you home."

"We have a killer to find, remember?"

"Whatever you planned to do at the office we can do at your place."

I couldn't argue that.

On the way home, I asked him about his date with Jessica.

"I got her to talk."

"And?"

Parks had one hand on the wheel and the other wrapped around a RaceTrac coffee he hadn't let go of since he grabbed it on the way back to my apartment. I sank into the passenger seat, wrapped in a hoodie from his back seat, my body sore and brain foggy, but at least I wasn't surrounded by beeping machines and interrupted by vitals checks every thirty minutes.

He glanced at me. "You good?"

"Better than yesterday," I muttered.

He nodded as his eyes flicked back to the road. "You had a hell of a night."

"Can we not talk about it right now?" I asked. "What happened with Jessica?"

"She had a lot to get off her chest, but she's not the worst dinner company, honestly," he admitted.

"And?"

He shifted in his seat, likely warming up to the intel dump. "She admitted it—she and Hoover. Said it started when he backed the early trial data, and then it turned into something more. Claimed they were getting serious until Evelyn put the brakes on it."

"Evelyn really had him under her thumb, didn't she?"

"If I had to guess, I'd say he wasn't willing to give up half his net worth."

"Good point. Was she upset about it?"

He turned off Highway 9 and headed toward my place. "Not as much as you'd expect," he said. "More annoyed she didn't win."

I stared out the window, watching the stores blur past. "I guess she needed a sugar daddy."

"I think she really cared about him," Parks said, his tone turning serious. "She looked genuinely upset when she talked about him."

I almost felt bad for her, but then I remembered she wasn't the only woman he had cheated on Evelyn with. "It amazes me that women think a married man will leave his family for them. Especially one with billions."

"Some do," he said.

"Rarely. What else did she say?"

"She mentioned that she and the rat king had a thing."

"Rat king?"

"Phillips. I'm assuming she called him that because of the testing on rats."

"Interesting."

"It was short-lived. Said he got weird fast. Possessive and controlling. Accused her of hiding trial data from him and messing around with other men."

"Did she?"

"She claims it was his paranoia. She broke it off when Greg showed interest."

"So, there was a love triangle brewing in the research wing."

"More like a messy petri dish of betrayal," he said. He laughed at his own joke. "She told me Phillips once went through her personal files at work. Said she walked in on it, and he claimed he was protecting her."

My stomach twisted. "Protecting her from what?"

"She said she learned Phillips was running the trial behind her back with Tellion and a few other PAC clients."

"Did she act like she wasn't a part of it?" I asked.

"Yep."

"Please tell me you don't believe her."

"I do not, but I think she thinks I'm more attractive than I am smart."

"I'm sure a lot of people think that."

"Nice."

Silence fell between us for a moment.

"Did she change her story about where she was the night of Greg's murder?"

"Nope."

"What about Evelyn's? Did you ask about that?"

"She claims she was with a friend."

"What friend?"

"She wouldn't say."

"That's not suspicious," I said. "Did you play this off as an interview or a date?"

"We're going out again tomorrow night. Does that answer your question?"

"Gross."

He laughed. "Phillips has access to everything, and she made it sound like he did it all behind her back, but she slipped up when she said she told Hoover."

"Because he would have already known, which he did."

"Right." Then he added quietly, "I was going to press for more, but dinner got cut short then because GBI called."

"Sorry I ruined your date, but thank you for being there for me, and for changing the emergency number in my phone."

"Any time."

"Don't touch my stuff again."

"I make no promises," he said.

"Okay, let's think this through," I said, though the fog still overwhelmed my brain. "Phillips had a thing for Moore, but she dumped him and started something with Hoover. That's motive."

"But we still have Bennett embezzling money and Hoover finding out."

"What if Hoover wanted out of the trial and planned to go public with it? That's motive for Jessica and Phillips."

"We'll have to find the answer to that," he said. "And I hate to be the one with the bad news, but Sullivan spoke to Bennett. According to him, Bennett was on a private flight home from a meeting in New York the night of Greg Hoover's murder."

"Private jet," I repeated. "That's convenient. I feel like we should have been the ones to talk to Bennett."

"It's Sullivan's investigation. We can't tell him what to do."

"I don't care."

He smiled. "I didn't think you did."

I exhaled. "Is he subpoenaing for the flight info?" I asked.

"Taylor is. Sullivan appears to be satisfied with the alibi, though I'm sure he'll demand more from Taylor."

"Seriously? That's shitty detective work."

"He's got his suspect. He's only doing this to check off boxes."

"What about during Evelyn's murder? He knows Riley didn't kill her, so was Bennett on a private jet that night too?"

"Wallace claims he was in Jackson Hole the night Evelyn died—at some hush-hush strategy meeting on a private estate with a group of overseas bigwigs. Off the books, of course. No itinerary, no digital trail, no names. Sullivan said he sounded smug, like he thought that was enough to shut us down."

"That oozes guilt," I said.

"My thoughts too."

"Any more bad news?" I asked.

"He spoke with Phillips as well."

"I'm assuming Phillips gave him the same alibi he gave us?"

"He did."

"What about for the night of Evelyn's murder?" I asked.

"Either Sullivan didn't have it or didn't want us to have it."

If I had the energy, I would have cussed like a truck driver. "He's trying to cut us off so his arrest doesn't get blown out of the water."

"He believes Riley is guilty. Working with us was just his way of solidifying that."

"He's wrong," I said. "And we're going to prove it."

18

Parks forced me into the shower, claiming the hot water would help burn off the effects of the fentanyl. Though it took a concentrated effort to undress and complete the task, I did feel much better. Not great, but better.

I walked out of the bedroom saying, "Thanks for helping me into the shower. I needed that."

Riley's mouth dropped open, and then she laughed. "Are we interrupting?"

I blushed at seeing Taylor shift in his seat, and I rarely blushed. "Oh, I didn't know you were here."

"Obviously," Tiffani said as she walked out of my kitchen. She flipped her long hair over her shoulder. "Darlin', don't be shy. I saw this coming during the Steadman investigation."

Saw what coming?

"I knew it," Riley said.

Parks practically spit out his coffee.

I shot Tiffani a look that could kill. "I'm not even responding to any of that."

She sat beside Riley and whispered, "That means I'm right."

"It means the exact opposite," I said.

Riley chuckled. "Whatever you say. Jack called Taylor and told him what happened." She walked over to me, placed her hands on my shoulders, and gave me a once-over. "Are you okay?" She pulled me into a hug. "I can't believe you almost died because of me."

"It tracks," I said, smiling. "First you nearly get me kicked out of law school, then you nearly get me killed. What's next?"

We locked eyes. I read the pain in hers and instantly felt horrible. She had taken responsibility for our past, and I shouldn't have joked about it. "Riley, I'm kidding. Harvard is long over, and I wouldn't be here, risking my life, if I didn't believe in your innocence."

That garnered me another hug, and I wasn't a touchy-feely kind of gal. "I don't know how I'll ever repay you, Jen. Really."

"That hourly fee is jacked up, so we're good." I dropped onto the couch and felt the pressure against my skin through my bones.

She laughed. "I'll pay more if I have to."

"We've requested the subpoenas for Bennett's travels. My assistant should have them here within the hour," Taylor said.

"Nice to have that kind of pull," I said.

He nodded. "It's helpful."

The sound of the gate buzzer jolted me. I pushed myself off the couch. "Excuse me." The room tilted sideways, like the ground had slipped beneath me.

Parks rushed to my side and guided me back onto the couch. "I'll get it." He checked his watch.

A few minutes later, Sullivan knocked on the door. Parks let him in while I controlled the urge to tell him where he could stick it and kick him out.

"We're no longer interested in or willing to discuss the investigation with you," Taylor said. "Should you want to request something, please defer to the legal process and the Assistant District Attorney, Zach Christopher."

"This is a courtesy visit," he said. "I wanted to check on Ms. Wyatt."

"Why?" I asked. "Are you hoping to manipulate the attempt on my life as something unrelated to our investigation?"

He looked straight at Riley. "We've already arrested our suspect, so, unless she somehow disconnected her ankle bracelet, your unfortunate situation is clearly unrelated."

"Unrelated, my ass. Someone followed me from my kid's home to the store and stuck me with a syringe full of fentanyl."

"I would expect you, as a former law enforcement officer, would notice being followed," he said. "Since you didn't, and you can't prove you were, it's clear to me this was a random event. Tragic and vile, but random."

"Right." I exhaled, knowing what I was about to say would sting. "Remind me of that when we catch the real killer and your career spins down the drain." I tipped my head back and groaned. "Thanks for stopping by, but get out."

He made eye contact with each of us, then pivoted and left.

"Same Jen," Riley said. "Thank God."

I jerked awake when someone knocked on my front door.

Parks patted my knee and rose from the couch. "It's fine. You fell asleep. It's just Taylor's assistant."

I fell asleep? Not at all mortifying.

I checked my mouth for drool and caught Riley smirking.

"You're good," she said.

I mumbled, "Thank you."

The guy was mid-thirties, business casual with a military buzz cut and a practiced expression that said he wouldn't hesitate to elbow someone in the throat if they got too chatty. He walked in and handed Taylor the envelope, then turned around and left.

Parks locked the door behind him. "He's a talker." He glanced at his watch.

Taylor, coffee in one hand and reading glasses perched on the edge of his nose, opened the envelope without a word and scanned the document inside. "The subpoena's been delivered to the FBO at Brown Field and to the charter company directly." He moved to the counter, pulled out his phone, and hit the speaker icon. "I'll call the FBO first, then the charter company. We'll see if Mr. Bennett's flight even existed."

The phone rang twice before a woman answered with polished Southern efficiency. "Fulton County Executive Jet Services, this is Reesa speaking."

"This is attorney Harris Taylor. I'm calling in reference to a subpoena delivered to your office this morning regarding a charter flight the night of March 5th. I need confirmation of receipt and access to the requested passenger manifest, departure logs, and billing record."

"Hold, please."

We waited.

Parks leaned over and whispered, "We're going to have a field day with Bennett if this turns out to be bogus."

Reesa returned a minute later, her voice tighter. "Yes, Mr. Taylor. We did receive the subpoena via courier about an hour ago. I can confirm we have no record of a PAC Health executive flight on March 5th under Wallace Bennett's name. In fact, there were no departures or arrivals listed between eight p.m. and midnight from our charter wing. Only one private jet landed during that time frame—coming in from Charlotte, not New York."

Taylor's brows rose. "And who was listed as the client for that flight?"

"I'm afraid I can't disclose that without an additional clearance request. But I can confirm it was not Mr. Bennett, or any PAC Health employee listed."

"Understood. Can you verify if he was on any flights that day?"

"He was not."

"Thank you, Reesa. Expect formal follow-up shortly." He hung up. "One down."

Parks and I exchanged a look.

Taylor dialed the second number. A man answered. His raspy voice said he'd either smoked since birth or inhaled too much jet fuel.

"Jet Southern Dispatch," the guy said. "This is Martin."

"This is Harris Taylor, attorney for Ms. Chatsworth. You received a subpoena this morning regarding charter flight 11JX, supposedly departing Teterboro and arriving at Fulton County on March 5th?"

Long pause. "Yeah, got the subpoena right here in front of me."

"I need confirmation that this flight existed, who paid for it, and if Wallace Bennett was listed as a passenger or coordinator."

Martin let out a low breath. "That flight ID was filed, but no physical aircraft departed under it. It was registered, scheduled, then canceled twenty minutes before takeoff. Reason listed as 'client delay.' No reschedule noted. In fact, no invoice either. No payment ever processed."

Taylor blinked. "To confirm, you're saying the flight was logged but never flown?"

"That's right. It's his plane. He's listed on the paperwork, but he never got on. The crew stayed on standby at the Teterboro hangar all night and left without a client."

"What about the flight to Teterboro? Was he on that?"

"No, sir."

Parks tilted his head. "He ghost-booked a jet." He checked his watch again.

Taylor's eyes narrowed. "Thank you, Martin. Please hold that documentation. You'll receive an affidavit request later today." He hung up and looked at us. "Bennett staged a flight he never took and counted on the charter company not cooperating or being too buried in private-client secrecy to confirm it."

Parks whistled low. "Classic executive sleight of hand."

"He gave Sullivan just enough to tick the box," I said. "A scheduled jet, no passenger list, some puffed-up story about a New York meeting, and Sullivan bought it."

Taylor sat and rubbed his temples. "This proves he wasn't in the air. But it doesn't place him anywhere else."

"Yet," Parks said. "We'll find out where he was that night."

Taylor looked at Riley. "This is how we flip the narrative. Tiffani, will you please send over a few men to keep an eye on PAC and Mr. Bennett?"

She stood and removed her phone from her Louis Vuitton purse. "My pleasure, Harris."

"I'll call Drew," I said. "Maybe he can cross-reference his IP logs with Bennett's devices. If he pinged anything from a private server or remote log-in, we might catch him screwing up."

Taylor pulled out his tablet. "I'll get the affidavits filed. We'll have sworn statements from both companies within the hour. In the meantime," he looked at me, "you need to rest. Keep me posted on what happens next, but only when you're feeling better."

Parks walked them to the door and checked his watch once again after closing it.

I sat cross-legged on the couch. "What's going on?"

He strutted over and sat beside me. "With the investigation? You really are tired."

"No, with you. You've checked your watch a dozen times since we got here. Are you late for something?" It hit me then. "Do you need to get ready for your second date with Jessica Moore?"

"Jenna, I went out with her last night. You don't remember me telling you about this earlier?"

I nodded. "You also said you had a second date. I just can't remember when it is."

He laughed. "That's right. I can't believe you fell for that. I was kidding."

"I literally almost died. Forgive me for being a little vulnerable." I had to turn and block my face so he wouldn't see me smiling.

"You're right. I'm sorry about that."

"I can't believe you fell for that. I was kidding." I busted out laughing.

He flipped me the bird. "I asked her a lot of questions about the murders. Would you want to go on a second date after that?"

"So, you're saying you didn't charm her?"

"I'm sure I did, but I can't say it was enough to go another round."

I cringed. "Go another round? That's disgusting."

"You know what I mean. I did give her my number, but only in case she remembered something."

"She won't remember anything unless it's disguised as a booty call."

He laughed and checked his watch. The laughter died. "My commander's memorial is in two hours."

My lungs deflated. "Damn it, Parks. Why didn't you tell me?"

"I'm telling you now."

I checked the time on my cell and gave him a once-over. "You can't go like that."

"I'm not leaving you. Nash would understand."

"I saw your face when Tortoise called. You have to go."

The sides of his mouth twitched. "Turtle, and I'm not comfortable leaving you alone."

"You've got clothes in that bag you always keep in your truck, right?"

"Yes, but—"

I carefully pushed myself from the couch. "Go get it. I'll change into something that doesn't make me look like I'm coming off a fentanyl high."

He stood and stared at me. "You can't—"

"Just get the damn bag."

We sat in the truck for a long moment, parked near the back of the Carmichael-Hemperley Funeral Home lot. Only ten cars dotted the pavement, all spaced apart like grief needed breathing room, which I knew to be true.

Parks stared through the windshield, his jaw tight, knuckles pale where he gripped the steering wheel. He hadn't said much since we pulled off the highway. He'd driven there without a radio, and we had barely talked.

I turned slightly toward him. "You okay?"

His lips pressed together before he responded. "Yeah."

He wasn't. Anyone with half a pulse could see that. His shoulders were too stiff, his eyes too distant. He wasn't looking at the building—he was looking through it, lost somewhere behind the brick and glass, probably in memories of his time with NCIS.

"You sure?" I asked softer.

He didn't look at me. "Let's just go in."

He popped his door open before I could say more. I stayed still for another breath, watching him walk around the front of the truck and brushing his hand against the hood. He opened my door and offered a hand, which I gladly took.

"Thank you."

"Are you sure you're able to do this?" He asked like we weren't at his commander's memorial service and that I was somehow more important.

"I'm fine," I said, even though I wasn't. Not really. My legs ached, my ribs twinged when I breathed too deeply, and my body still felt like it had been wrung out and left to dry on a rusted clothesline. But it wasn't about me. He needed to focus on Nash and his team.

Parks didn't argue, but he stayed close as we walked. I moved carefully, deliberately, with no sudden steps, no deep breaths. I caught him watching me.

I gave him a look. "Don't even think about it."

"Yes, ma'am."

Inside, the air smelled faintly of fresh lilies and wood polish. Muted gray carpet stretched down a wide corridor leading to a small chapel on the left with multiple visitation rooms lining the side. The door to one stood open.

"There," Parks said.

Several people stood and talked in small groups, most wearing navy, black, or a military uniform.

"Cowboy?" someone called from ahead. A man with silvering temples and a crooked grin called out to Parks. He wore a sport coat over a faded NCIS polo. "Damn. Is that really you?"

Parks managed a smile and walked over. I followed, staying just behind him. The man pulled him into a hug and clapped him on the back hard enough to jolt me just watching it.

"Thought you weren't going to make it," the man said. "Figured the legend forgot his roots."

"Wouldn't miss this," Parks said. "You know how much Nash meant to me."

"To us all," the man said.

I lingered near the aisle to let him have his moment. Another man joined them, shorter and rounder than Parks, with wire-rimmed glasses and a face I could only describe as kind. He stuck out his hand.

"Name's Turtle," he said to me. "Don't ask why. Long story involving tequila and a very bad decision on a beach in Bahrain."

"I'll take your word for it," I said as I shook his hand.

Two women came over next, both early forties, with the calm, efficient energy of military women. The one with short dark curls and warm brown eyes introduced herself as Casey.

"This is Micki," she said.

I smiled at her. "Nice to meet you. I'm Jenna Wyatt."

Micki's eyes trailed up and down my body. "You must be Parks's woman."

Before I could say anything, Turtle let out a belly laugh. "Hell froze over. Parks settled down. Someone get me a drink."

"Didn't think he had it in him," Casey added, bumping her shoulder against Parks. "I had money on him going full hermit by fifty."

I didn't disagree, knowing denying would result in more ribbing, and Parks didn't need that.

Parks rubbed the back of his neck and muttered something about bad bets and stubborn women. I just stood there, watching him squirm and letting the warm wash of old friendship wrap around us both, wondering if Riley and I could ever get to that point, where the good memories outshone the bad.

We took seats together near the back. The room quieted as a man in a pressed Navy uniform stepped to the front. He cleared his throat and talked about Nash. Not the man in a box up front, but the commander. The leader. The quiet professional. Someone who gave more than he took and never talked about it.

More people spoke, telling small stories and anecdotes about how he remembered everyone's name, even the enlisted. How he checked gear personally before every overseas op. How he never raised his voice but never needed to. How his heart had started giving him trouble a few years back, but he'd ignored it—never letting on that anything was wrong.

One man said, "He didn't even tell his sister. That was Nash. Always carrying more than he should."

I looked at Parks, noting his neutral face, but caught the twitch at his temple and the slight flare of his nostrils.

Turtle leaned across the aisle and whispered to me, "Nash saved his life. Kabul, 2011. Cowboy never talks about it."

We left a short time after that, but Parks didn't head toward my place or the office. He headed toward Midtown instead.

"Where are we going?"

"PAC, to talk to Bennett. Unless you're not up for it?"

"No. I'm up for it."

19

Wallace Bennett sat behind a massive slab of a desk, flanked by two monitors and a branded decanter set that probably saw more action than a hooker on Buford Highway. A glass of amber liquid sat on his desk next to a stack of papers. He didn't stand when we entered, just looked up. His eyes flicked between us, narrowing slightly, then blinking twice, as if recalibrating. His eyes registered surprise first, then irritation. "I wasn't aware we had a meeting."

Parks closed the door behind us, slow and deliberate. "We just have a few more questions for you."

I watched Bennett carefully, studying everything from his facial features, his micro-expressions, and his tight beard. I just couldn't recall the image of the man at Publix. I couldn't guarantee it was him, and that ticked me off.

He gave Parks a tight, professional smile. "I'm not sure why I need to speak with two private investigators when I've already spoken to—what's the detective's name? Sullivan, I believe."

"You don't have to speak with us," I said. "But there is a licensed process server with a subpoena for deposition waiting outside your door. We thought we could move the process along."

He hit a button on his landline and asked his assistant to bring in the person waiting.

The same man who delivered the subpoenas to Taylor at my place walked in. "Mr. Wallace Bennett?"

"Yes."

He handed Bennett the envelope. "You've been served."

Bennett's jaw twitched. He glanced at the envelope like it might bite him, then forced a breath through his nose.

"Shall we talk now?" I asked. Though still groggy from being shot up with a lethal substance, I stood strong. If Bennett had anything to do with my near demise, I wanted him to see how poorly he had failed. I sat in front of the desk.

Bennett eyed the envelope. "What is this about?"

Parks sat in a chair beside me. "You were on a flight home from New York the night of Greg Hoover's murder, correct?"

"Yes. I had traveled there for business. Again, I already discussed this with Detective Sullivan. Can't you get his notes or something?"

"We've already spoken to the detective," Parks said. "We're just clarifying some things."

"Riley Chatsworth has already been arrested for Mr. Hoover's murder. While this is all tragic, it has nothing to do with me."

"You sure about that?" I asked. "Because we're not."

"I'm not interested in talking with you. I'll have my lawyer contact whoever's on this subpoena. You may leave."

Parks placed a file on the desk—slim, but dense with meaning. "You might want to reconsider that. I'm sure you wouldn't like the media finding out what we know."

His hand jerked toward the glass on his desk but stopped short. "What are you saying?"

"You ghosted that plane," Parks said. "You set it up to make it look like you used it, but you didn't."

Bennett's smile froze mid-formation. His brows pinched together, and his nostrils flared.

He shifted in his chair, his spine suddenly rigid. "I've already discussed it with the police. They have no concerns about my whereabouts, and I'm confident they verified."

"See," I said, "that's the thing. Claiming you were out of town only works if no one checks."

His eyes darted to the door, then to the file on the desk. "The police checked."

"Nope," Parks said.

He laughed too loudly, too quickly. His laugh ended in a dry cough, and he cleared his throat. "Then they're going to. I understand it might require a subpoena for the records, considering they're private."

"They didn't, and they don't plan to," I said. "But as I'm sure you know, Riley's got an amazing attorney with connections, and he verified. We know you weren't on that plane."

The color drained from Bennett's face. His hand moved to his tie, loosening it a half inch. He opened his mouth, closed it, then walked to the decanter. His hand trembled as he poured a splash of amber into a glass. His other hand braced the edge of the cabinet, steadying himself. "Why are you asking me this? Mr. Hoover died from a heart attack. The shooting happened afterward."

"Interesting that you mention that," Parks said. "Let me explain how the law works in these situations. When a cardiac event is caused by a stressful situation, for example, someone holding a gun pointed at your head, that is considered a forced cardiac event followed by execution, and it is a felony."

"Think of it as a death by terror," I said, "sealed with a bullet."

"He didn't survive the heart attack," Parks added, "but the bullet made sure there was no second chance, and that's still a felony, Mr. Bennett."

"Why would I want Mr. Hoover dead? He owned our biggest client."

"Maybe," I said, "because you were mad he pulled his business?"

Parks disagreed. "Naw, that happened months before his death. It had to be something else."

Bennett stilled. His eyes narrowed, his breathing slowed.

"Oh," I said, feigning excitement to have pieced together the puzzle. "Embezzlement! That's right. How could I forget?" I winked at Bennett.

He swallowed hard. The muscle in his jaw twitched like a ticking clock. "Are you accusing me of stealing from my company?"

"That," Parks said, "and your clients. I guess you didn't want to pick favorites."

"This is ridiculous. I've worked hard to get where I am. Why would I do something so stupid?"

"The richer you are, the more money you spend," I said. "Maybe you have debts to pay."

"I'm not going to sit here while you accuse me—"

I cut him off. "It shouldn't surprise you that PIs do their due diligence, Mr. Bennett. If someone wants to hide money, they'll do so somewhere with strict banking secrecy laws, low or no taxes, and limited cooperation with foreign investigations. Does that sound right?"

He pressed his lips together. A bead of sweat rolled down his temple, and he didn't wipe it away.

"The Cayman Islands is highly popular for shell corporations and secret banking and is known for low taxes and financial privacy, and as I'm sure you're aware, the Panama Papers leak made it infamous for hiding wealth through complex legal structures." Parks paused, then added, "Evelyn Hoover showed us the emails. We know Greg was going to report you. But you couldn't have that, so you killed him."

I looked him straight in the eyes. "Then, when you realized his wife might find out, you killed her too."

"I didn't kill anyone. She didn't know what she was looking at," he snapped. His voice cracked halfway through. He ran a hand through his hair, ruffling it out of its stiff part.

"But you did," Parks said. "And we did a little digging. We have a digital footprint. We know how you did it and where the money came from."

Bennett dropped into his chair, the glass of liquor forgotten on the desk. His face had gone gray. His breathing was shallow and uneven.

"Wallace," I said, quieter, "how long were you stealing from your own clients?"

His eyes shimmered—no longer with confidence, but with something close to defeat. He shook his head. "You don't understand. PAC was hemorrhaging. The expansion into oncology trials—we couldn't afford it. Greg didn't listen. So, I made it work."

"Oh, come on," Parks said. "That's BS, and you know it. You stole millions for yourself, not to save the company."

He stood again. Too fast. His hand knocked the glass, which shattered on the floor, but he didn't react. His chest heaved. His hands clenched and unclenched. "I didn't kill anyone," he said. "I didn't—"

"Why keep denying it?" I asked. "We know the facts."

Bennett's mouth worked, but no sound came. His gaze went distant, unfocused. He gripped the edge of the desk. His knuckles turned white. Finally, he whispered, "Why are you doing this? It's not true."

"You were desperate," I said. "Because someone, maybe Evelyn, was finally willing to tell the truth. And because you panicked. Just like you're panicking now."

He opened his mouth to reply and then staggered back a step. His eyes went wide, unfocused, then flared with fear. His left hand clutched at his chest. The panic in his eyes intensified.

"Oh, shit." I knocked my chair over and climbed over his desk.

He gasped, then a wet, rattling sound came from his mouth. He dropped to the ground.

Parks dialed 911 from the landline.

I dropped to my knees beside him. "Wallace, we've got you! Can you hear me?" He was seizing, eyes wide, face drained of color. "He's having a heart attack," I said.

Parks pulled me back as the PAC staff burst in from the hallway, Dr. Phillips included.

It took ten minutes for the EMTs to arrive. Ten minutes of Dr. Phillips performing CPR and keeping him alive. The EMTs finally wheeled him out, unconscious but alive.

Monica Bennett barred us from her husband's hospital room and wouldn't share a single detail about his condition. Instead, she unleashed on us, furious and unapologetic, blaming us outright for nearly killing him. Sullivan showed up mid-outburst—and backed her up without hesitation.

After a doctor called her away, he hit us harder.

"What the hell were you thinking? I've already cleared Bennett as a suspect. You're fucking with my investigation."

"Don't act innocent, Sullivan," I said. "You cleared him without even mentioning the embezzling or linking him to the weapon. That's BS."

"There is no link to the weapon, and we don't have enough on the embezzling to move on it."

I laughed. "Do you hear yourself right now? No proof? We have the money trail. Oh, wait. We. Not you. Since you didn't find it, it doesn't exist. Is that it?"

Parks rested his hand gently at the small of my back, anchoring me in the chaos. His voice, calm but edged with conviction, broke through the haze.

"Detective, we've done what any capable investigator would—we followed the truth. We uncovered the lie Bennett told about his whereabouts the night Greg was murdered, and we exposed the quiet theft he orchestrated from his company and its clients. If the weight of his own deceit crushed him in the end, that burden belongs to him—not us."

"You can't prove he murdered Evelyn."

"Give us a minute," I said. "We'll connect him to the gun."

He scrubbed his hand over the top of his head. "Get out of here. You've hurt this family enough."

I smiled. "Whatever works for you, though I'm sure your chief won't like seeing the evidence from us instead of you."

He took a step back, dropped a trail of cuss words, then walked away.

Parks and I looked at each other, both silent for a moment before he finally said, "That guy's not long for the law enforcement world."

"Good. He sucks at it." I dug my phone from my bag and dialed Drew's cell.

"Hey, Jenna, 'sup?"

"Are you still at work?"

"No, but that doesn't stop me from helping you if you need it."

I clicked the speaker icon when we reached Parks's pickup. "Good. I need a deep search on Wallace Bennett. I dropped the ball—"

"We," Parks said. "Hey, Drew. We dropped the ball."

"Hey, Parks. Got it."

"Okay, now that that's settled, Bennett's in the hospital. We think it's a heart attack, but we don't know. He can't talk to us now, and we need to know if he's got any connection to a weapon. A carry license, trips to a range, purchases, anything."

"When do you need it?"

"The sooner, the better," Parks said.

"I'll see what I can get, but you know the odds of connecting him to the weapon aren't good."

"I know," I said. "What about traffic cameras? Can you check for his vehicle around Hoover's home on the night of both his and his wife's murders?"

"Sure thing, Jenna. I'll get back to you as soon as I've got something."

"Thanks, Drew. I'll tell Leland to give you a raise. You deserve it."

"Hell, yeah, I do, but I'll take another two-week vacation if that doesn't fly."

"It's worth a shot."

―――――

We sat in my apartment, as usual, eating a deep-dish Rosati's pizza that smelled like comfort and extra days at the gym. The deep-dish box lay open between us, sauce-smeared and half empty. Parks chewed thoughtfully on a crust while I spread the case files across my coffee table like a crime scene mosaic—emails, interview notes, printouts from Evelyn Hoover's stash, Chandra's download logs, everything we'd pulled for the investigation. The lamplight softened the edges of the chaos, but my mind felt jagged and restless. Bob planted himself by my side and fell asleep within seconds.

Parks dipped his crust in a small container of sauce. "You can't take a break, can you?"

"We can't afford one."

"You nearly died, Jenna, and you look like it. You need to rest."

"I'll rest once Bennett's in cuffs. There's got to be something here. Something we're missing that will give us a hard link to Bennett and the Hoover murders."

"Christopher wants a link to the weapon. You won't find that in there. Wait for Drew to call. He's a genius. He'll find something."

"Maybe not," I said.

"We're not going to find the smoking gun tonight," Parks muttered. He wiped his fingers on a napkin and eyed the stack of papers.

I sifted through Evelyn's meticulously ordered email printouts. "I just need something, anything, to set this whole thing on fire."

"Are you questioning Bennett's guilt?" he asked.

"I'm questioning everything."

"His ghosted private jet had cracked the surface of his alibi, Jenna, and the embezzlement scheme gave us motive. A connection to the gun will seal the deal."

"What if we can't link it?" I shook my head. "I don't know. Something feels off about it now, but I can't put my finger on it. It doesn't feel personal enough."

"The murders don't feel personal enough?"

"I don't know how to explain it, okay? It just feels off. Let me run with it."

"Yes, ma'am."

I handed him a stack of files. "Let's go through what we know about the night Greg Hoover died."

Parks took the files but didn't open them right away. He scanned the rows of papers and email printouts spread between us. "We've seen all this already."

"Not like this," I said. "Let's pull Riley's emails with Bennett first. Maybe there's something buried in the tone. Something that shows anger, or pressure. A shift. We have to make sure we didn't miss something."

He hesitated, then nodded. "All right."

"Focus on anything that might've felt off. Passive-aggressive language. Demands. Odd phrasing."

We worked in silence for a while, the only sounds the turning of pages and the occasional shuffle of paper as Bob sighed in his sleep beside me.

Finally, I glanced at Parks and noticed the deep frown carved into his cheek. "Anything?" I asked.

He shook his head. "Mostly business stuff. Trial discussions, the loss of

Tellion as a client and the consequences of that. Staffing. She challenged him on performance metrics once, but he didn't take the bait."

I flipped to a flagged thread—Riley to Bennett, dated two weeks before Greg's death—and read through it twice, hoping something would crack open.

"Riley says Greg was worried about liability since PAC's board denied paying the additional claims for the trial. She tells Bennett she's working on softening him, and that she's making progress but needs more transparency across the board. Bennett responds with, 'I trust you'll find a way to manage him. Greg has a history of overthinking.'"

"Dismissive," Parks muttered. "Not enough to be angry. But enough to be annoyed."

I tossed the emails to the top of the "nothing" pile and continued.

We tore through two more conversations. One where Bennett deflected his concerns about rising healthcare costs and their impact on PAC. Another where he cc'd Jessica Moore about following up with Hoover one more time to encourage him to bring Tellion back under their fold, but neither responded.

I leaned back and rubbed my face. "If he wanted to frame Riley, wouldn't he have planted something? Leaked something from her account? There's no fingerprint of that."

"He's too smart to leave one," Parks said. "And maybe he didn't need to. She was close enough to Hoover for her emotions about Tellion dropping PAC to play into it. She was an easy fall girl."

I looked back down at the pages as the pressure built behind my eyes. I grabbed another stack and scanned them. Finally, a faint thread clicked. "Where are the notes from Phillips's interview?"

He flipped through the file and handed them to me.

I read through it. "Phillips said he'd just finished a call with their West Coast team and stayed up late reviewing draft protocols for the trial." I read the notes out loud. "He said he uploaded the protocol summary to PAC's server around 9:45."

"And?" Parks asked.

"He said he emailed Hoover, and he responded."

"Which gave him a window of activity," Parks added. "Home, working, helpful."

"Do you remember reading anything like that in Hoover's emails?"

He sat forward. "No."

I sifted through the stack of emails Evelyn had copied for us, scanning thread after thread. Hoover and Jessica Moore went back and forth on trial budgets, treatment plans, even PAC's crumbling ethical line—heated debates that all took place in the days leading up to his death. There were a few messages from Riley, too, professional on the surface but tinged with something unresolved, like regret edging into resentment. But Phillips? Nothing. Not in those final days. Not the night Greg died. Nothing from him at all. My gut shifted.

"There's nothing."

Parks exhaled, then asked, "Could it be missing?"

"He told us he sent Hoover the draft protocols around 9:45. That it was requested. That Hoover responded. But nothing here shows that."

Parks let out a low whistle. "Then Phillips lied."

I flipped open our notes from the Phillips interview and read through the highlighted sections out loud.

"Yes. I sent him the protocols. He requested them earlier in the day…"

"Did he respond?"

"Yes, with a thank-you."

There it was. On record. Clear. Direct.

"He invented the email," I said, my stomach hollowing. "Greg never got that file. Phillips never sent it."

Parks stood and started pacing. "But why lie about it? If he was home working, uploading to the server, why build in a false email?"

"Because he needed us to think he was in contact with Hoover," I said slowly. "That he was alive and engaging with him after 9:30. But if that communication never happened—"

"He never sent it because he wasn't home." He stopped pacing. "Holy shit."

My fingers drummed against the edge of the couch. "If he lied about talking to Hoover that night, then his timeline's wide open."

I turned back to the files Evelyn had labeled *Trial Discussion – Private.*

One thread stood out. Jessica Moore had emailed Hoover a list of trial modifications. Phillips was cc'd on the discussion.

And in one email—dated a week before Hoover's murder—Phillips detailed a revised draft protocol, referencing projected patient outcomes and specific dosage adjustments. It was the same file he claimed to have sent Greg Hoover the night he died.

I handed it to Parks. "Same email. He just repackaged it later. The trial hadn't changed. The data hadn't changed. Just the time stamp."

"So, he used a file Hoover already had and pretended it was new."

"To establish a nonexistent email chain," I said, breath catching. "To create the illusion of communication. Of life."

We both fell silent.

Then I reached for Evelyn's last stack—the files labeled *Notes: Why?*

Her handwriting scrawled across sticky tabs in the margins. One note circled a quote from her husband's internal email:

I won't let Phillips push this through without review. I want this off PAC's table entirely.

And beneath it, Evelyn's note:

Greg canceled their involvement. Killed the trial. What did that cost him?

"We know what it would cost Phillips," he said. "His entire model depended on PAC backing the trial. Without it, he had no footing. No funding. No leverage with pharma partners."

"And if Hoover went public?" I asked. "Exposed the trial for what it was, an unauthorized scheme run behind PAC's back."

"He'd take Phillips down with him," Parks said. "Along with Jessica. Maybe Riley, too."

"But Phillips had the most to lose," I whispered. "Reputation. Career. Maybe even criminal charges if the trial hurt someone."

"We already knew this," he said. "And so did Sullivan."

"But we never confirmed the emails. We dropped the ball on that, and so did Sullivan."

"Or," he said, "Sullivan chose to ignore it."

"Christopher's going to want him linked to the gun as well," I said.

Parks ran his hand through his hair. "Did we screw this up? Did we just accuse the wrong man?"

I didn't know how to answer that. Had we been so intent on nailing Bennett that we overlooked other suspects? Especially one who had a lot riding on the trial? I pinched the bridge of my nose as I thought it through.

Parks cleared his throat.

I looked up at him.

"What are you thinking?" he asked.

"Even if Phillips didn't kill Greg or Evelyn Hoover, he still committed a crime. Running an unauthorized cancer treatment trial without FDA approval, without IRB oversight, and under the false pretense of PAC's support isn't just unethical, it's illegal. Fraud, wire fraud, potential negligence. He gambled with lives and hoped no one would notice. He'll go down for that.

"Bennett's not innocent of other crimes, either. He embezzled millions through a shell billing scheme, falsified internal financials, and laundered company money through dummy corporations. He's built a quiet empire on theft. One way or another, they both have blood on their hands. One just more literally than the other."

He breathed in and out through his nose. "Valid points, but we need that smoking gun."

"Literally."

Parks chewed on a fingernail. "What if, and work with me here, one killed Greg and the other killed Evelyn?"

"That's a stretch."

"Not really. The first killer left the gun at Riley's. The news reported it everywhere. What if, worried Evelyn would learn the truth, the other decided to kill her, thinking the blame would fall on Greg's murderer then?"

I licked my lips. "Two killers, two motives, and two murders." I sat on that for a second. Link one gun to Greg Hoover and figure out who the hell had murdered his wife. "There's got to be something else we've missed. Something important."

And so we started over, reading every single paper we had, looking for that golden nugget.

20

I woke to the low buzz of a phone vibrating on the table, followed by the quiet creak of Parks shifting on the opposite side of the couch. The cushions dipped slightly as he stood, but it was the intentional silence in his movement that pulled me fully awake. My body protested as I sat up, every muscle stiff from being folded into the same position.

Parks stood by the window, his phone in his hand, staring at the screen.

"Everything okay?" I asked, my voice still thick from sleep.

He didn't answer right away, and that pause told me more than any explanation could. Something wasn't right.

"Parks."

He turned slowly. "It's from Jessica."

"Ah, the booty call. I knew it."

He walked over and handed me the phone. "Not quite."

The message was short: *I found something. I'm scared. Can you come alone?*

My pulse kicked up. "That's vague."

He nodded. "Too vague."

I caught the look in his eyes that said what I felt. Something cold was curling in my gut, not fear exactly, but instinct. A warning we'd learned to trust.

"She knows you and I are working this together," I said. "If she really found something, she wouldn't ask for you alone."

"You think she's trying to get me in bed?"

I rolled my eyes. "Parks, contrary to what you think, not every woman wants you."

He raised an eyebrow. "Are you sure? It sounds like you thought it."

"I just think it's odd that she's asking for you alone, but you did go out with her, so maybe she feels comfortable doing that. Do you even know where she lives?"

"Roswell. Off Sandy Plains. I've got the address." He grabbed his cowboy boots and slipped them on. I made the connection to his nickname then. "She might really be scared. I'm going over."

"We should call Roswell PD," I said, but even as I said it, I didn't reach for my phone.

"If this is a setup and Jessica's in danger, flashing badges might get her killed before I ever get to the door," he said.

"And if it's not, and she really is just scared?"

"Then I look like the one who overstepped."

I exhaled, low and controlled. "We, Parks. I'm going with you. That's what partners do." I shoved the files into my bag without bothering to organize them.

Parks checked his Glock, cleared it, and holstered it like he was brushing his teeth—routine, automatic, necessary.

I didn't bother changing clothes. There wasn't time or room in my head for vanity.

Parks angled his chin toward a dark two-story house half a block ahead. "That's hers."

I spotted the car in the driveway first, parked clean and undisturbed. Not a single window showed light or movement. "We don't stop," I said. "If someone's watching, they'll expect headlights."

He nodded and kept driving. We passed slowly, both of us staring without turning our heads.

"Circle around and park down the street. If someone's in there—"

"We want them to think I left. I know the deal, Jenna. I'm not a virgin at this kind of thing."

"Noted."

Parks pulled into a driveway and backed out to head the direction we came, then parked down the street. "We're not splitting up," he said. "We'll check the perimeter before going to the front door. If we're clear, then I'll knock, and you have my six."

I nodded once.

We eased out of the car and quietly shut the doors. Parks headed across the street and moved through the grass toward the back of the property. I scanned every window we passed, each one blacked out with either curtains or blinds.

He kept low along the side, stopping at the deck steps and carefully climbing up them to try the door. I waited. Locked. He gave a quick shake of his head, then moved toward the closest window. Also locked. No sign of forced entry, no lights on timers, no music to fill the silence.

I checked for security cameras along the way but hadn't seen any. My heart hammered in my chest. One of the basement windows caught my attention. A faint line of light edged beneath the sill—sharp, narrow, and barely visible. I froze and stared. A shadow moved past, blocking the light temporarily.

Someone was inside.

I motioned for Parks to look and whispered, "There's a light, and a shadow moved across it."

He didn't ask questions. Just nodded once, held up his hand, and moved to the opposite end of the house. I crept closer to the window, each step slow and deliberate, until I reached its edge. My breath hitched. The angle gave me no easy way to look inside. Any lower and I'd lose the line of sight. Any higher and I'd risk being spotted. I inched down, knees flexed, fingers sinking into damp earth, until my eyes aligned with the narrow gap. The shadow passed again.

My pulse hammered in my ears. No aimless pacing. The steps carried weight and purpose. I narrowed my focus, eyes locked on the movement.

Whoever it was wasn't female. Silence gripped the room beyond, but my instincts fired like alarms.

I locked my eyes on the corner where Parks had vanished and waited for him to reappear. Seconds passed. Then he stepped back into view and crossed the yard to meet me.

"Nothing else," he said. "Everything's shut tight. No motion. No cameras. If someone's watching, they're doing it from inside."

I looked at the basement window again. "Whoever's in there walks like a man. I can't see anyone else."

We moved along the edge of the house, close to the siding, quiet as we could manage on wet grass and uneven ground. The side door sat recessed beneath a narrow overhang. Paint peeled around the edges. The knob showed wear, but nothing recent. No new scratches. No damage. Just locked.

Parks studied the frame, then glanced at me. "Whoever's in there didn't come through here, but we can. Glass panel. We crack it, reach in."

He pulled the Glock from his holster and used the barrel to tap the glass gently. It held. He shifted his grip, angled the steel just right, and struck once. The pane shattered inward with a muffled pop. Shards hit the tile inside with soft clicks. I stepped back as he reached through, flipped the lock, and pushed the door open. He looked at me once before stepping in and gave me a slight nod. I followed.

Darkness seeped into my bones, pulled tight around my shoulders, and whispered that something waited just past the edge of vision.

I stepped over the threshold, Glock in hand, my body tight with the raw, electric edge of awareness that only settled in when something felt deeply, dangerously wrong. Parks moved in behind me, the soft snick of the door closing at his back sounding louder than it should have. We didn't speak. Didn't need to. The air already told us everything.

The place reeked of copper.

Blood.

We adjusted to the black. Moonlight filtered through partially closed blinds, throwing slanted patterns across the hardwood floor. I kept low and swept left. Parks took right. Our movements mirrored, deliberate and controlled. Each shift silent and measured. Every step an unspoken agreement to survive. Every creak of old flooring shot through my nerves like a wire trip. I clenched my jaw and tightened my grip on my weapon.

No flashlight. No talking. Total stealth.

Signs of a struggle greeted us immediately. A lamp shattered on its side, its base splintered like bone. A chair flipped near the corner, one leg splintered. A bookshelf leaned at an unnatural angle, paperbacks spilled across the rug like bodies. A shattered photo frame crunched under my boot, and I froze. I stopped breathing. Parks paused too. His eyes cut toward me. We waited and listened, but the silence held. No footsteps. No breathing. Just the weight of something unseen pressing harder with each second. Then we moved again.

Parks touched my elbow. His head tilted toward the hallway.

I nodded.

We moved.

Doorways yawned open on either side of the corridor, each one a potential threat. I cleared the kitchen first. Empty, but in disarray. A drawer hung open with silverware scattered like shrapnel on the counter and floor. Cabinet doors gaped. Someone had been searching for something, or they'd fought like hell. A bottle of juice lay on its side, bleeding a red stream across the tile that looked too much like blood.

A knife block sat on the counter near the sink with one slot empty. I scanned the area. No blade in sight. Nothing on the counter, nothing on the floor. Whoever took it hadn't dropped it. I prayed they hadn't used it.

The copper smell slammed into me. Close, raw, and wet, as if it had just hit the air. It thickened in my throat, soaked the back of my tongue and coated every breath I took. Fresh blood, not dried.

I caught the glint of it streaked across the floor. A smear dragged down the hall and disappeared around the corner. Another trail led in the opposite direction, toward the bedroom.

Parks raised two fingers to note we needed to split.

I nodded again.

He took the blood that veered toward the bedroom. I tracked the second path, stepping over a toppled picture frame and a torn throw pillow. Each step took conscious effort. I steadied my breathing. Primed my body to react at the slightest movement or faintest sound.

The hallway narrowed as I moved. Family photos hung crooked on the walls, some with the glass cracked. I reached the bathroom just as Parks moved in beside me.

The door hung half open, nudged by a smear of blood thick against the tile. The smell punched me full in the gut. It saturated the air enough for me to taste.

Parks and I made eye contact. He nodded. I pushed the door with my knuckles.

My stomach lurched.

It wasn't Jessica.

Chandra Martin lay twisted between the toilet and tub. One arm bent backward under her torso, the other flung out like she had tried to crawl. Her throat gaped open, skin peeled wide from the cut of a large blade. Blood pooled beneath her, too dark and too much to let her live.

No breath. No twitch. Eyes wide and glazed, mouth parted in shock. She never saw it coming.

Her fingernails carved shallow trails across the tile, barely visible but frantic. Crimson smeared in arcs where she had tried to push herself forward. Small spots of blood had dried in some places, but the puddles of it still glistened. I dropped to a knee and hovered my hand over her shoulder. Her body had cooled but not enough for rigor to set in. She hadn't been dead long.

Long enough to kill her. Short enough we might stop the next.

I crouched beside her. My breath caught in my throat.

I pulled my phone and thumbed a text to Leland. *Need backup. Jessica Moore's house. One confirmed dead. Basement occupied. Armed.*

Three dots appeared. Disappeared. Reappeared. *Hold perimeter. No lights. No sirens. Team en route. They're nearby. Ten, tops.*

Ten minutes felt like ten years. Long enough for someone to bleed out. Long enough for the killer to bolt. Not long enough for us to wait.

I showed Parks the text.

A female scream split the silence. Muffled but raw, and clearly Jessica Moore.

Parks spun. We moved around the corner toward the basement door.

He pressed his hand against it. I followed suit but felt nothing. No vibration, no footsteps vibrating off the floor.

He pointed to the doorknob, then pulled a small mirror from his back pocket and angled it under the door.

No movement. No feet.

We couldn't wait for the agents. Ten minutes could mean life or death. Sweat trickled down my spine. I shifted my grip on the Glock. We moved to either side of the door. Guns raised. Breaths slow. Muscles coiled.

He met my gaze. He counted down with his fingers.

Three.

Two.

One.

We moved.

21

Parks led, yelling, "You're surrounded!" Two-thirds of the way down the basement stairs, we froze.

Phillips stood with one arm wrapped around Jessica Moore's neck and the other holding a syringe.

His eyes locked on mine, dry, flat, vacant. "Take one more step and she's dead."

We didn't move but kept our guns aimed at him, neither getting a clear shot.

Parks took a slow step down. "Let her go."

Sweat poured down Phillips's temples. "I said stay where you are!" He pulled her closer.

She stumbled. Her arms shook. Her knees buckled slightly. Tears streamed down her cheeks. "Help me! He's crazy!"

"Shut up!" He tightened his grip around her neck, forcing her head to bend to the side even more.

He'd cut off her airflow if he tightened his arm any more.

"This is fentanyl, just like I used on you. Enough to shut her down before she hits the ground." He kept his eyes trained on me. "I should have given you more."

Jessica's face twisted. Blood streaked along her temple. Her lower lip had split at the corner and swelled. Whatever had happened, she'd put up a fight, and from the looks of Phillips, Chandra had too.

"You don't want this ending here," I said. "Things are already bad enough for you, Phillips."

"It's *doctor*, and trust me, I do. This bitch deserves to die for what she did to me!"

"Don't listen to him!" Jessica yelled.

He jerked her neck and picked her off the ground. "Shut up!"

"Drop the needle," Parks said. "You're not going to win this one."

"I've already won." He glanced at the window with the small opening under the shade. "No one's coming to help you. Drop your guns now, or she's dead."

Parks shifted and inched left.

"Don't," he warned. "Don't you get it? I want her dead, and I'll die making it happen. Guns on the floor! Now!"

"Let her go, and we talk," I said. "You still have time."

"It's too late," he said. His jaw tightened. "She knows the truth. Now put the damn guns down, or she's dead!"

We slowly placed our guns on the stairs.

"What truth?" I asked.

"He killed Greg!" Jessica said through sobs. "He told me! Shoot the bastard!"

He sneered and growled into her ear. "Because of you, Jessica. He died because of you. Did you think he loved you? He couldn't, not the way I do. No one will."

My skin crawled at the sound he made. High, jagged, and full of something cracked and furious.

"You're crazy," she said. "You don't know anything!"

"Dr. Phillips," Parks said. "We can help you, just let her go and drop the syringe."

"You weren't there. You didn't see them. The way she looked at him. The way he said her name. You think it was about research? You think I gave a damn about data?"

Jessica whimpered. "I didn't—"

"You did. You loved him." He shook her once. "I saw it in your eyes every time you pretended not to care."

"You murdered him," she said. "You took an oath to save lives, and you murdered him!"

"I erased a problem." His voice hollowed out. "He didn't deserve you. I did."

"She was never yours," I said. "But your wife is. What about her? Do you want to do this to her?"

"My wife?" he snarled. "I gave her everything, and she just wanted more."

"What about Jessica?" I asked. "If you love her, why want her dead? It doesn't matter now. We know you killed the Hoovers and Chandra Martin. You don't need another murder on your conscience. Let her go."

"You don't know anything," he said. "Why would I kill Evelyn Hoover? She meant nothing to me. But this one?" He breathed into Jessica's ear. "I gave you the trial. I gave you notoriety. Your name in the paper. I gave you that lab, that salary, that title. And you gave him everything instead."

Parks moved half a step.

Jessica hadn't texted us. Phillips had. He wanted us there. Wanted us to know everything.

"No one walks out alive," he said.

I checked the window and saw the bodies move outside. "You're too late."

"It's never too late."

I shifted just enough to reach for the backup tucked at the small of my back. "You can't fix this. But you can stop it from getting worse."

His mouth twitched.

"We're not the only ones here," Parks said. "They're surrounding this house right now. If you let her live, they'll listen. You'll still go down, but maybe not forever."

He laughed. A soft, broken sound. "You think I care about prison?"

His lips pressed thin. His jaw clenched hard enough to twitch. The syringe trembled slightly. Not his hand—just the pressure in his fingers.

Jessica's eyes found mine. Panic flooded them. Tears spilled. She shook her head once, barely. Her lips mouthed something I couldn't make out.

Phillips's stare snapped back to me. "You said you'd listen."

"I am."

Parks shifted. I didn't move. He looked at me from the corner of his eyes. Just once. A beat passed.

Outside, movement shifted again. I caught a shape at the window. A slow drift of shadow—two, three figures. Agents in place.

Phillips saw it too. His hand jerked. The syringe punched into Jessica's neck.

She screamed.

My arm shot back. I grabbed the backup Glock. Parks moved the same second. We fired—one, two, three shots in unison.

Phillips dropped. The syringe flew from his hand and skittered across the floor.

Jessica collapsed to her knees. I caught her under the arms and pulled her back. Her hands clutched her throat. She gasped. Her eyes rolled back. I dragged her out of the way, flattened my palm against her sternum. "We need Narcan!"

Parks kicked the syringe down the hall. Blood pooled under Phillips's body, the liquid slowly spreading. His mouth opened, but no sound followed. His chest stopped moving.

The stairwell door slammed open. Boots thundered down the steps. GBI agents flooded the basement, weapons drawn, voices tight.

"Hands up!"

"Narcan," I screamed, "now!"

One agent bolted back up the stairs. Two rushed to Jessica. Another dropped beside Phillips and checked for a pulse.

He shook his head.

"He's gone," Parks said. He stayed at my side, breathing heavy, eyes locked on the dead man across the floor.

We didn't speak.

Seconds later, the agent raced down the stairs, jabbed Jessica in the arm with another syringe, then turned her on her side. Her eyes shot open, wild and unfocused. She coughed hard, a wet, hacking cough. Her whole body jerked as she gasped for air, and she tried to sit up.

"It's okay," I said. "We've got you."

"He," she mumbled. "Is he dead?"

I exhaled. "Very much so."

The rhythmic beeping in Jessica Moore's hospital room echoed low beneath the fluorescent lights, steady but irritating and a constant reminder of how close she had come to dying.

Parks leaned against the wall, silent but locked in. I knew that look. He was tracking everything—her words, her micro-movements, her breathing. We had questions and needed answers, but she needed time.

Detective Sullivan stepped into the room. "I'd like a minute alone with her, please."

"Ain't happenin'," I said. "If you want an interview, you'll need to talk to GBI Special Agent in Charge Leland Seymour."

He scowled at me. "This isn't over, Wyatt." He pointed his finger at Parks. "With you either."

"You're right," Parks said. "We'll chat about your failures and cover-ups as soon as the DA drops the charges against Riley Chatsworth."

Sullivan strutted out as if he thought he might win the battle, but we knew he wouldn't.

Jessica licked her lips and tried to sit up but winced. "Please don't make me talk too fast. My head feels like a bowling ball full of razor blades."

"Fentanyl will do that to you. You're lucky to be alive."

"Fentanyl?"

I stepped closer. "Do you remember what happened?"

She nodded slowly. "I think so. My mind is so fuzzy right now." Her hand twitched toward her temple. Her voice cracked. "It's so loud in here. Why is it so loud?"

I smirked. "That'll fade. I promise."

She closed her eyes. A tear slid from the corner of one. "God. I thought he was going to kill me. I saw it in his eyes."

"You're safe. For now. But we need to know everything. Can you handle talking with us now?"

Jessica gave a shallow nod. "Okay." She exhaled like it took everything she had just to get air in her lungs. "Greg and I were in love. We were together for over a year, maybe closer to two if you count the months we pretended we were 'just business associates.' It wasn't casual. It wasn't some affair we stumbled into. We planned a future."

I hated that for Riley. Hoover had played her. He'd played them all, and he paid the ultimate price for it.

"He said he'd leave Evelyn. He promised. We were supposed to go public after Tellion terminated the contract with PAC. Everyone assumed that decision was about the premium increases, but it wasn't. It was because of us."

Parks shifted his stance. We exchanged a weighted look, knowing we'd have to tell Riley everything.

Jessica turned her head toward him slowly. "Greg hated having the trial under the table. He knew what it could do to Tellion, to PAC, and to me. He wanted to walk away before it imploded."

"Did he say that to you?"

She nodded weakly. "He said he couldn't risk my career. That if PAC went down over it, I'd be caught in it whether I was involved or not. Which I was, but only because Phillips pushed it. He promised to keep me safe from any fallout, which is why I participated."

"Hoover or Phillips?" Parks asked.

"Phillips. But Greg wanted to keep me safe too."

"Tell us about Phillips," I said.

She looked at me like the name alone made her nauseous. "He was obsessed. With the trial. With himself. Maybe with me, but I hadn't taken that seriously. In the beginning, I was starstruck. He's a genius. I was so excited to work with him. I learned so much, and I couldn't believe he was willing to spend so much time helping me grow in our field."

"But it wasn't that, was it?" I asked.

She shook her head. "At first, he started out respectful. Brilliant, even. But the closer we got, the weirder he became. I thought I had feelings for him, and when he approached me in that way, I couldn't help myself. I was so wrapped up in his, I don't know, essence, I guess. I think I confused my attraction to him with awe. The more intimate we became, the more unhinged he became, so I ended it. But that got worse when PAC denied the trial for Tellion."

"How so?" Parks asked.

"He had always been possessive, but when I ended it, he backed off. Or so I thought at first. Then he noticed me spending more time with Greg. I told him it was about the trial, and initially, it was, but he didn't like it. He tried to convince me to give him another chance, but I wouldn't. I told him I had fallen in love with Greg, and that he and I were over, but we had a job to do, and we needed that trial to be a success. When we couldn't get PAC to support it, he lost it. Lawrence didn't like delays. He hated that the board denied the trial, and thought they were idiots." She drew in a breath. "He pushed it through for Tellion anyway. Off the books. He wanted to be the one to deliver the next major breakthrough in oncology. Not for the patients. For his résumé."

Parks exhaled. "Did he use your relationship with Greg to make that happen?"

Jessica turned to him, her eyes glossy but focused. "He didn't need me. He needed Greg, and Greg wanted his team healthy. He wanted to take care of his employees and their families. But Greg realized the risk was too great, so he backed out of the trial and terminated the PAC contract. Phillips freaked out because he saw it all slipping away. It was like he'd been betrayed. Personally. Like Greg didn't just end a contract. He ended *his* future."

"He said he didn't kill Evelyn. Do you believe him?"

Jessica's voice dropped to a whisper. "I don't know. I don't know what she knew about the trial. Greg didn't talk about her. But I think she found out about me and made him choose. And when he chose her, he lost everything else."

"Riley saw him with someone at his Midtown apartment," I said. "Was that you?"

She blinked. "He preferred coming here. He was probably with his wife."

"I'm sure that's who it was," I said, though I didn't believe it.

"I loved him," she said softly. "For all his flaws. For everything he did wrong. I wanted *him*. And now he's dead because of me."

Greg must have memorized a things-to-tell-mistresses script. I wanted to tell her about Riley. To say she wasn't the only one, but I couldn't do that to her in that state, and she would find out eventually. Besides, it wasn't my story to tell.

"None of this is your fault," I said. "No one can control how another person handles things. Don't take on Dr. Phillips's mental illness."

"He really was an amazing medical scientist. He'd done so much for medicine. I just can't believe he threw it all away."

"People do things others can't understand," Parks said. "But the choice is theirs, no matter how much they want to put it on us."

"Jessica," I asked, "why was Chandra at your house?"

She sighed. "I asked her to come. I needed everything I could get on Lawrence because I knew he murdered Greg."

"What made you realize that?"

"I don't know. Something clicked inside me, and I wanted to prove it. I wanted justice."

"How did Phillips find out?" Parks asked.

"I don't think he did until he showed up at my house. He's done that before. I guess he carried that damn syringe around just in case or something."

I rubbed the back of my neck. We would have to tell Riley about Chandra. Somehow, for the time being at least, Leland had made sure the media sat on the story, but Jessica had neighbors. Someone saw the EMTs carting out two body bags, and the connection would be made. We needed to get to Riley before someone else did.

"What happens next?" she asked.

"GBI has taken over the investigation. You may see Detective Sullivan, but he's not running the show, so you don't have to answer any of his questions," I said.

"What about Riley? Will they drop the charges against her?"

"I'm sure it's already in the works."

We left the room quietly to give her time to rest. I finally sent Tiffani and Taylor a text asking them to shelter Riley from the news. We wanted her to hear it from us, not some reporter looking for an award. Parks and I didn't speak to each other. We didn't need to. Until the elevator dinged and the doors slid open.

We stepped inside, but instead of pressing the button for the ground floor, I hit the button for the fourth.

When the doors opened again, we walked out into the quiet corridor lined with frosted windows and muted signs. At the far end, a familiar woman leaned against the wall outside room 418. She sobbed quietly.

Wallace Bennett's wife. She glanced in our direction, wiped her eyes with a tissue, and walked toward us. I braced myself for another verbal beating, but it didn't come.

"I was just about to call you."

I raised an eyebrow. "Why?"

"He's ready to talk."

22

Wallace Bennett sat upright in the hospital bed, looking like he'd lost a fight with a freight train. He wasn't cuffed yet, but with his multiyear white-collar crime spree, that was only a matter of paperwork.

In a groggy, hoarse voice, Bennett confessed his embezzling transgressions like he was up for an award. "I have been embezzling. It wasn't supposed to go this long, but..."

"But the money was good," Parks said.

Bennett's wife stood just inside the door, arms crossed, and a look of complete disgust plastered on her face. I assumed she meant it for her husband, not us.

"I wanted to stop, I really did, but then the people that helped me threatened to report it."

"That doesn't make sense," I said. "They would have been charged too. They will be charged as it is."

"They said I coerced them, claiming they were afraid of losing their jobs if they didn't help me."

Given the evidence, his crimes were easily proven. "We already have proof," I said. "I'm not sure your statement will go far with the DA's office."

"That's not all," he said. "Evelyn Hoover spoke to me at her home after the funeral. She told me she knew about the embezzling, and she planned to tell the police."

My breath caught. "You killed her."

Sweat dots formed on his forehead. "I didn't have any other choice."

"You always have choices," Parks said. "And murder should never be one of them."

His wife finally spoke. "He's been so stressed. That has to mean something, right? Maybe he's too sick to be tried for this?"

"Mr. Bennett," Parks said. "I suggest not saying anything more until you consult with an attorney."

I stepped out of the room and called Leland, apologized for the late call and explained the situation, leaving out the murder confession. Since we weren't officially law enforcement, Parks and I didn't need to share the information, but we would eventually be deposed, and it would come out.

"Is this about the embezzling only, or is there more?"

Leland could read me better than anyone. "More."

"Evelyn Hoover?"

"You know I'm not going to answer that right now."

"Noted. I'll contact Sullivan," he said. "His PD has the case, but I think I can swing this entire thing to GBI. I'm sending someone now to cover the room. Can you stick around until they get there?"

"Only if you follow through with that home-cooked meal."

"Already in the works." He killed the call.

I made one more call, to Taylor, again. "We'll be at Riley's first thing. Can you keep this all from her until then?"

"I think you should come now. The media's all over her place. Atlanta PD isn't happy."

"On our way."

23

We pushed our way through the crowd of reporters at Riley's.

Parks shoved a cameraman out of our way. "I thought they were strong-armed into sitting on this?"

"I guess they didn't listen. Hopefully Taylor's kept it from her. She doesn't need to hear about Jessica from anyone but me."

The police escorted us to the elevator.

He turned to me and smirked. "You've forgiven her, haven't you?"

"What's the point in carrying that baggage anymore? I've already got enough issues to fill the cargo hold of a jet."

"I can't argue with you on that." He bumped my shoulder with his. "I'm proud of you. Now you have two female friends."

"Who's the first?"

"Tiffani."

"I wouldn't call us friends, but maybe one day." I chuckled. "I could have my own little high school clique."

"Let's not go that far."

Tiffani met us outside the elevator.

"Are your ears burning?" Parks asked her.

"Should they be?"

I rolled my eyes at Parks, then said to Tiffani, "We're just glad you're here for this."

"Riley's going to have mixed feelings about all this." She opened the door to Riley's. "We're here."

Riley didn't wait for the door to close. "They won't let me look at my phone or listen to any media. What's happened?"

"Lawrence Phillips is dead," I said.

Her eyes widened. "Why?" She gasped. "Oh, my God. He killed Greg? Why? Because of the trial? That makes no sense."

Parks led her to the couch. "We need to sit down for this. It's not a short story."

A woman walked out of the kitchen with a tray of waters and coffee. Did Riley keep someone on staff twenty-four-seven or something?

"No, thank you," I said. I almost asked for a shot of whiskey, but I wasn't about to travel down that road again.

"May I have my phone now? I'd like Chandra to be here for this," Riley said. Her voice carried a flicker of relief, and I hated I had to rip that to shreds.

Parks shifted beside me. I looked at him, and in that brief silence, the truth passed between us bright enough for Riley to notice.

Her expression tightened as she glanced between us. "What? What's going on?" Her voice rose in pitch as she searched my face for the answer. Then something in her broke. Her body stilled, but her eyes widened with sudden, terrible understanding. "No," she said. Her breath caught hard in her throat. "No, please, God. No."

She backed away from us, one step, then another, before her legs gave out. Parks reached for her and helped her onto the couch. She wrapped her arms around her middle. Tears fell without restraint. She blinked hard. "She can't be dead. Not Chandra."

I knelt in front of her, knowing she needed a friend more than anything. "I'm sorry, Riley. She—" My throat closed around the rest. I couldn't finish it. Tears filled my eyes.

We stared at each other as the reality of her loss sunk in as much as it could then. Finally, she looked to the glowing Atlanta skyline. "She was my constant. Even when I didn't deserve her."

"I know," I said. I sat beside her on the couch. "I'm so sorry."

"Why? Why her?"

"Jessica called her and asked for help. She believed Phillips murdered Greg. Unfortunately, she was there when Phillips arrived. We don't know for sure, but we think Phillips had been watching Jessica's house, and when he saw Chandra, he knew he had to do something."

"I don't understand. Why would he be watching Jessica? How would he know what she thought? All for this trial that likely wouldn't have worked anyway."

Tiffani sat on her other side and handed her a box of tissues.

"He wasn't there because of the trial," I said.

"Then why did he kill Greg and try to frame me? This doesn't make any sense."

I hated what I had to say, but I knew Riley well enough to know the best way to do it was to rip off the Band-Aid. "Jessica and Greg had been having an affair for at least a year."

Her eyes bulged. "What? No. That's impossible."

"I'm sorry, Riley, but it's true. Evelyn even threatened her."

"But Greg said he wanted to marry me." She leaned back into the couch. "Did he tell her that too?"

"He said he was going to divorce Evelyn for her."

She sat there for a moment, her face contorted into something I couldn't define. Finally, she said, "Is Jessica dead?"

I shook my head.

"Good." I recognized the scowl. "Because we're going to have a talk." She looked at Taylor. "When can I get this anklet off?"

"I'll make the call at eight a.m."

She looked at Tiffani. "I want to go to the hospital."

"No," Taylor and I said in unison.

I motioned for him to go first. "Things must be done before you talk with anyone. We can't put your freedom at risk, Riley. Do you understand that?"

"Yes," she said through gritted teeth.

"It's not Jessica's fault," I said. "Greg played you both, and honestly, there could be more women we don't know about."

"Phillips killed him because of her."

"No," Parks said. "Phillips killed him because he was mentally unstable."

"Did he confess to it? Maybe it was Jessica who killed Greg. Maybe he dumped her because he wanted to marry me. Maybe she killed him because she was jealous."

"No," I said. "Riley, listen to me. You know I don't BS people. Phillips admitted to the murder. It had nothing to do with the trial. He was jealous of Greg. Jessica couldn't have stopped this from happening."

"But he loved me."

"I'm sorry."

Parks picked me up later that morning. I'd barely slept and wanted to kiss him when he handed me a large coffee from RaceTrac. "You're amazing."

"I know." He winked. "You ready?"

I nodded, then pushed past him and out my door. "Is it weird to you?"

"What?" he asked.

"Giving statements to law enforcement."

"Not really. Why?"

"Because we're former law enforcement. I don't know, it's just odd. I guess I prefer the other side of the table."

"I don't. Too many restrictions and people to report to."

"That's a good point."

"I'm smarter than I look."

I grabbed the pile of mail in his passenger seat. "You're a smart guy, Parks. You called it on the double-killer theory."

He pressed the start button, and his engine roared to life. "You would have gotten there eventually."

"I don't think so." I sifted through his mail. "Do you ever read this stuff?"

"Sometimes. Just toss it in the back."

I straightened the pile and tucked it between the seat and center console. "I've been thinking about something. Something I know I'm going to regret."

His eyes flicked to me. "You're going to be nice to Heather?"

"I am nice to her. Most of the time."

"Then what?"

"You need a printer."

"I know. What're you going to do, buy me one?"

"Something even stupider than that."

His lips twitched. "Are you asking me to move in with you, Jenna?"

I leaned my head back and groaned. "Of course you'd say it that way. Let me be clear. I'm suggesting we share office space."

That twitch progressed into a full-blown smile. "Will you stock up on Wite-Out?"

"You can handle that."

24

Alyssa glided across the stage with the grace of a butterfly. Sort of. She carried herself well, even nailing the facial expressions she said she had been practicing. My heart swelled with pride.

I leaned toward Nick and whispered in his ear, "Did they switch our baby at birth? We both know she didn't get those dance skills from us."

He laughed. "I was thinking the same thing."

I moved back and continued to watch my daughter convince me to drain my bank account for ballet lessons until she made it big on Broadway.

"She's really good," Parks whispered. "Thanks for inviting me."

"I didn't invite you. You insisted on coming."

"To protect Heather."

I smiled. "Okay, I'll give you that one."

The recital lasted thirty minutes. After it finished, the girls and their families met at Taco Mac for dinner. I asked Parks to tag along.

Somehow, I ended up sitting next to Heather. "Hey, I've been meaning to ask you about the guy at the coffee shop. Did Alyssa point him out to you?"

"Oh, gosh. I'm so sorry. She did." She dug her phone out of her purse. "I took a photo of him for you." She handed me her phone.

I scrutinized the picture. I didn't know the man, but I wouldn't forget his face. I handed Parks the phone. "Do you know this man?"

He studied the picture. "I don't think so."

"Thanks." I handed Heather her phone. "Would you send me that?"

"Absolutely. Is everything okay?"

"It's probably just a coincidence, but watch for him when you're out with Alyssa, okay?"

"Of course, and I'll let you know if I see him."

"Thanks."

Parks squeezed my knee, and I practically jumped out of my chair.

"Don't do that."

"Watch out," he said with a grin. "Or Heather will wind up in that new friend circle of yours."

"That's never gonna happen, Cowboy."

Before the Next One Falls
Jenna Wyatt Book 3

A killer's revenge plot unfolds in the shadows of Atlanta's landmarks, leaving a trail of bodies and cryptic clues—each one more personal than the last.

A chef floating in Lake Lanier. A man pushed from Stone Mountain. Two deaths connected by a single thread: Jack Parks.

Private investigator Jenna Wyatt ignored the first unsettling message. Now bodies are dropping. And both victims are tied to her partner—a former NCIS agent with secrets he won't share.

As they decode the killer's taunts, Jenna questions everything about Jack. Who's targeting his inner circle? What past sins have returned to haunt him? The closer they get to answers, the more dangerous the game becomes.

With each new victim, the killer draws them deeper into Jack's buried history. Old enemies. Powerful secrets. Betrayals worth killing for.

When the hunter becomes the hunted, Jenna faces an impossible choice: trust the partner she barely knows, or become the next target on a murderer's list.

USA Today bestselling author Carolyn Ridder Aspenson delivers a pulse-pounding thriller packed with shocking twists and relentless suspense. Perfect for fans of Robert Dugoni and Allison Brennan.

Get your copy today at
severnriverbooks.com

30% Off your next paperback.

 SCAN ME

Thank you for reading. For exclusive offers on your next paperback:

- **Visit SevernRiverBooks.com** and enter code **PRINTBOOKS30** at checkout.
- Or scan the QR code.

SEVERN ⚬ RIVER
PUBLISHING

ABOUT CAROLYN RIDDER ASPENSON

USA Today Bestselling author Carolyn Ridder Aspenson writes cozy mysteries, thrillers, and paranormal women's fiction featuring strong female leads. Her stories shine through her dialogue, which readers have praised for being realistic and compelling.

Her first novel, *Unfinished Business,* was a Reader's Favorite and reached the top 100 books sold on Amazon.

In 2021 she introduced readers to detective Rachel Ryder in *Damaging Secrets*. *Overkill*, the third book in the Rachel Ryder series was one of Thrillerfix's best thrillers of 2021.

Prior to publishing, she worked as a journalist in the suburbs of Atlanta where her work appeared in multiple newspapers and magazines.

Writing is only one of Carolyn's passions. She is an avid dog lover and currently babies two pit bull boxer mixes. She lives in the mountains of North Georgia as an empty nester with her husband, a cantankerous cat, and those two spoiled dogs.

You can chat with Carolyn on Facebook at Carolyn Ridder Aspenson Books.

Sign up for Carolyn's reader list at
severnriverbooks.com

Printed in the United States
by Baker & Taylor Publisher Services